Beyond the Break

a novel

Blessings!

Bonnie J. Hopkins

D1385109

OTHER BOOKS BY BONNIE HOPKINS

SEASONS
(The Riverwood Series)

NOW AND THEN, AGAIN

DESTINY
(The Riverwood Series)

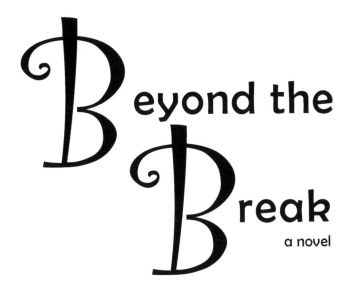

Beyond the Break

a novel

Third story in Riverwood Series

Bonnie Hopkins

Bonnie Hopkins Publications
Houston

Bonnie Hopkins Publications
Houston, Texas

For more information:
www.BonnieHopkins.com
BonnieHopkins@Yahoo.com

First Edition: April 2015

ISBN: 978-0-9962644-0-2

Printed in the United States of America

dedication

To our Gracious Heavenly Father,
Who began this work and gives the grace to
Continue it,
All Glory, Honor and Praise to Your Name;
To the readers, book clubs, churches, retailers, and all
Who contributed, supported, prayed or assisted in any way,
To bring this book to fruition,
A gigantic, heartfelt 'THANK YOU'
And may God bless each of you!

note to readers

I am so delighted to bring you the third of four stories in my Riverwood series!

Although each story stands alone, you will gain a deeper insight and appreciation for the series and the Winslow cousins by reading each story –

Jaci, who journeyed through *'Seasons'* before finally realizing that God charts our course and controls all of our seasons;

Nita, who endured years of abuse and hardships before arriving at the *'Destiny'* God had prepared for her;

And now, walk with C.J., whose life falls apart in a matter of hours, causing her to endure countless struggles in her effort to reach *'Beyond The Break'* to a new beginning.

It is my hope and prayer that God will bless as you read these stories of deliverance, renewed hopes, and new beginnings, and that you will be entertained, encouraged, inspired, and most of all, that your faith in God will be increased as they point you to the Author and Finisher of life.

Blessings!

Bonnie

Prologue

THE BEAUTIFUL, SUNNY MORNING WHEN C.J. SINGLETON LEFT HER LARGE luxurious home located in a southwest suburban neighborhood of Houston, Texas, she had nothing more pressing on her mind than her regular Friday morning salon appointment, a little shopping, and running a few errands.

She had no idea it would be the last day she would share the home with her husband—former NBA player, Randy Singleton; no idea that it would only be the grace of God that would keep her from committing murder; and no idea that a chain of events was about to begin that would change the course of her life.

Surprise, devastation and burning anger engulfed her when she returned several hours later and stood in her bedroom doorway, gazing in shock at her husband, in her bed with another woman.

She snapped! And in hot-tempered 'C.J.' fashion, ran downstairs, expertly loaded her deer rifle, grabbed her camera, and headed back upstairs.

She took aim—first with the camera—capturing the engrossed couple who were unaware of her presence. Then she raised the rifle and started shooting. Finally . . . she had their attention.

Randy jumped up high and fast as though going for a basketball re-bound and yelled, "Woman, are you crazy?"

Without a word, C.J. took aim again, spraying bullets all around them.

Randy dropped, grabbed his head and screamed, "Oh, God, help!" while the hysterical woman beside him cowered, and tried to find a hiding place.

"So now you finally call on God!" C.J. said and shot again, then turned and left the room. Her twenty-year marriage was over—or was it?

Chapter One
Randy

RANDY CROUCHED AGAINST THE HEADBOARD, YELLING AS BULLETS whizzed past his head—one so close he felt the heat of it near his ear—and the woman in bed with him screamed and scrambled to the floor beside the bed, frantically searching for a place to hide.

After his wife stopped shooting and walked out of the room, Randy grabbed his pants and tossed an irritated look at the woman who was still screaming and crouched on the floor beside the bed. "Shut up, and get out of here before she comes back," he yelled, struggling to get into his pants.

"But what about the money?" she whimpered. "Remember, you promised to give me some money."

Randy threw some bills at her. "Now get out!" He rushed out of the room and down the stairs. A few minutes later the woman cautiously followed him down the stairs, grabbed the purse she'd left in the family room, and stuffed parts of her outfit into it, not caring that the clothes she wore were inside out. She ran to the door and took off barefoot with her shoes in her hand.

Randy, who was filled with rage, went looking for C.J. He found her in the office, calmly pulling files from the desk and packing them into a briefcase.

"Have you lost your doggone mind? You could have killed me!" He screamed at her. "Well, this is the end of the road for us. I'm not living with someone who is subject to blow my head off. You are getting your behind out of my house today."

C.J. rose and stood toe to toe with him. "And I won't tolerate a low down, dirty sucker like you who has sunk so low that you would bring another woman into our home and bed. How dare you do something like this, Randy! You're lucky I didn't shoot both of you."

Enraged, Randy angrily slapped her so hard she stumbled backward. Before she could regain her balance, he was on her again with a back-handed slap to the other side of her face, causing blood to spurt from her lips. His hands closed around her throat, choking her, as he snarled, "I'll tell you how I dare. This is my house and I'll do anything I want to do in it. You gon' find out that without me, you're going to starve 'cause you're not getting another cent from me. Now get out!"

With more strength than he expected, C.J. violently brought her fingernails down both sides of his face and neck. He groaned in pain and filled with rage, slapped her several more times. As he reached for her throat to continue to choke her, he heard her yelling. . .

"Help me, Lord! Oh God, please help me!"

Before he knew how it happened, she had grabbed a heavy figurine from the desk and sent a hard whack up side his head with such force that it stunned and knocked him to his knees. She then swung the figurine like a baseball bat, knocking him all the way to the floor. Before he could think about trying to get up, she swung again, delivering an excruciating blow to his groin. He screamed in pain, crawled away from her and somehow struggled to get to his feet determined to go after her again. But he stopped in his tracks when he realized the rifle was in her hands—aimed and ready to shoot.

"I told you to get out of my house!" he yelled, holding his head where she had struck the blow. "Now get out, or I will throw you out!"

"I have as much right here as you do," she answered. "But I'll leave because if I don't, one of us is going to die, especially if you hit me again. And you'd better be thanking God for keeping me from filling you with bullets right now, she said, keeping the gun pointed in his direction. I'll be out of here as soon as I get some of my things together. I'm leaving, but I'll be back to get the rest of my stuff."

Randy nervously eyed the gun. "Don't bother!" he snarled, as he backed closer to the door. Even in his drug-dazed mind, he knew he would be dead if she'd wanted to kill him. She was an expert shot. "What you leave here with today is all you're getting. Think about that the next time you want to shoot at me."

"Unh, unh, buddy-boy," C.J. responded hotly. "This house and everything in it is community property. I will be back, and I will bring the police with me if I have to, so don't even think about doing something stupid like destroying my stuff or trying to lock me out." She raised the rifle, said, "Come to think of it, I should go on and end this right now. With my face bruised and swollen like I know it is, I can claim self- defense for killing you today."

As she took aim with the gun, fear made Randy yell and run through the house to his man cave – his place of pride, filled with years of basketball trophies and paraphernalia from his years in the NBA. He slammed and locked the door, and slumped down on a sofa where he inspected his various wounds. He listened as C.J. made numerous trips to the garage. "Good riddance," he mumbled, arrogantly. "I'm sick and tired of her anyway, and might as well start the rest of my life without her constant nagging."

He jumped fearfully when she banged on the door and said, "I'll be back for the rest of my things and to discuss how we're going to settle everything."

"You're not getting another red cent of my money, you . . ." a string of derogatory words flew out of his mouth as he continued with, "Just get your behind out of my house."

He breathed a sigh of relief when he heard her SUV back out of the garage. The reality of what had happened hit when he considered how close he had just come to dying. *I'll make her regret all she did to me today!* He vowed.

Chapter Two

C.J.

As C.J. drove away from the house with as many of her belongings as she could get stuffed into her SUV, the thought of all she had left behind sickened her. But she was extremely thankful for her life. She trembled when she recalled the absolute rage on Randy's face as he attacked her. It was terrifying and sent several disturbing messages: The man was angry; the man was out of control; the man had lost his mind; the man would have no problem killing her. Somehow, she had not shown Randy the pure terror she'd felt while the fight was going on, but she'd been gripped by it, and in desperation, had cried out to God for help. "Praise You, Father, for delivering me," she mumbled through her swollen lips.

She wiped at the perspiration running down her swollen and bruised face despite the full force of the SUV's air conditioning. The above normal temperature coupled with the high humidity in Houston was bad enough, but the added trauma-induced heat brought on by the fight with Randy made her feel as though she was in a furnace.

She looked nervously in her rearview mirror, expecting to see flashing lights bearing down on her, thinking her neighbors had to have heard the gunfire and commotion coming from her house and called the law. *Nothing!* She sighed in relief.

But her relief was quickly replaced with gigantic problems. *Where am I going to go? What am I going to do?* Her frantic need to get out of the house had crowded out practicalities, but now, these critical questions brought distress and caused tears to fill her eyes and run down her face.

C.J. wiped at her eyes and glanced in the mirror again. *No flashing lights.* She aimlessly slipped in and out of traffic, finally inching over to the right lane when she saw the sign for the interchange from Highway 59 South to the 610 Loop. She took the Loop, still unsure where she was going. Too late she realized she should have taken 59 North and headed to her hometown of Riverwood, Arkansas, but she quickly nixed that thought—how could she show up in her home town with her face messed up like this?

She had taken the time to call Kyle Bingham for help in between her trips to load her things into the truck, but ended up leaving a message. Kyle was a former teammate of Randy's who had tried to talk to him about his lifestyle.

Now, she asked desperately, "What am I going to do, Lord?" Her cousin, Jaci, the obvious person to call for help, was knee deep in her own issues and didn't need any more on her plate. But she had to go somewhere, talk to somebody and regrettably, that meant Jaci.

Sweat and tears mingled and rolled down her face, obstructing her vision, and causing a flash of common sense to finally break through. It was difficult enough to keep from colliding with the crazy drivers on the freeway without the problem of not being able to see clearly. She worked her way over to the exit lane and got off the freeway, turned onto the first street she got to and whipped into a convenience store parking lot. The weight of her situation became so heavy that her silent tears became loud sobs. "Lord, why did I grab that gun? Why didn't I just get my things and leave? Shooting at Randy and that woman solved nothing, and look at where it got me."

A look in the mirror showed that her right eye was almost swollen shut, her face was badly bruised, and her lips were nearly twice their normal size. She lost track of how long she sat there crying and condemning herself before she dug into her purse, found her phone, and dialed her cousin's number.

"Jaci! Need help! Randy— big fight!" She choked out enough for Jaci to understand and ask, "Can you drive?"

When she walked into Jaci's house an hour later, her cousin gasped.

"C.J.! Oh my God! Do you need to go to the hospital?"

"No, I'm okay," she answered through painful lips.

Jaci ran and got her first aid kit and cleaned up her face, all the while fussing because C.J. hadn't called the police. "He needs to be in jail for this, Cij."

Later as they were sitting at Jaci's kitchen table with a cup of tea, Jaci frowningly looked at her face and said, "So tell me what happened? From the looks of your face it was a heck of a fight. I'd hate to see how Randy—" She suddenly stopped and gasped loudly. "Oh. My. God! Cij? Where is Randy? You didn't . . . shoot him, did you? I know you and that temper of yours and no way did you let him do this without retaliating. Oh Lord!"

C.J. took a sip of her tea, and as everything came crashing back into her mind, started crying again. She re-lived the trauma as she haltingly recounted everything to Jaci.

Randy

Randy rubbed at the areas that still throbbed painfully and hobbled to a mirror to see the damage his wife had done to his head and face. Big knots were forming on his head and he looked for some antiseptic to apply to the deep gouges she had left on his face and neck with her fingernails. "Dang! That woman whipped my behind!" he mumbled to himself.

He shook his head, trying to clear the lingering fog left by the alcohol and pills he'd consumed so he could deal with the horrendous fight between him and C.J. He sat down and tried to remember how it had all unfolded . . .

He had been in a bad mood when Willa Tisdale had called him shortly after C.J. left that morning.

"Hey, you big handsome rascal! You're home alone so why don't I come by and let's have some fun?" She asked in a merry voice.

Despite his foggy mind, Randy had vaguely wondered how she knew his wife was not there, but what the heck! With all that was going wrong in his life, he'd take his fun wherever he could get it, but he did make a weak effort. "Look, I'll meet you somewhere. My wife will probably be back before long."

"Hey, it won't bother me if it won't bother you," she smoothly replied. "If you've got some money, I've got some pills that'll have you feeling real good. You're going to love me."

So she came. They hit the liquor and took some of the pills she had brought and before long, Randy was so high he could hardly see and Willa was leading him up the stairs to the bedroom. It was definitely a horrifying moment when bullets started flying and he realized his wife was standing over them shooting.

Now he was wondering how he could've been so stupid. But maybe it was a good thing. C.J. was gone and good riddance—no more hassles from her—and he would make sure she suffered. He grabbed a bottle of scotch and headed upstairs to the bedroom—not the one his wife had shot up.

But his plan to get drunk again was short-lived. The doorbell rang and he loosed a string of not so nice words when he saw it was his friend, Kyle. Doggonit! C.J. must have called him. He considered not answering, but when Kyle kept ringing and knocking, Randy relented and opened the door.

Chapter Three

C.J.

I LET MY TEMPER GET THE BEST OF ME," C.J. CONFESSED AS SHE DABBED at the tears streaming down her bruised face. "But no, I didn't shoot him, Jaci, even though I did come close more than once. But look where it got me—beaten up and forced out of my home. Things have been bad but I just didn't see this coming!"

Jaci sighed. "Well don't be too hard on yourself," she consoled as she handed C.J. a box of Kleenex. "A lot of women wouldn't have missed with that rifle. That was despicable of Randy. Did he even apologize or show any signs of regret?"

"Are you kidding? He was too busy cussing and hitting me," C.J. answered, rubbing her tender face, which she knew would be black and blue with bruises the next day. Her shoulders shook as she sobbed. "Twenty years gone, Jaci! And look what I have to show for it," she said, pointing to her face.

She continued in a sad voice. "I don't know what I did, or didn't do to bring this on, but I must have failed somehow. And I can't understand the kind of woman who goes to another woman's house and gets into bed with her husband? I didn't think even Willa would sink that low."

Jaci looked shocked. "You mean you know this woman?" She shook her head at C.J.'s nod, then said, ". . . the most evil, low-life kind that should be shot! Unh, unh, Cij, don't even think you're in any way responsible for this."

C.J. nodded agreement to Jaci's words. "Willa was married to one of the other players on the team but he got rid of her when he found out what she was about. She's no more than thirty, really pretty, and has a reputation for going after money. If Randy had any sense he would realize she's only a gold digger and not interested in his old behind." She started crying again. "Lord, when I think of all I've endured with that man—only to have it come to this."

She covered her face and mumbled between sobs, "I have no idea what I'm going to do, Jaci. This is so . . . out of left field, that I'm just not ready to handle it." The brave front she had put up for Randy a few hours ago had crumbled.

Jaci hesitated before answering, then said, "You don't have to deal with it right now. Just be thankful you're out of there. I still think you should've called the police."

C.J. dabbed at the tears running down her face. "Well, to tell the truth, I was afraid they would arrest me for shooting at them, and I didn't want to go to jail."

"I doubt that," Jaci said, with a disgusted look. "The woman was trespassing, and as far as Randy is concerned, all they had to do was look at your face to conclude that it was self-defense."

In frustration, C.J. said, "All I could think about was getting out of there alive. I've endured humiliation and worse with his constant affairs and all the trouble he got into, but never imagined he would go crazy like this. We got married right out of college, just after Randy went to the pros, and he was never able to handle the instant fame, money and notoriety. He was into one mess after the other and when things got too hot he would run home to me, beg forgiveness and throw money at me while playing the role of loving husband until it was safe to resume that lifestyle."

Cleah's mind worked desperately. "I'll think of something. It's not like this is the first time. He found out about me being at a clinic in another city a couple of years ago and I talked my way out of that. I still don't know how he found out about that one."

"Well, really, Cleah, this is crazy. You should just go ahead and get your tubes tied? Then you wouldn't ever have to worry about this again."

"Trust me, I would do that, but the day may come when having a child could come in handy. Marc could get crazy and demand we have a child or else, and you know how the public is about people in politics. They want to see happy little families with fat little babies."

"Okay then, I'd say this is the time to make that a reality. So you better get Marc in the bed and get yourself pregnant, because otherwise this might be the end for y'all."

"Hmmm. Marc hasn't slept with me since he found me in a hotel room with that rich dude. Really, Marc can be so dense. I need that guy and others like him to finance my political treasure chest if I'm going to win that state senate seat next year. But you may have hit on something. I'll work on getting him into bed and getting pregnant. Being married to the chief of police can be very useful in numerous ways and being a glowing, pregnant little wife won't hurt either." She paused a second, then confidently said, "I've got this. I know just how I'm going to work it, and I'm sure I can coerce him into bed. He's like any man and won't know what hit him."

Her mouth fell open when Marc walked into the room with a furious look on his face. It was obvious he had overheard her conversation. He snatched the phone out of her hand and threw it across the room.

"Oh yeah, I'll definitely know what hit me, and there's no way I'm going to let you make a mockery of marriage and family or destroy everything I've worked so hard for, Cleah. Now you can put that in your treasure chest."

Cleah's mouth hung open as she watched him walk out again.

19

Chapter Five

Marc

MARC HAD WANTED A WIFE AND CHILDREN, AND A WARM, LOVING home for a long time. But all he had was a cold house, an unfaithful wife and no children. In addition to her infidelity, this made two abortions that he knew about, but there could have been more. Cleah's life was dominated by such a whirlwind of activities geared toward her political future that she forgot to take care of practical things like birth control. Easily obtained abortions were her answer to that. To Cleah, the end justified the means and it was time he faced the fact that she could potentially destroy both of them.

Marc's first inclination was to pack a bag and leave that night. But then his logical mind started working. He knew his very public position as police chief made him media fodder and he couldn't afford any negative publicity in his personal life. He needed to talk to someone he could trust and his sister and brother-in-law were the ones he went to. He sat in their family room for long minutes, releasing frustrated sighs and groans, but no words.

"Okay, what's wrong?" his sister, Roz, finally asked quietly. "You wouldn't be here sighing and groaning if something bad wasn't wrong."

him—and me— in the media, and that is interfering with me being able to hold on to a job. So I'm in a rough period."

Gina sighed. "I'm just wondering how you managed to put up with him so long. He's due for a good butt whipping and you know our cousins, Big Ben, Buddy and Dusty are anxious to give it to him. If Randy's smart, he'd better be watching his back."

After chuckling over the fact that their male cousins were indeed capable of hunting Randy down, C.J. exhaled heavily. "Yes, he needs a good whipping and he'll get it in God's own time and way. But you know what, Gina? I've been doing a lot of thinking about this. Maybe this is God's way of pushing me out of there."

"But He shouldn't have had to push you out. You couldn't have been happy dealing with Randy and all his mess."

C.J. was quiet for a moment. "Well, that's something I have to figure out for myself. I can't blame Randy if I didn't have sense enough to leave. I sure do hate to think I stayed just for the money and the comfortable lifestyle, but so far, those are the only reasons I've come up with and that's not saying a whole lot about who I am. It's not like I'm in the same kind of situation as Nita. I can understand why she stays there with Frank beating on her. I mean, he threatened to take her children and destroy her if she tries to leave."

"Well, don't be too hard on yourself. Sometimes we can just get stuck in a place that takes too much effort to get out of. But our loving God is all-wise and all powerful and all in control. He gave you the strength to stay there until it was in His plan for you to leave. It's strange how Randy suddenly went crazy like that. I mean he'd always run women, but he knew not to bring one into the house and he certainly never beat on you before. No, God's timing is always perfect and He's always in control. Grab your bible and read Isaiah 40:28-29."

C.J. picked up the bible that was always close by, looked up the scripture and read, *Have you not known, have you not heard? The everlasting God, the Lord, the Creator of the ends of the earth, faints not, neither is weary? There is no searching of His understanding. He gives power to the faint; and to them that have no might He increases strength."*

29

C.J. read it again, then said, "Gina, this hits it on the head. It gives me a whole different perspective. He did give me the strength to stay and when it was time to leave and I didn't have the sense to do it, He made Randy throw me out." They both cracked up laughing.

Gina finally stopped laughing and said, "That's not to say Randy's not due for some justice. So do you need anything to tide you over? I can send you some money, or a gun and a knife, or something to do that sucker in."

C.J. groaned. "No, girl! It was my deer rifle that got me into this fix. I'm okay for now. I just have to figure out a way to hold on to the next job I find. There's this one reporter in particular, who must be trying to make her career on the backs of professional athletes and their messy lifestyles. They must have some kind of tracker on me. And you know with this red hair and green eyes I'm not hard to find. As soon as I get a job, they show up with cameras, and there goes the job."

"Hmmm. Well, it may be time to take some drastic steps. Ditch everything that ties you to that creep and makes you easy to find—his name, your red hair and green eyes . . . everything. And there must be some legal steps you can take against those reporters."

"You know, that's a great idea. I'll start working on that immediately. And in the meantime, girl, keep sending up those prayers, please."

"Will do," Gina answered, cheerfully. "You know, sometimes it seems as though I can still hear Grammy praying for us, and I believe many of her prayers are still out there in the spirit, waiting for us to get our acts together so God can answer them. I don't know why we keep blowing it."

"Oh, Lord, Gina. I do remember her praying that God would send us godly husbands and give us the privilege to raise godly children. It would break her heart to see how we've blown it in one way or another. I really hate that."

"Just keep praying and trusting that God is already working to get us in the right place for it to happen. He's already doing it for Jaci, so hopefully, that means He'll do it for the rest of us. Look, I have to go, but let me know if you need anything, Cij. I mean that."

"I will. And thanks, Gina."

As soon as she hung up, C.J. started praying. "Heavenly Father, I need Your help and guidance in this situation." The first thing she did was call her attorney and asked for help with the reporters.

"I'll call the stations right now and let them know I'll take whatever legal action necessary to stop their stalking of you," the attorney said, hotly. "You should have informed me about this a long time ago."

Another call to Randy, pleading for a resolution only led to a fight and his reiterating that she would get nothing from him. *Forgiveness Lord.*

Chapter Eight

Randy

RANDY'S HOUSE WAS PARTY CENTRAL TWENTY-FOUR-SEVEN. FILLED with people—many he didn't even know. Drug raids became frequent occurrences during which the cops arrested everyone, including him. Even his parents were coming down hard on him.

"Randy, I'm tired of having to get you out of jail and tired of this whole mess you've made with your wife," his dad complained.

That rubbed Randy the wrong way. After all, they were using money he sent into their bank account every month. "Well, it's all C.J.'s fault. We could've worked it out if she hadn't tried to kill me."

"Randy, you know doggone well if C.J. had wanted to kill you, you'd be dead. That woman can shoot better than any man I know," his dad argued. "Now if you don't want to be married to her, you need to be man enough to do it the right way and stop all this foolishness. You're just about to worry me and your mother to death."

"Well, I don't like C.J., and never have," his mother stated heatedly. "I think she married you for the money she knew you were going to make and you should've gotten rid of her years ago. It's always been obvious to me that she was wrong for you."

Surprisingly, Randy was annoyed on C.J.'s behalf when he

remembered all C.J. had done for his parents over the years, including when they'd both been hurt in a car accident and C.J. had been the one to spend a month with them, nursing them back to health. He knew his mother didn't like his wife but it had always been his dad who tried to keep the peace between them—never Randy.

His mother continued her tirade against C.J. "I'm glad she's gone. What you did was wrong, but she had no right to shoot at you."

"Well, I bet she's sorry now," Randy said. "I didn't waste any time stopping her access to everything. I meant it when I told her she was not getting another cent from me," he boasted proudly.

"Son, you're crazy if you think it's going to be that easy. C.J. is nobody's fool," his dad stated. "She is not going to take this lying down. She's going to file for divorce and fight you for everything you've got and she's probably going to win because of your stupidity."

Curiously, Randy hadn't thought any further than making his wife suffer. It hadn't crossed his mind that she would fight him about the money, or that she would file for a divorce—which was why he was so upset a week later when the divorce papers were served.

Randy was furious when he stormed into his attorney's office and threw the document on his desk. "What is this supposed to mean?" he yelled.

The attorney perused the document a few minutes, then looked at him and said, "Your wife has filed for divorce and wants half of everything and she also wants living expenses until the divorce is settled. You need to tell me everything that happened and don't leave out anything."

In a prideful manner, Randy recanted all that happened the day of the break-up – even chuckling about it.

"Well, it sounds like your wife has a valid case," the attorney said.

"A valid case? For what?"

The attorney calmly said, "Basically, everything she's . . ."

"No way!" Randy interrupted him. "Hell will freeze over before she gets a penny! That woman tried to kill me." He shook his head. "Dang! I wasn't expecting this. She's just doing this because she's hurting for money. Besides, I don't want a divorce so she can forget that."

The attorney looked at him in astonishment. "Randy, let's get real. By your own admission you cheated on her by bringing another woman into her home; then, you beat her, put her out of her home and froze all financial resources against her. Based on these facts alone, I have to tell you, she could be asking for a lot more than half. My recommendation is that we offer her a settlement. You don't have to agree to half, but twenty years of marriage and community property laws dictate that she deserves a significant share. But understand that if you don't agree to a settlement now, she's going to place a restraining order on everything so that neither one of you will have access. And it sounds like she left with all the documentation she needs, so it won't do any good to try to hide anything."

"What! She can't do that can she?"

"Yes, she can, because she has the grounds to do it."

"Contest everything. She's not getting a dime and I'll fire your behind if you don't get her and that shyster lawyer of hers off my back. You're supposed to be finding a way for me to win, not telling me why I'm going to lose."

He missed the look of intimidation when the attorney noted who the opposing attorney was. He had been defeated by her countless times and knew any tricks he might have pulled to assure a win for Randy would be to no avail. The woman knew them all and didn't play.

Randy walked out the door, an ugly expression on his face and even uglier thoughts. Dang! Nothing was going right for him.

He was disenchanted with how his life was going, and beginning to realize—much to his disgust—that his troubles had only increased since C.J. had left. He'd discovered he didn't like having to fend for himself; he didn't like having to figure out all the things that had to be done to keep the big house functional and the finances in order. His clothes were in disarray—dirty most of the time—and as easy as it was to send them to the laundry, he didn't like doing it, because he then forgot they were there.

Unsure of what else to do, Randy grabbed a big chunk of money out of his account before C.J. could file her restraining order and disappeared.

C.J.

Because of the traveling C.J. had done with the team, her church attendance had been irregular, and when she was at home, there was always a hassle with Randy, because he didn't want her to go. But now, she not only attended weekly church services and bible study, she also joined the church's grief and loss counseling program. She was still having those ungodly thoughts about Randy, which she wanted to get past. If God gave her another chance to fulfill Grammy's prayers for a godly husband and a chance to raise children, she wanted to be ready. Anger and unforgiveness toward Randy was not the way to get ready.

C.J.'s desperation was growing. Randy had contested the divorce, refused to pay support, and disappeared. She watched her meager savings dwindle and increased her fervent prayer.

Thankfully, God came through. Jaci, along with her friend, Lena, who both worked for city government, managed to get C.J. an interview with the human resources director. Using Gina's suggestions, she used her maiden name, covered her red hair with a short black wig, and her large almond shaped green eyes with dark brown contacts and large framed glasses with plain glass lenses.

She explained her situation to the human resources director and filled out an employment application using her full name, Catherine Joy, with her maiden name, Stroman. A week later, she was offered a position as an administrative assistant and promised that information about her marriage would be placed in a sealed file with limited access and few others would know her entire story. She was fingerprinted and told that they would have to run a routine background investigation on her to assure she had no criminal record, and the head of the department she was assigned would have to be informed and approve everything. She was informed that it could take weeks or even months, depending on how quickly they processed her application.

Randy

Randy spent the next six or seven months roaming around the Caribbean islands and only returned after hearing that his dad was having health issues. He flew straight into Little Rock, Arkansas, where his parents lived and stayed a couple of weeks before heading home to Houston, where he found numerous things needing his attention. The utilities in the house had been turned off and there were posted violations of neighborhood and city ordinances. The house was a mess both inside and outside. Plus, the taxes were overdue and the insurance had lapsed.

These were things that C.J. had always taken care of and the accounts he had frozen against her had also stopped automatic payments she had set-up on everything else. But his biggest problem was the restraining order his wife had placed on all his accounts. He angrily called his attorney.

"Randy, you can't run from this. Your wife has one of the best divorce attorneys in the business and she's blocked every way we can win. The most pressing thing is to decide what you're going to do about the house. Do you know?"

"Heck no, do you? Just what am I paying you for?" Randy responded, nastily.

"Well, my advice is to sell it. Even after taking care of everything, you'll probably come out ahead, although it's going to be an IRS nightmare for you." He chuckled. "That's why they say it's cheaper to keep her."

"To heck with you, the house, and the IRS," Randy told him, and went out and leased a condo.

But before long Randy was running so low on money that he decided selling the house could keep him going until he could decide what to do about his wife. He still refused to pay her anything, and a disquieting thought crept in. *Maybe it was indeed cheaper to keep her.*

He grudgingly called his attorney. "Hey, look, is there any way I can sell the house and keep all the profit?"

"No. That house is community property and both of you have to sign off on the sale. By law she's entitled to half unless otherwise ordered by the courts, and honestly, I've worked all the magic I can for you. I suggest you offer her half."

"Dang!" was Randy's reply. "Okay, go ahead and tell that witch attorney of C.J.'s that she can go ahead and put the house on the market."

Randy resented the desperation he was feeling. Why should he be in this kind of financial crunch with all the money he had? Why couldn't he and C.J. simply go their separate ways and be done with it? He was quite happy to live as a "free" married man, who could have all the women he wanted without the hassle of a wife. But strangely, the thought of C.J. with another man didn't sit well with him.

Chapter Nine

C.J.

WAITING. WEEKS PASSED AND HER FRUSTRATION GREW AS THE waiting continued—waiting on the call about the job; waiting on the call that Randy was ready to agree to a divorce settlement, or at least pay her living expenses; waiting to move on with her life.

C.J. hated waiting, especially when she couldn't do anything about it. Thank goodness one of the principles she was learning in the counseling group was how to wait effectively. The secret was to remember who you were waiting on and trust His timing. Isaiah 40:31 was a favorite Scripture. *"They that wait on the Lord shall renew their strength. They shall mount up with wings as eagles; they shall run, and not be weary; and they shall walk, and not faint."*

Just when she thought she could wait no longer, she received a call from her attorney who stated that Randy had finally surfaced and wanted to put the house on the market. C.J. joyfully praised the Lord and lost no time in contacting Realtor, Jason Gilmore, who happened to be Jaci's finance.

But she had to fight to hang on to her joy when she and Jason went to check the house. Her mouth dropped open in shock when they saw the chaos. Randy had simply taken what he wanted and left the house in a mess. She made arrangements with Jason and Gilmore Realty to work things out with city and county governments regarding the taxes and violations and to have the house cleaned up and prepared to put on the market. They used the furniture Randy had left to stage it and make it attractive to potential buyers.

So another element was added to C.J.'s waiting mode. Not only was she waiting for the divorce or living expenses, and for the job to come through, but now, she waited for the house to sell. "Lord, I know You know what You're doing, and I know Your timing is perfect, but I sure do need some "suddenly" happenings!"

She started praying and meditating on another principle on waiting from Psalm 27:13-13. *"I would have fainted, unless I had believed to see the goodness of the Lord in the land of the living. Wait on the Lord; be of good courage, and he shall strengthen your heart. Wait, I say, on the Lord."*

She was meditating on that verse when Jaci's friend, Lena, called with a request.

"Hey, C.J., the State Conference of Municipal Attorneys is being hosted in Houston this year, and we need volunteers for the reception. You interested? It'll be a great opportunity for exposure and networking."

C.J. groaned inwardly. "I guess so," she answered reluctantly; it was the last thing she was in the mood for, but hopefully, something good would come from it.

The following Wednesday night, she donned her 'other' persona and arrived at the reception hall where she was assigned to work the registration table. While checking people in she noticed a name tag for someone from Texarkana. After registration closed, she strolled through the large reception room toward the food and drink tables. On the way, the wearer of the name tag from Texarkana, Texas caught her eye and she stopped to introduce herself.

"Hi, I'm Catherine Stroman, originally from Riverwood, Arkansas which is very near Texarkana."

"Hello, I'm Todd Fletcher and I know where Riverwood is."

The man seemed happy to meet someone from near his hometown

and soon they were involved in a lively debate about the twin city of Texarkana and which side of State Line Avenue that separated Texas from Arkansas had the most advantages.

C.J. was telling him about her dad, who had just bagged a large deer during deer hunting season. "I hate I missed it this year. I'm certain I would have gotten one or two myself," she was saying, when Todd looked over her shoulder and exclaimed, "Marc! I was hoping to see you here."

C.J. turned and her mouth literally fell open when she saw that the good looking guy standing there in full dress uniform, was none other than Chief of Police, Marcus Carrington.

"Excuse me," the Chief said. "I just wanted to say hello and welcome you to my city while I have the opportunity," the Chief responded to Todd, but his eyes and interest were on C.J.

"How's it going, Chief?" Todd said, giving the Chief a hearty handshake. "Now you know I wouldn't come to this city without finding my old law school classmate who I credit for helping me get through," he said. "Who knows, I might need your help again if I can't manage to leave this city without getting a ticket."

"Well, you know I will extend every courtesy, but I don't fix tickets, I only show you where to pay them," he answered with a smile. He turned to C.J. "By the way, I'm Marc Carrington, Chief of Police of this great city."

Another couple joined the group, more friends of Todd's, who began a new 'let's get caught up' conversation. "Excuse us, Chief," the new guy said. "We didn't mean to interrupt you, just wanted to holler at Todd."

"It's always good to see the great Bradshaws and hear about how things are going over at Connection Communications, but I don't know who this lovely lady is," the Chief said, looking at C.J. again. "What fair city do you hail from?"

C.J. smiled. "Right here in Houston. I'm Catherine Stroman," she said, smiling at the Chief and the Bradshaws and shaking their hands. "Wow! I can't believe I'm actually talking to the Chief of Police. I'm not familiar with Connection Communications, but it sounds intriguing."

"We are always happy to introduce our company to new people, but you can find information on the web also," Mrs. Bradshaw said, as she pressed a card into C.J.'s hand.

"Are you in the legal field?" the Chief asked, still looking at C.J. with interest.

"No, I just happen to be volunteering tonight."

"Ohhh? Who do you know in the legal department?" His eyes went to her bare fingers.

"Lena Hinton," C.J. answered, noting his attention to her hands.

"Yes, I know Lena. Good attorney."

She decided to move on so the group could get reacquainted. "Well, I was heading to the food table, so I'll move on so you all can catch up."

"I was headed that way too," the Chief said. "I came straight here from work so I could do with a little sustenance."

"Okay, that makes it unanimous," Todd added and fell into step with them. "You might as well follow us," he said to the Bradshaws. "It'll give us all time to catch up."

They all got plates and drinks and luckily found a table to sit down.

"Did I hear you say something about being a deer hunter?" Chief Carrington asked, looking at C.J. with a dubious look on his face.

"Absolutely," C.J. answered. "Have been since I was just a girl. I love sitting in that deer stand freezing my butt off, taking a bead on a deer and seeing him fall. There's been an overabundance of them the last few years and they cause so many accidents on the roads; otherwise, I would feel guilty about killing them. Unfortunately, that's the only way they can keep them under control."

"I can't believe a beautiful lady like you would even think about stomping through the woods to go hunting."

C.J. laughed. "Now see, that's where people go wrong, looking at someone and making judgments about who they are. You of all people should know better. I love to go hunting."

"Do you even know what it means to take a bead on something, or someone?"

C.J. squashed the thoughts that went directly to Randy and the woman who had most recently been in her rifle sight. "I would happily demonstrate if we were not in a room full of people."

The Chief bit into a piece of fruit before he asked, "So, what do you do when you're not volunteering, Ms. Stroman?"

"Please call me Catherine, and well, actually my life is in transition right now and I'm between jobs, but I manage to stay busy," she hedged.

"So, are you a friend of Lena's?"

"Yes," she stated without elaborating.

"I'm just wondering why I hadn't run into you before. Lena and I sometimes hang out with the same crowd." His eyes swept over her face again and lingered.

Was that interest she saw in this man's eyes? She thought with a sinking feeling, but answered, "Oh well, it happens like that sometimes. I guess—" She was interrupted by Mrs. Bradshaw.

"I'm sorry, but you do look familiar, Catherine. I'm sure we must have run into each other somewhere before. Did I hear you are between jobs? Where have you worked before?"

C.J. was saved from answering when a photographer started snapping pictures of them, which caused others nearby to rush toward them with cameras and cell phones and start snapping.

Oh no, this is not good, she thought. She hurriedly gathered her purse and the still full plate. "I suppose I must be in the company of some famous people since everyone wants to get pictures of you, so I'm going to get out of the way. It was nice meeting you all. Todd, maybe I'll look you up when I'm in the twin city area again."

Todd handed her a card. "I'll be disappointed if you don't."

Marc also handed her a card. "I'd like to continue our conversation. I want to hear more about your deer hunting experiences. Will you call me?"

"Yes and me too," Mrs. Bradshaw said. "I'd love to tell you about our company and if you're looking for a job, we're always looking for good people."

"Good night, everyone," C.J. said, over her shoulder, in a rush to get away from the cameras. She set her plate on a waiter's tray, found Lena and said goodnight then headed for the parking garage, thinking, *interesting night!*

Marc

For some reason, Catherine Stroman still lingered in his mind days after he had met her. He had enjoyed talking to her and had been disappointed when she'd left the reception so abruptly. He hated he didn't get her contact information, but at least he knew who he could get it from. He made the call.

"Lena, how are you? It's been a while since we talked."

"Hi, Chief Carrington, I'm fine and I'm wondering what I should attribute the pleasure of this call to today," she bantered.

"Well actually, I met a lady at the conference reception who told me you are a friend of hers. I gave her my card and asked her to call me, but unfortunately, I didn't get her contact information."

"Oh! So you want some intervention, I take it."

"Right. Her name is Catherine Stroman. Please say you'll help me."

Lena hesitated for a beat. "I'm sorry, Chief. The best I can do is pass the word that you're waiting on her call. It's up to C.J.—uh, I mean Catherine, to make that call."

"I know I'm probably getting ahead of the game and haven't given her enough time, but can you tell me if she's attached or in a relationship?"

"Nope. That too, must come from her. I'm sorry I can't be more helpful, but I hope you understand."

"Yes, I do. But thanks anyway."

He knew he wouldn't rest until he found out more about Catherine—like if she was married. She didn't wear a ring but these days that didn't mean anything.

It had been well over three years since his divorce. He had prayed, had some sessions with a counselor to make sure he was ready to be a husband again, and had quietly been searching for the right woman. He had been hopeful a few times, but strangely, they all fell through for some reason. Catherine Stroman stirred excitement in him and he was anxious to find out more about her.

Chapter Ten

C.J.

THANK GOD! TWO "SUDDENLY" BREAKTHROUGHS! INTERESTINGLY, the same day C.J. finally got the call to report to the personnel office to be processed for a job, she also received a call from Jason Gilmore telling her there was an offer on the house. When he told her how much it was, she almost jumped six feet into the air. "Yes, I accept! Let's do it as soon as possible."

Overjoyed, she called Lena and Jaci to let them know and to thank them for their help in getting the job and told them the good news about the house.

"I've been planning to call you," Lena told her. "I don't know what you did at that conference reception, but I've received no less than three calls about you. You really impressed some people."

"Like who?" C.J. asked curiously.

"Well, the Chief of Police, for one. He wants you to call him and told me to give you his number just in case you lost the card he gave you. And the Bradshaws, because you mentioned something about looking for a job, and Todd 'whatshisname,' the Assistant District Attorney from Texarkana, who was just basically asking questions about you. I think he's interested but just so you know, he's married."

C.J. smiled, thinking, *Something good did come from that night!* "Wow! Well it's certainly an ego booster to know people are interested. And if I hadn't heard from the city I'd be looking those Bradshaws up."

"Well, I would have called before now with that piece of information from them, but I checked with city personnel and found out they were processing you. I mean, you can still check them out, but you might have more stability and benefits with the city."

"So what exactly do they do? It seems they know just about everybody."

"They do. They own a community newspaper and at least two radio stations. They do a lot of business with the city, which is why they are at just about every city function. But why don't you go on their website and read about them. Who knows, they might come in handy later on."

"I'll do that, but I'm going for the position with the city because like you said, that sounds more stable."

She found out she would have a position in the Legal Department—probably Lena's doing—although not in the section where Lena worked. Thankfully, she was able to delay her start date until after the closing on the house.

It was a wonderful, victorious day when she received the check for her half from the sale of the house. The only negative cloud over the day was at the closing when Randy managed to catch her on the way out.

"C.J., wait; I need to talk to you!" Randy yelled, as she was leaving.

C.J. starred at her husband. This was their first face to face encounter since their break-up. She had expected a feeling of loss, a wave of loneliness from missing him, some kind of connection or link of familiarity, but it was almost like looking at a stranger. She fought off the sadness this caused. After all, they had lived together as man and wife for twenty years, had a baby together, and shared many peaks and valleys. Surely there should be something between them other than memories of the final traumatic events that led to the end of their marriage.

"Randy, we don't have anything to talk about unless you're going to tell me you're ready to finalize the divorce. I hope you realize I could've already legally forced the issue, but I decided to let God take care of everything."

"You're crazy! I'm not going to let you take half of what belongs to me. And why are you so gung-ho about a divorce anyway? I mean we've been together a long time. Why end it now?"

She looked at him in astonishment. "Randy, you ended it when brought that woman into our home, then beat the crap out of me, threw me out of our house and added insult to injury by freezing me out of all our accounts."

"That was *your* fault! If you hadn't shot at me, I never would've done that," he said, angrily.

"That's ridiculous, Randy! And you're lucky. A lot of women wouldn't have just shot *at* you."

"Well, you could have killed me," he grumbled.

"Yes, I could have if I had wanted to and since then I've often wished I had. It would have made life a lot simpler and easier for me. I've struggled for months to survive and you haven't given a rat's behind about whether I had food and shelter. That tells me a lot. I don't regret the struggle I've had, but you should, because you'll be in the same predicament soon unless you do right by me. So I'll send you a care package in prison because from what I've seen on the news, that's where you're going to eventually end up." She walked away with him spouting something about hell freezing over before she got anything from him.

C.J. praised God all the way to the bank. "Thank You, Heavenly Father! Thank You so much for answering my prayers for some things I've been waiting on. I have a job and no reporters will show up, and the house has been sold."

The day after the closing, she reported to her new job. She was careful to guard her identity, wearing the dark wig, brown contacts and glasses, and using her full maiden name. Other than extreme nosiness from her co-workers, she thought she was going to like her job.

47

The way things had happened all at once, she was overwhelmed—trying to learn her job and pack up everything in the house at the same time. But she refused to complain. God had blessed!

While the house had been on the market, C.J. had been looking at houses and dreaming of the day when she could move into her own place. So when Kyle's wife told her about a house that was for sale next door to Kyle's parents, she was reluctant to go see it, thinking it was probably more than she could afford. But when she saw it, she fell in love with the beautiful lakefront house.

Although it was larger than she wanted and more than she had planned to pay, the price was actually a bargain because ironically, it was being sold by a couple who was calling it quits and wanted a quick sale. She agonized, prayed, and wore out her dollar store calculator trying to figure out if she could get the house and still have enough left to live on if things didn't work out with the job. She finally decided to take the risk; after all, things would be resolved with Randy eventually—one way or another.

On the advice of her attorney, who reminded her she was still legally married to Randy, she made an agreement with Jason Gilmore to purchase the house in the name of his Real Estate Company to avoid confusion over community property laws. She would lease the house from him until she was free to purchase it.

She wasted no time hiring a moving company to make two moves—one from her small apartment and one from the storage facility where she had stored everything from the old house—to get everything moved into her new house. Even with what Randy had taken, there was still an over-abundance of furniture for the much smaller house. She and Jaci worked like crazy making the house livable. Her parents came to help a few days and her brother, Chuck, who had moved to Houston with his wife, Tara, a few months ago, came by for a few hours while they were there, but even after a couple of weeks, there were still boxes stacked up in most of the rooms, and the garage was filled with furniture and boxes waiting for her to find a place for them inside the house—or maybe someplace else.

But if she thought her plate was already full, she would soon find out it was about to overflow.

Randy

A few days after getting his money from the sale of the house, Randy decided to take a trip to Vegas. Maybe he would get lucky, win a lot of money, and be able to tell C.J. to take her restraining order and go take a hike. But before he left, he received a letter from IRS that almost spoiled his excitement. It was a huge bill for past due income taxes—another thing C.J. had always taken care of, and another reason he needed to win big in Vegas.

He started feeding the slot machines as soon as he landed. For a while things looked good. One day he would be on top, the next he'd be down, but overall, still coming out ahead. But then he was more down than up. He kept hitting the ATM account where he had stashed his house sale money, hoping things would turn in his favor, but his luck had changed, his money dwindled down, every credit card account was frozen, and he was nearly broke. He cashed out his return plane ticket, still hopeful that he would hit it big. That didn't happen. When he was down to his last few dollars, he went to a dive and ate, and ended up with food poisoning. He couldn't pay his hotel bill, couldn't get back home, and was sick as a dog.

He had been in tough spots like that before and a call to C.J. was all it took to rescue him. But this time, he ended up having to call his parents; otherwise, he was going to jail.

Instead of trusting him with the money, his parents paid the hotel bill and booked his flight to Little Rock.

It took several days at his parents' home to get over the effects of the food poisoning, but when he felt better he was ready to leave.

"Randy, is this the kind of thing C.J. had to put up with all these years?" his dad asked. "If so, I can't blame her for getting rid of your behind. Heck, she's got to be tired."

Randy chuckled. "Aw, C.J. is tough. She can handle it. And anyway, she was living the life of luxury, so she had to do something to earn her keep. Look, I need to get back to Houston. Can you get me a flight home?"

"No," his mother answered. "We're going to drive you back. As irresponsible as you are, who knows? You might not even have a place to stay, especially since C.J. is not looking out for you anymore. I'm starting to see that girl in a whole new light."

He hated to admit it but they were right. Between his losses in Vegas and the IRS bill, almost all the money from the sale of the house was gone. C.J.'s last words to him floated through his mind. He was almost in the same situation he had placed her in.

Chapter Eleven

C.J.

IT WAS SATURDAY MORNING TWO TOUGH WEEKS AFTER STARTING HER job and she had every intention of sleeping late before she started unpacking boxes.

She felt as though she'd just closed her eyes when an incessant noise penetrated her sleep. When she realized it was her doorbell, she turned over and mumbled, "Go away!" It really hadn't been that long since she'd gone to bed. She'd been up unpacking and trying to get things organized until well after midnight. She was in the process of separating what she would keep from what she would get rid of, which in some cases, was a hard decision. She struggled to get an eye open to look at the bedside clock. "Five o'clock!"

Her truck was parked outside in the driveway because she couldn't get it in the garage—an indication to the person now banging on her door that she was inside the house. The banging and ringing continued, and she groaned again. Apparently the persistent person wasn't going away. She struggled out of bed, stumbled over a pile of stuff she had left on the bedroom floor, and nearly tripped trying to get down the cluttered stairway. She snatched the door open without a thought to her safety. She dared anyone to mess with her.

"Hey, Sis, can we come in?" Her brother, Chuck, stood there holding a baby carrier and a baby bag.

"Chuck! What in the world are you doing here with the baby before the crack of dawn? Where's Tara? Don't tell me you're finally coming to help me at this hour."

"Nah, Sis, you know how it is. I just haven't been able to get over here."

"Well what are you doing here now?" She asked irritably.

"Uh, Tara's gone on an assignment, and I got called in for a flight this morning. So, I need to leave the baby with you."

"Oh no, you're not! Look around, do you see all the work I have to get done in this house. And I have a job now. I'm sorry, but you're going to have to find someone else to keep him. And wait a minute, Chuck, this baby is only what . . . a month old? How could Tara go off and leave him?"

"No, he's six weeks, and well, you have to help me, I don't have anybody else."

"Big deal! So he's two whole weeks older than I thought, but like I said, I can't keep him, so goodbye." She tried to push him out the door.

He didn't budge. "I have to go to work, C.J.! Please, help me, I'm desperate."

She heard his desperation and sighed. "For how long, Chuck? When will y'all be back?"

"Just a couple of days. Please, Sis! I'm in a real bind and I have to get to the airport."

"Didn't y'all think about all this before you decided to have a baby? Didn't you realize you would have to make some adjustments?"

He groaned. "All I can say is it's just a bad situation." He placed the carrier and bag down on the floor and rushed out the door.

C.J. looked at the tiny, sleeping baby and shook her head. It had been nearly fifteen years since she had taken care of a baby. "Lord, help! Life just keeps dumping new stuff on me."

She picked up the carrier and bag, walked into the family room and sat down for ten minutes, feeling overwhelmed. She finally got up and moved slowly into the kitchen where she started a pot of coffee. While it was perking, she went through the baby bag which was so light it couldn't have been enough of anything in there for the two days Chuck had said he would be gone. What she found was a half-full bottle of milk and a six pack of readymade formula, a small package of pampers and a onesie. There wasn't even a blanket covering the baby or in the bag.

She wasn't a cussing woman, but right then she wished Chuck and Tara were there so she could give them a good cussing out.

The baby was starting to squirm and make whimpering noises. "Lord, I need help," she groaned, as she went into the kitchen and poured a cup of coffee. She took a few sips and looked at the clock. Not six o'clock yet—too early to call anybody with this kind of issue. "Hey, Geordi!" She said, as she went and picked the baby up from the carrier and hugged him. "It's just you and me, kid, so you need to understand that Auntie is way out of practice with this baby stuff."

She noticed the onesie he had on was dirty and wet and wanted to cuss again. She quickly stripped him, ran to the hallway bathroom and washed him down in warm water—the little rascal didn't smell like he'd had a bath lately—then grabbed the bag and ran upstairs, thankful she kept powder and Vaseline on hand. She rubbed Vaseline on his irritated little bottom and powdered him down, then dressed him in the other onesie.

Back downstairs, she took a few more sips of coffee, then pulled the bottle of milk out of the bag. From the way he guzzled it down, he was hungry. Before long he was sleeping again, and since she didn't have anywhere else to put him, she laid him back into the baby carrier.

She looked at the clock again. Six thirty. She sat down and tried to figure what to do. One thing she did know was that the baby would need more milk, diapers and clothes real soon. Could she manage a trip to the store with a newborn baby?

She waited until eight to call Jaci and ask for help. "Oh God!" C.J. said, shaking her head at the list of things Jaci was telling her she needed.

"Just hold off on some of that stuff and get the essentials for now," Jaci said. "I'll call my daughter. I'm sure she has plenty of extra baby stuff, and hopefully, Chuck will be back to get him when he promised."

It would have been comedy at its best for anyone watching as she struggled to get the baby carrier secured in the truck. She was sweating profusely and her head hurt from bumping it several times during the process. It was the same again when removing it and then replacing it once she had done her shopping. But she felt better knowing she had enough for him to eat and keep him dry.

Now though, she not only wanted to cuss the baby's parents out, she was also ready to strangle them when she thought of what the money she had spent had done to her tight budget.

Later that evening, when Jaci came by with her daughter to drop off some things for the baby, she said, "Oh, Lord, C.J., this is the last thing you need at this point."

C.J. held back tears of frustration. "I know. I just . . ." Her voice trailed off, because she didn't know what to say.

Jaci continued, "Since you have a job, you're going to need a babysitter or daycare if Chuck and them don't get back before Monday. And you'll have a problem getting him into a daycare without his birth certificate and medical record."

C.J.'s spirits sank and she grabbed her head with both hands. "I hadn't thought about that."

"Well, hopefully, it won't be an issue but it's something to keep in the back of your mind, just in case."

"I am going to kill Chuck and Tara," she exclaimed. "They need a baby like they need a hole in their heads."

"That's for sure." Jaci agreed. "Well, you know I'll do what I can to help you so don't let it get you down," Jaci said, before she left.

It wasn't long before Geordi was crying for a bottle and a diaper change. C.J. went to the bassinet that Jaci had brought and picked him up. She was exhausted, and wondered what to do about her own tears.

Chapter Twelve

Randy

BROKE AND UNABLE TO ACCESS THE ACCOUNTS THAT C.J. HAD put a restraining order on, desperation eventually won and Randy met with his attorney to finally work out the support payments he would be paying C.J. When the restraining order was removed and he had money, he was more than ready to party and decided to go to a sports bar he frequented.

He was sitting at a corner table having a drink and checking things out, when a woman walked up to the table and struck up a conversation. Randy was glad for the company, and turned on the charm, hoping it would lead to something more than talk. He was enjoying himself until someone else walked up to the table.

Willa. Randy groaned in frustration when he realized who it was. Of all the people in the city, why in the world would the one person who had caused him nothing but trouble be seeking him out?

"Thanks for the heads up, Courtney. I'll take it from here." The other woman got up to leave, and Willa said, "Oh, and Courtney, hang loose, I'll probably be calling you later on, and don't worry, you'll get paid well, okay?"

"Wait! Courtney!" Randy yelled. "Don't leave. I was enjoying our conversation." But the woman kept going.

"Well, well! Randy Singleton." Willa said. "You know, I should've filed charges against that wife of yours for shooting at me, but I decided to just let it go after I heard you threw her out. I've been seeing you in the news a lot, and wow, you've been busy."

"What do you want, Willa?" He asked in an unwelcome tone. "That lady and I were having a pleasant conversation. Why did you run her off? And my wife had every right to shoot you since you were trespassing, and just so you know, she missed on purpose." Randy knew he should have gotten up and left. After all the trouble this woman had caused, he should have been running. But since wise choices had never been his strong suit, he stayed, deciding to see where it would lead.

Not surprisingly, Willa had a stash of her little pills, and they partied all night, finally ending up at his condo. He was so high and out of it, he didn't even know when she left.

It shouldn't have come as a surprise when, still half stoned out of his mind, he was shaken from deep sleep as police officers stormed through the door of his condo the next day and arrested him. Willa had filed charges against him for assault and rape.

His first thought was, *why didn't I follow my mind and run from that woman?* He was handcuffed, thrown in the backseat of the police car and taken to jail. The next day he realized that the troubles he'd had before were nothing compared to what he had now. He was the headline in all the news sources, who showed a battered and bruised Willa appealing for justice as she repeatedly told of being brutally raped by him. He didn't think he'd done that, but when he recalled his violence against his wife when he'd taken those pills before, he couldn't be sure and was definitely worried.

His attorney wasn't encouraging. "Randy, needless to say, this rape case is serious. You could definitely end up in prison because this woman is not like your wife, who's been going easy on you. This woman is out for blood and obviously wants to get paid."

Randy didn't respond to what the attorney said. "Can you just get me out of here? I'm about to lose my mind."

"Yes, I can bail you out, but you can't pull anymore disappearing acts. You have to stay in town until this goes to trial."

Randy groaned. "Aww, man! My dad is having some health problems. You mean I can't even go see him until I can get out of this mess?"

"A mess of your own making, Randy," the attorney reminded. It was obvious the attorney was weary of dealing with him, despite the money he was making.

"That's your opinion," Randy angrily answered. "I did not rape or assault that woman. She's lying and trying to get some easy money."

"Well, to be honest, it is your word against hers, and with all the trouble you've been in lately, it looks pretty bad for you. You could do some time."

Randy broke out in a cold sweat and felt himself actually shaking. There was no C.J. to get him out of this mess, and he needed her more than he'd ever needed her. He wiped at the sweat running down his face with a shaky hand. "How soon can you arrange the bail and get me out of here?"

"It might take a day or two to get the paperwork through." The look on the attorney's face said he wasn't going to put forth the effort to rush anything.

As soon as Randy got a chance, he called C.J. and almost cried with relief when she answered. "C.J., do you know where I am? I'm in jail! You know I didn't rape Willa. You have to help me."

C.J. chuckled. "Of course I know where you are, Randy. It's all over the news. Didn't I tell you no good was coming your way? And you can expect more of the same. I suggest you talk to your attorney, who will in turn talk to mine. All I want to hear is that you're going to do the right and legal thing and agree to a divorce settlement. Otherwise, I'm really not interested in anything you have to say."

Randy cussed and said, "See, there you go. I don't want to hear that mess. I have to wait in line just to use the telephone in here. And another thing, I don't want a doggone divorce. I know you've been having a hard time making it, and I know I need you with me. So when I get out of here you better be ready to talk about getting things straightened out between us because—" He suddenly realized the line was dead. She had hung up on him. He felt like crying because he was starting to get the message. His wife wanted nothing to do with him.

Chapter Thirteen

C.J.

C.J. HAD BEEN WATCHING NEWS STORIES ALL WEEKEND ABOUT HOW a great talent like Randy Singleton had declined to the point that he would commit rape. She could only muster a faint bit of compassion for him.

Thankfully, her attorney had taken steps to prevent reporters from stalking her, otherwise, they would have tracked her down by now and would've been pushing cameras and microphones in her face. Lord, have mercy—her job! Panic hit until she gratefully remembered that no one on her job knew Randy was her husband— at least she hoped not.

Suddenly, she remembered something that had gotten lost in her mind. She ran and found her camera and looked at the pictures and recording of Randy and Willa in her bed. Thankful God had given her the presence of mind she needed that eventful day, she made a note to call her attorney. Hopefully, this was the leverage she needed for her divorce settlement.

But now, back to her immediate problem. It was Sunday afternoon and she was stressing over the fact that Chuck and his wife were not answering their phones. "Help me, Lord!"

Her neighbor, Ms. Maggie, came over to meet the baby. When she heard about C.J.'s potential babysitting dilemma, she offered to babysit the baby until C.J. could make other arrangements.

Ms. Maggie wrote her telephone number on a pad and said, "Now you just call me if you need me, C.J., I'll be happy to help you out."

C.J. called Kyle's wife as soon as the woman left and filled her in on the situation. "Ms. Maggie has offered to keep him but what do you think? I mean, I don't really know her."

"Oh, girl! Ms. Maggie is great. She kept my kids when they were little. I definitely recommend her."

She tried to reach her brother again with no success and finally called Ms. Maggie. "Thank you for your gracious offer to babysit the baby, and I would like to accept, if you're sure you still want to."

"Oh, baby, of course I'm sure. It'll give me something to do."

They agreed on the amount she would be paid, and although C.J. thought it was a little low, she didn't argue, but thanked her profusely. An answered prayer!

Two weeks later, there was still no word from Chuck or Tara. She was managing to get her and the baby out of the house and make it to work on time, but having to get up with the baby at night and work all day, had her functioning on sheer adrenaline.

Her encounter with Chief Carrington had long been pushed so far to the back of her mind that she had almost forgotten it. She had been on the job a little over a month, and it had been almost four months since she had met him. So she felt a jolt of surprise when he walked past her cubicle on his way to the Director's office. A little while later, C.J. was asked to deliver a file to the Director. She gave a brief nod of recognition to the Chief as she was doing so.

But after his meeting ended, he sought her out.

"Hello, Ms. Stroman, the deer hunter. Welcome. I see you managed to find a position with the city. Do you like working here?"

"It's a job, which I desperately need; so yes, I do like it," she said with a smile.

"Well, you're in a good department, so you should be okay. Do you still have the card I gave you?" he asked in a lower voice.

She looked embarrassed. "Yes, I probably have it."

He gave her a disappointing look, then said, "Those numbers still work, and I'd still appreciate a call."

C.J. lowered her eyes, but finally said, "I'm sorry, my life is really crazy right now."

His eyes softened and he looked concerned. "No, it's okay. I didn't mean to pressure you. Anyway, welcome to city government. Have you seen Lena and the Bradshaws lately?"

Before she could answer, Betty, one of the paralegals, and C.J.'s immediate supervisor, rushed over to C.J.'s cubicle when she saw him standing there. She looked at the strained expressions on their faces. "Chief, is everything alright? Can I help you with anything?"

"No thanks, I'm fine," he answered.

Betty tossed another quizzical look between them and said, "Well, I need Catherine's help on a project now, so if you'll excuse her I'd appreciate it."

"No problem. We were just making small talk about some mutual acquaintances."

Betty's eyes narrowed in curiosity again. "Oh, so you have mutual acquaintances? It's a small world isn't it?"

As soon as the Chief walked away, Betty didn't hesitate to ask, "So who do you know that the Chief knows?"

Wondering why she was so curious, C.J. said, "The Bradshaws. Why?"

Betty's curiosity was satisfied. "Oh, everybody in town knows the Bradshaws. That's their business, knowing people."

"So I've heard," C.J. said. "Now what did you need me to do?"

"I just realized I need to get some more information together. I'll buzz you when I'm ready. In the meantime, there's some filing that needs to be done, so why don't you take care of that."

"Ok." Although C.J. had already filed everything, she went into the file room anyway and started straightening out the files and praying.

"Lord, I need this job, at least until my finances get more stable, so help me get along with these people."

While she was busy working and talking to the Lord, Agnes, another co-worker came in. "So, where did you work before coming here, Catherine?"

"At a book store, but of course, the pay wasn't that good and I didn't have benefits. Why?"

"What did you do there? And didn't I see you at the Legal Conference reception?"

"Much like what I do here. Whatever I was told. And yes, you did see me at the reception. I volunteered that night."

"Who asked you to volunteer?" She was bursting with curiosity. "Someone you know who works here?"

"No, just a friend of someone I know. And since I didn't have anything to do that evening I said, why not?"

"Do you remember who it was?"

Nosey! "No, but why is that important anyway?"

"Are you married? Have children?"

Super nosey! "You know, I think I'll run to the ladies room while Betty gets my next project ready. I'll talk to you later." She walked away praying, "Lord, help me deal with this nosiness."

When she got back to her cubicle, she found an inter-office memo on her desk informing her she was required to attend a city-wide informational meeting being hosted by the mayor the next week. Citizens were invited to come and receive information about the services each department provided. She remembered being advised during orientation that she would have to attend after-hour meetings occasionally, and saw no problem with it then. But now, foremost in her mind was, *Oh Lord! I need a babysitter!*

Betty finally showed up an hour before it was time to leave with several legal briefs for her to work on. As tired as she was, C.J. worked her butt off to get them done.

That night, after she got Geordi ready for bed, she called both Chuck and Tara. She loved baby Geordi, but his parents needed to show up.

Her message to them was abrupt and to the point. "Chuck and Tara, I've had your baby way longer than the two days you asked me to care for him. I have to work, and therefore have to pay a babysitter. Plus, I have to feed, clothe and buy diapers for him. I can't get him into a daycare because I don't have his birth certificate or his medical records, nor can I get medical care for him if he gets sick because I don't have the authorization to do so. I will not keep waiting on you. If I don't hear from you very soon, I'll have no choice but to call Child Protective Services and report him as an abandoned child because I can't continue to keep him under these circumstances. Bye."

Chapter Fourteen
Marc

PEOPLE WOULD NEVER GUESS HOW MUCH MARC DREADED GOING to that community meeting that night—a clear indication that it was time for a change.

He caught sight of Catherine Stroman handing out pamphlets about the functions of the Legal Department soon after he arrived. Later, when he saw her talking with members of a civic group, Marc walked up and joined them. Feeling honored to have him join them, the members of the group smiled and thanked him for the good job he was doing.

Mr. Clem Washington said with a wide grin, "Chief, this lady was just telling us that she's a new employee with the city in the Legal Department. I'm glad I know someone else in that department I can call when I have a question about something. She was just saying she might not know the answer, but would get it for me. I like that."

Not to be outdone, Cy Ratner put in, "Yeah, but she also said, she's a country girl. And that's what country girls do."

Marc looked down at Catherine and grinned. "Well, I'm happy we have that kind of employee working for the city. Catherine, I'll have to find out if you're violating any of our hunting laws in the city." He winked at the private joke they shared.

The president of the group's organization rushed up and said, "Excuse us, Chief, but we have a possible sponsor for one of our neighborhood projects." He gestured urgently and said, "Come on, folks, we can't miss this opportunity. We'll catch you later, Chief."

They left him and Catherine standing there looking at each other, totally unaware of the attention they were drawing or the pictures being taken of them. "It's good to see you again," he said with a smile. "So, should I stop hoping to get that call?"

She looked at him with regret. "Well, actually, I have a lot going on in my personal life right now so that may not be a bad idea."

His hope crashed and was replaced with disappointment. He wanted to ask her to explain, but thought better of it and said, "So tell me about your hunting. How often do you go? Do you go back to Arkansas to hunt?"

"Yes, most of the time." She described her small community of Riverwood, and how her dad, grandfather and cousins all loved to hunt and fish. She, unlike her female cousins, loved to tag along with them.

"So you actually know how to take a bead and hit something?"

Catherine grinned. "Of course I do!"

"Demonstrate how you do it," he said, a dare flashing in his eyes.

"I would, but I've already explained it wouldn't be a good idea in a roomful of people."

He laughed. "I suppose you're right, but hopefully I'll get that demonstration sometime in the future, and I'm expecting bull's eye accuracy."

Before she could answer, Betty and Agnes swooped down on them. "Chief, how are you? We saw you standing here alone after those people from the Tenth Ward Civic Club left. Did you know they are about to change presidents?" Betty asked.

Standing here alone! Was Catherine invisible? He quickly hid the flash of irritation in his eyes and said, "Yes, I did, but it's all good. I've known the incoming president for years." He turned back to Catherine, wanting to continue their conversation.

But Agnes stepped between them and said, "Yeah, the new

president is a go-getter. He's coming in with a bang, with sponsors for projects already lined up."

Then Betty said, "Chief, you probably know this already, but I ran into your wife, Cleah, the other day. I'm helping with her campaign for state senator and it's looking real good for her. She would have been here tonight but had a fund-raising function." She threw a look in Catherine's direction, then stepped closer to Agnes, effectively shutting Catherine out of the group, and kept talking about how great it would be to have Cleah win.

Marc reluctantly watched when Catherine turned to walk away, and said, "We'll continue our conversation later, Catherine." She gave a little wave and walked away from them. He wanted to follow her but couldn't appear to be rude, even though he was thinking, *Man, these women are vicious.* No doubt, that interruption and deliberate exclusion of Catherine had been calculated to do just what it had done. He battled the irritation that filled him. Maybe he could have found a way to ask her about the personal issues she was dealing with and if they were the cause of her not calling him. But those women had stolen that opportunity.

C.J.

C.J. didn't want or need any more battles. When she walked away from the Chief and her co-workers, she headed toward the door to leave since she had fulfilled her duties. Someone called her name and when she saw it was Mrs. Bradshaw, she walked over to greet her. She was blown away when the woman said, "Those women are friends of Chief Carrington's ex-wife, that's why they're blocking."

"Oh, it's okay, Mrs. Bradshaw, good to see you. Good night." She continued her trek to the door, but the incident with the Chief and her co-workers left uneasiness in her spirit—on several levels.

It was obvious the Chief had more than a passing interest in her. Granted, he was a good-looking, intelligent man, who seemed to be nice enough, the little she knew about him. But she was still a married woman and the Chief could complicate matters for her very easily.

But what was up with her co-workers? She needed to pray, and like her pastor always said, "Don't just say you're going to pray, start praying! God is Omnipresent. There's no place you can be that He is not." So that's what she did.

"Gracious Master, I have an unsettled heart about many different things, but topping the list right now is Chief Carrington and my co-workers. I don't know what's going on, Father, but I sure do need You to take control and cause it to work for good and not for evil. Lord, I'm already fighting battles with Randy and Geordi's parents. I certainly don't want any battles on the job, but if they come, please be with me and give me the victory."

Her prayer continued until she reached home. She ran next door to get Geordi, then gratefully entered her home. She got Geordi into his bed, then undressed, showered and got herself ready to call it a night. It was only when she was going through the house making sure everything was locked up and the alarm was set that she noticed the message light blinking on her phone.

She was happy to see she had several calls. She listened to Chuck apologizing and promising everything she needed, including money, by the end of the week.

The next message was from her mother. "C.J., we talked to Chuck, and he told us what was going on. I know you're in a bad situation, but I sure hope you didn't mean what you said about calling those children protective people. Give Chuck a chance to do the right thing, and let us know if we can do anything to help out."

The last call was from Tara's mother. She had met Tara's mother when Geordi was born and she had come to help Tara several days.

C.J. was surprised as she listened to the woman's message. "This is Tara's mother, Lois Smith. I want to apologize, first for my daughter, and also for myself. My daughter is somewhere overseas. I'm ashamed for not calling to check on Geordi like I should have been doing. But when Tara told me what you said, I had to call and let you know I appreciate everything you're doing for my grandchild. Please call me back when you get a chance."

"Wow! I should have gotten angry enough to make that call a lot sooner. Funny how people will ride a free horse for as long as it will carry them. Well, I'm going to wait and see what's going to happen. Guess it's time to draw the line with Randy too."

Chapter Fifteen

Randy

RANDY WAS OUT OF JAIL, BUT STILL CONSIDERED HIMSELF IMPRISoned. He couldn't leave town, and he couldn't go anywhere in town because he was persona non grata since the story about him raping Willa had hit the news. It was embarrassing!

He felt like seven kinds of idiots and the possibility that he wouldn't be able to fix the mess scared him to death. He wanted . . . no, *needed* his wife back. He figured if they got back together it would help solve all his problems. But when he told C.J. all of this when she finally answered one of his calls, he didn't like what she said.

"Randy, for years we were obviously trying to row a boat with holes in the bottom. Sinking was inevitable. I have faced the fact that we are not meant to be together, that we want different things out of life, and to stay together will only lead to destruction. I don't want to kill anyone, Randy, but I can't promise that won't happen if I ever walked into my bedroom and found a woman in my bed with my husband again, or if my husband ever laid a hand on me again."

"Okay, I admit I was wrong to do that, but I promise that won't happen again."

"And how is this promise different from the others you've made over the years, Randy? You and I both know you'll promise anything to get yourself out of a jam and then it's back to business as usual."

He wiped at the sweat rolling down his face. "Okay, I lost my mind for a while when things started going wrong, and I just forgot everything good in my life. When you tried to point it out I just lashed out at you because I wasn't in my right mind. But this time apart has shown me how much I need you. We married each other and promised to be married until death. We've stuck it out this long, so why throw in the towel now?"

"Because I'm tired, Randy, and because you have apparently lost respect for me and for our marriage. Otherwise you would never have brought another woman into our home, and into our bedroom. There were six other rooms you could have used in the house, for goodness sake! No, that was your way, even sub-consciously, of calling it quits to our marriage."

"Why do you keep bringing that up? That's in the past . . . Forget it! We can make it from here if you would just forget all that. You can do whatever you want to do like always. Babe, we've had a good life."

"No, Randy, *you've* had a good life. We can't piece this back together because it's too frazzled and rotten. You want to go back to the way things were, and I can't accept them as they were. I don't believe God requires that of me. He knows how hard I tried to be a good wife to you. He's probably jumping up and down, and screaming at me saying, 'Don't you understand that man does not want a wife?' No, as you so violently told me, you don't want to be married to me any-more, so I'm giving you what you want. As far as I'm concerned, you have your freedom. Now sign the doggone divorce papers, Randy, and give me what you owe me. It's time for both of us to move on."

Randy cringed, squirmed and begged. "Baby, please, give us another chance." He wanted to promise he would never sleep with other women again and mean it, but the truth was, he wanted his wife—his security blanket, but he also wanted the freedom to live his life as he wanted—other women and all. But the day he had let that

floozy into his house and into his and C.J.'s bed was the day he had
totally lost his mind and told her through both action and word that
he didn't want to be her husband anymore. That was the day his mess
had caused a volcanic eruption in her that spilled over and almost
pushed her to commit murder.

"Randy, I could try to get beyond all the hateful things you've done
to me, but it's as simple as this—I dislike the person you've become.
You've always been weak, but you were never cruel and hateful, and
apparently, you like who you are now. I may have to ration food and
gas, and do without a lot of things I was accustomed to, but at least
I don't have to worry about you, what you are getting into, who and
what you're bringing into my home, and ultimately, into my bed. I
don't have to listen to your rants about it being your house and 'you
can do whatever you want in it, and if I don't like it I can leave.'
Having to suffer the humiliation of being beaten, thrown out of my
own house and shut out of our bank accounts killed everything I
ever felt for you, and any desire I had to stay in the marriage. Now, I
can go to my own house and enjoy sweet peace, the kind that money
can't buy."

"Then why are you trying to take half of my money?" Randy
asked, nastily. "Naw, that's just a bunch of hogwash."

"The fact is, I want what is lawfully and rightfully mine, and I also
want my freedom! There's nothing wrong with having both."

"So, you must've found some other dude to take care of you, huh?
Figures! Well, just remember that you're still my wife 'cause I'm not
signing no divorce papers and you got all you're going to get."

"I don't need anybody to take care of me because I'm perfectly
capable of taking care of myself. I just want what's mine. And I
wouldn't be too quick to say what you won't do. God is working.
Can't you see that?"

"Look! I need us together. We have too many years invested in this
marriage to throw it away. We can fix things, start over, and have a
good life together. I'm begging you to give us another chance."

"Fix it how, Randy? What has changed? I haven't seen any sign of remorse, or anything that indicates you're really sorry. You're sitting on millions of our money, if you haven't wasted it all, and I could be hungry right now, but you haven't even offered me a meal. That speaks volumes. It tells me you are nothing but a childish, selfish little boy who has no intention of growing up and behaving like a man. Well, I'm not playing mama to you anymore."

He felt his heart fall. Beside the fact that he desperately wanted his wife back because he missed her and needed her badly, his attorney's words echoed in his mind . . .

"Randy, you need to walk into that courtroom with your wife at your side, and get her to agree to testify that she saw this woman in your house and willingly in bed with her husband. That's your best defense to keep from going to jail."

The attorney had hesitated before he added, "C.J.'s attorney has dropped some hints that C.J. might have some evidence that might possibly help you with this case, but she'll provide it only if you agree to finalize the divorce settlement."

"What?!" Randy had yelled. "What has C.J. got? She'd better come up with it, because I ain't going to prison over that crazy woman." He sweated— hating the position he was in, then said, "okay, go ahead and get in touch with C.J.'s attorney, and let her know I might agree to her demands, but it better not be just a game she's running to get my money."

"Well, frankly, you're not going to have any money if you keep blowing it like you've been doing. In fact, I'm going to start billing you every month so I'll at least get some of what you owe me."

"Aw, man, I still got plenty of money." But he suddenly remembered something his friend Kyle had told him about how a leaking bucket that never got refilled would soon be empty. Kyle . . . he needed his friend.

"That may be," the attorney stated, "but this is not the time to play hardball with your wife."

"You just let me deal with my wife," Randy had said rudely, before hanging up.

Chapter Sixteen

Marc

TWO MONTHS HAD PASSED SINCE HE'D SEEN CATHERINE, AND during that time, he had put some thought into what happened with her coworkers. The fact that Cleah's name even came up in the conversation raised red flags and led him to do a little investigating. It dawned on him that every woman he had shown an interest in had inexplicably ended things with him. Now, he was wondering if they'd had a little help from his ex-wife. He recalled that Cleah often bragged that she had spies everywhere and the fact that Catherine's co-workers had made it a point to bring Cleah up in front of her stirred his suspicions that they might be among them. He got in touch with a couple of his former girlfriends and found out he was on the right track. His ex-wife definitely had her nose stuck in his business.

He had a task force meeting and luncheon with the director of the Legal Department and a citizens review group to discuss pending police cases that had been referred to the Legal Department. The director had promised lunch.

One of the first people he saw when he walked into the conference room was Catherine. She stood at the back of the room with the director and several other employees. When a group of people came through the door pushing catering carts, she moved to greet them. To his surprise she hugged some of them and began to give them instructions on where to set up. He loved everything he had seen her wearing, but today, she looked wonderful in the tailored black trousers, black wide-collared blouse, and red blazer. She wore red heels and all of her accessories were black and red. She looked great, and he had to restrain himself to keep from going over to her.

The caterers were good. They unobtrusively served the tender, juicy barbecue brisket dinners without disturbing the meeting. And the meal was delicious. He was so busy trying to keep an eye on Catherine that he had trouble following the flow of the meeting. When the meeting was almost over a dessert cart was pushed into the room and he gestured for Catherine, but Betty saw him and hurried to his seat.

"Can I help you with anything, Chief?" she asked, with a smile.

"Would you ask Catherine to step over here a minute, please?" The expression that crossed Betty's face was priceless, but she did as he asked. When Catherine came, he said, "What kind of dessert do they have? Is it as good as everything else?"

She smiled. "Peach cobbler and pound cake. You can't go wrong with either of them. What would you like, Chief?"

"The cobbler, please. And thank you."

He was playing devil's advocate, but he was curious to see if his suspicions proved correct. He hung around after the meeting ended, talking to some of the citizens and posing with those who always wanted to take pictures with him. When he had a chance to speak with Catherine, he made sure the official photographer got pictures of them when he spoke to her in a low voice. "I haven't given up on my phone call. Do you need another card?"

She looked flustered. "No, I don't need another card," she said sharply and walked away to help the others get the room in order.

If Cleah and her spies were up to something, he would know soon because they would make sure she saw those pictures. He just hoped they wouldn't give Catherine too hard a time because she had told him she needed the job. Before he left, he heard the director talking to the caterers. "I'm planning a fifty-year anniversary for my parents. Do you all do event planning as well as catering?"

"We just cater, but check with C.J. — uh, Catherine. Trust me, she'll do a good job for you."

Marc grinned and told the Director, "If she agrees to do it, I would like an invitation. And I mean that."

"Marc, are you interested in Catherine?" he asked. "I've noticed you always seem to seek her out."

"Yes, I am. And that's all I'm going to say right now," he answered, still smiling.

C.J.

C.J. really wished Marc Carrington would stop seeking her out. She didn't need his attention for two critical reasons—one being there was nothing she could do to reciprocate, no matter how much she might want to, and the other being that her co-workers had more than a little interest in the attention he showed her, probably for the reason Mrs. Bradshaw had mentioned.

On the way home that evening, she thanked God for coming through for her in a special way. Earlier that week, Betty had approached her about taking the lead on planning the luncheon. She could tell the woman hoped she was going to blow it, and probably had another plan on standby. But she knew Jason Gilmore's friend who owned a restaurant and catering company, and had in fact, used them several times. She wasted no time in calling them, and thankfully, they were happy to do it. She spent a lot of time with them, planning the menu and explaining how she would like things done.

But she had other reasons to be grateful. Chuck had kept his promise and delivered Geordi's birth certificate, the name of a pediatrician, and some money. Sadly, Geordi was three months old and hadn't even started his shot regimen. Chuck also brought a statement he'd had drawn up by an attorney, giving her permission to act as Geordi's guardian in the absence of his parents.

When she tore into him, he apologized. "I'm really sorry, Sis. I know we've blown it, but there's a lot going on with me and Tara that I'm not ready to deal with, so I just took the coward's way out. The fact is, we're stuck with a baby that neither of us wants."

"Oh. Lord. Have. Mercy." Tears filled her eyes and ran down her face. She thought of all the times she had resented having to care for Geordi, when all this time, he had probably been in the only place where he was loved and cared for. "Well, how long is this situation supposed to last?"

He gave a frustrated sigh. "I don't know, C.J. I've told Tara we need to make a decision, but it hasn't happened. When she got your message about Geordi, all she said was, 'Whatever.' But she did call her mother and tell her what you said."

"I know. Her mother called me, and we've talked a few times since then. In fact I've emailed some pictures of Geordi to her. She really wants to see him."

"Yeah," Chuck stated. "She's been calling me too. Look, I know this is not fair to you, C.J., but I'm just hoping you can continue keeping him for now. I promise to kick in some money on a regular basis from now on."

"I'm glad to hear that, but you know I was never going to turn Geordi over to Child Protective Services. I just had to say something to shock you into action."

"But you were right. Geordi's not your child, although I have to admit, it seems like he's more yours than mine. I don't feel any kind of Daddy connection to him."

"Chuck, that's because you've never bonded with him. I bet if you started coming around more and spending time with him, that would change."

Chuck looked disinterested. "Maybe. I don't know."

"Well, my neighbor has been happy to keep him until other

arrangements can be made, but she does have other things to do. I'll probably have to put him in the church daycare center."

So between her job, Chuck's promise to kick in some money for Geordi's care, and the support money Randy was paying her, C.J.'s financial crisis had finally eased up. But she had no intention of leaving her job—yet.

It bothered her that the baby situation was so uncertain, because her long-term desire was to eventually get married and have a family. And she had to consider that her future husband, whoever it might be, may take exception to her raising someone else's child. For some reason thoughts of Marc Carrington's interest in her entered her mind and she wondered what his attitude about it would be.

Chapter Seventeen

Cleah

CLEAH FROWNED AS SHE PICKED UP THE COMMUNITY NEWSPAPER she made a habit of reading to keep up with what was going on in the community. "What the heck is this?" On the front page was a story about the Legal Conference held in Houston, and the benefits it had brought to the city in terms of the economy and exposure. But it was one particular picture that caught her attention. Along with the Bradshaws and a man she didn't know, was Marc and some woman looking at each other and laughing. Since she didn't know the woman, she assumed she was from out of town—until she picked up the stack of pictures on her desk that had been sent by one of her spies.

Her campaign was in full swing and from all indications she would be elected state senator. The only thing still incomplete in her plan was the situation with her husband. What he had probably forgotten was that she had people everywhere, watching everything and reporting to her. People who were as power hungry as she was, and dumb enough to believe she was going to repay them by giving them a high profile position on her senate staff. Whenever she heard about a woman he was showing interest in, she used various ways to quickly and discreetly get rid of the woman.

Cleah sorted through the pictures, found some of Marc and a woman—the same woman in the picture with him in the newspaper—who were looking at each other in a certain way. It was disturbing, and her instincts told her it was something to be nipped in the bud.

She picked up the phone and dialed the person who had sent the pictures to her—one of her spies in the Legal Department.

"Hi, Betty. I just received the pictures you sent me. Who is this woman in these pictures with the Chief?" She listened as Betty gave her a run down that ended with, "I know you said to keep you posted on anything out of the ordinary, and personally, I've never seen the Chief pay so much attention to a woman before. He seems to seek her out whenever they're in the same room."

Cleah felt the tips of her ears begin to burn. "How long has this been going on?"

Betty cleared her throat and said, "Well, as long as she's been here. A few months."

"So who is she? Where did she come from?" Cleah asked. "Did she transfer in from another department or is she a new hire?"

"A new hire. She's very secretive, and won't talk about herself much. All we've been able to gather is that she once worked at a bookstore."

"Hmmm. What's her full name? I'll find out more." She hung up after getting the information she needed from Betty, and sat there for a few minutes, fuming. No little fly-by-night clerk was going to mess up her plan to get her husband back. She had worked too hard to get to this point to have it messed up. Marc's presence in her life was important. He was a golden boy in the city now—liked and respected across most demographic lines. He'd been appointed Chief of Police four years ago, and his popularity had only grown. The buzz in political circles was that he was a person of interest to run for mayor in the next few years. That fit perfectly in her plans. She looked at the pictures again, thankful that one of her spies was on top of things. This Catherine person was definitely a threat. During their short marriage, Marc had never looked at her like that—*never*. This woman had to go.

She picked up the phone and called the director of Human Resources. "Hey, Oliver, how is the best department director in city government?" She schmoozed.

"Councilmember Fields, I'm doing fine. What can I do for you?"

"I need a gigantic favor, Oliver. Some discrepancies have come up regarding hiring practices. I'm specifically interested in your file for a person by the name of Catherine Stroman, hired as an administrative assistant in the Legal Department. I just have some questions about how she came to be hired."

"Okay, but have you spoken to Legal about this?"

"No, not until I've checked it out. You know I like to stay on top of things even when no one else is doing so."

"Yes, well, I'll get that file over to you myself, but you know I'll have to notify the department head."

"Can't that wait? I don't want to stir up things if there's not a problem."

"My point exactly. I have to follow protocol."

"Darn," she mumbled, but said more clearly, "Good, Oliver. I certainly hope you'll be able to do this today," she smoothly issued the order wrapped up neatly in her friendly tone.

"Sure thing. I'll see you soon."

Her meeting with Oliver was extremely enlightening. She scrutinized the file on Catherine Stroman, but noticed it didn't reveal much. No husband. No children. Not much of a job history. Something didn't add up. Oliver reluctantly admitted there was confidential information about Catherine that was sealed, stating it was a quality of life issue and had nothing to do with her qualifications for the job. She recognized special treatment when she saw it.

After Oliver left, she felt the beginning of triumph. "Confidential my foot!" She called her assistant, Carl, to her office. "I need you to start digging into employee, Catherine Stroman's life. Her file is not telling everything, and I need to know what's missing. If it's hot

80

enough, we can make something big out of it, and I'll accomplish more than one victory—great media exposure which will not only help seal my election, but will also get this Catherine Stroman away from Marc, and I'll be closer to getting my husband back where he belongs."

After her assistant left, Cleah looked at the pictures of Marc and Catherine Stroman again, then leaned back in her high back chair, thinking *I've got to think carefully about how to proceed with this. But in the meantime, I'll harass this heifer and kick her behind away from my husband.*

Chapter Eighteen

Marc

MARC'S DISCONTENTMENT WAS GROWING. NOTHING HE COULD put his finger on specifically, but just a nagging sense that things were off in his life. A good case in point was his dread of attending community events and meetings. He had never felt that way before, but always had excitement for meeting people and hearing about what was going on in the city. But now, he was ready to be out of the spotlight and away from the ever present media, and people who were always watching and speculating on his every action and word. He wanted the freedom to live his personal life without the whole city tuning in.

But the main thing bothering him was the fact that he was lonely and wanted a wife. He wanted children before he got too old to enjoy them. It was time to start seriously thinking about his future.

While Marc was pondering these things, he got a call from Ryan Whitfield, the Director of the Legal Department. He groaned, immediately envisioning a police issue that had gotten to the Legal Department. He was wrong, but the issue hit right on top of what he had been thinking about and confirmed that it was time for him to make a move if he wanted a life without Cleah trying to manipulate it.

"Marc, I hope I'm not overreacting when it might be nothing. It seems small and inconsequential, but truthfully, it could blow up if we don't nip it in the bud now, and . . ."

Marc impatiently interrupted him. "Ryan, whatever it is, I'm sure between us we can handle it."

"Well, it involves Cleah." Ryan paused to let that sink in, then added, "and a woman who happens to be an employee in my department."

Marc felt a sick feeling in his stomach. "Tell me what's going on."

"I received a call from the personnel director. He had a meeting request from Cleah regarding city hiring practices, specifically as it relates to Catherine Stroman."

The sick feeling in Marc's stomach increased. "Oh my God! You just confirmed something I suspected was happening. Anyway, what is it Cleah is looking for?"

"Who Catherine is, her credentials, how she got hired, and her personal information. Basically, I think she's digging into Catherine's life to find a reason to let her go, and see if there's a way she can use this to benefit herself and her campaign. And since I am privileged to some confidential information about Catherine, I know if someone starts to dig into her life, they're going to find some things she doesn't want to go public. It has nothing to do with the job or her qualifications for the job."

Marc squirmed in his seat. "Well, can you share that information? Nothing illegal I hope."

"No, I prefer to keep it confidential, and of course it's nothing illegal. I will tell you it's of a domestic nature."

"That explains a lot about why she's so reluctant to talk about herself. I hate to admit it but I think this might indirectly be my fault. Darn! I hate for Cleah to mess with that woman! Catherine mentioned the first time we met that she needed a job."

"She's a great addition to my administrative staff, and I would hate to lose her. In fact, she's agreed to plan my parents' anniversary party for me."

"I hope you remember what I said about wanting an invitation," Marc threw in before continuing with the matter at hand. "Anyway, I would hate for her to lose her job over Cleah's mess, especially when I know I'm at the bottom of it. I suspected some time ago that Cleah actually has people spying and feeding her information about me and any woman I show interest in. For instance, a lady and I will be dating and things are going well, then all of a sudden, the woman breaks it off. I'm now convinced that Cleah is behind that. I know she's plotting and planning for us to get back together because she has some cockeyed notion that we can become a political power couple. It's not going to happen."

"So you think that's what this is about?"

"Hopefully, I'm wrong, but I have to confess that ever since I met Catherine at that Legal Conference, I've been showing her considerably more attention than I usually show to women employed by the city. She wasn't an employee when we met. Anyway . . . I've noticed some rudeness toward her by some of your other employees and I tested my suspicions using them. I think Cleah is acting on information they are feeding her. "

Ryan paused before saying, "I'll keep my eyes open on that. Although we haven't done anything wrong, you know any kind of investigation into hiring practices will provoke a media firestorm, and I don't need that. So what can we do?"

"I'll get with Oliver and see what else I can find out. If Cleah is planning to use Catherine to get media exposure for her campaign, and in the process, cause detriment to Catherine's job and her private life, I may have to deal with Cleah myself."

He called Oliver and got the whole scoop. Then he called Cleah and the conversation confirmed his suspicions about her intentions to target Catherine—all for her own selfish purposes.

His next call was to his mentor and old friend, Harry Beckman, now an independent investigator and consultant, who he could trust to handle things discreetly. Marc explained the situation.

As expected, when anything came up about Cleah, Harry exploded. "That's the one thing you've done that I didn't agree with. She's never brought you anything but trouble. It doesn't surprise me that she's still messing around with your life even though you divorced her years ago. I did just enough to shut her up during the divorce, but I'm going to dig deeper this time—unless you don't want me to."

"No," Marc said, "do what you need to do. It has to be done."

"Okay, good," Harry answered. "Just remember you might not like what I come up with."

Chapter Nineteen

C.J.

WHILE C.J. HAD BEEN GOING THROUGH HER SEASON OF TROUBLE, life had moved on for her cousins, Jaci and Nita, both of whom had experienced life-changing events. Jaci took the plunge, married Jason Gilmore, and much to everyone's surprise, was pregnant with twins after a few months. Nita's womanizing, abusive, husband, Frank died suddenly. And Nita later agreed with C.J.'s suggestion that she move from Dallas to Houston, resulting in shocking, surprising and joyous turns in her life.

C.J. was happy for her cousins, but wondered when her change was coming. However, her drama just kept coming. Case in point, a call she'd been expecting and dreading finally came . . .

"Hi, C.J., this is Lois, Tara's mother. Listen, Tara is finally back in the states and she's spending some time with me in D.C. and we were wondering if you would be willing to bring Geordi to us? Tara and Chuck will take care of your travel expenses, of course."

C.J. was slow to respond. "Well, I guess so, but I'll have to get back to you to let you all know when to make my flight plans though."

She called Nita to get her help planning the anniversary party. Her cousin had been successful in putting together a foundation for victims of domestic violence, so C.J. knew she was good at that kind of thing.

It was with mixed emotions that she prepared for the trip. A week later, on the morning of her flight, she was a nervous wreck—fearing the worst—that she was about to lose the baby she had grown to love. Jaci and her husband, Jason, took her to the airport. "Thank y'all so much," she told them. "I would have been hard pressed to carry Geordi and these bags by myself."

"Glad to do it," Jaci answered.

Normally, C.J. enjoyed people watching at airports, wondering where they were going, and why. But not today. Today, she hated the crowds and the reason she was there.

Jason carried the wriggling Geordi, whose dimpled smile was in place as usual. He giggled as Jason threw him into the air, and she could hardly believe the baby was almost six months old.

"C.J., why don't you tell those jerks to kiss off?" Jaci said, angrily. "Somebody needs to do it. And from where I'm sitting, you're the one to do it, since it's you and Geordi getting hurt in this mess."

"I can't, Jaci. He's their baby and I went into this with my eyes open."

"No, you got suckered into it because you didn't stop to consider the fact that you were dealing with some selfish, immature and irresponsible people. I would punch Chuck myself if I could get my hands on him right now. He's taking terrible advantage of you!"

"I'll be okay," C.J. said quietly.

"Look, you mentioned you wanted some gum to take on the plane. Why don't I run over to the concession stand and get you some. Do you need anything else?"

C.J. shook her head no. "I guess I'd better get in line and check in while you guys are here to watch Geordi."

Chapter Twenty

Marc

MARC LEFT THE CHECK-IN COUNTER AND STARTED WALKING through the airport terminal toward security, but a familiar looking man holding a fat little baby caught his attention. Marc walked over to him and said, "Aren't you Jason Gilmore?"

Jason smiled and said, "Yes, I am. How are you, Chief Carrington? Getting ready to do a little traveling?"

"Yes, unfortunately I am. No matter how I plan, it always comes up at the worse time. I planned this trip weeks ago, and now, I really don't have the time, but it's too late to cancel at this point although I sure did consider it."

"I certainly understand. I know you have all kinds of hot items to keep you busy here, with most of them needing your immediate attention. I've been following the story on your request for new patrol cars. Are the mayor and council still giving you a hard time about that?"

"You better believe it! I don't know what more I can do to make them understand that we can't catch crooks in old, broken down cars. Right now, the crooks are laughing at us while we're eating their dust."

Jason laughed. "Just give it a little time and make the most of it when the next high speed chase happens, and the officers are left in the dust. It's going to happen sooner or later, and then they'll be trying to wipe the egg off their faces, and pointing fingers at each other."

Marc nodded. "You know, I've been kind of praying for something like that to happen. That would certainly be better than trying to make my case on paper."

While they were talking, a woman walked over to them and said, "While C.J. is checking in, I'm going to run over to the concession stand to pick something up for her. Will you be alright with the baby?"

"Honey," Jason said in an urgent voice, "we've got to be leaving real soon or we're going to be late."

She gave him a look that said, 'I don't want to hear that now' and walked away.

They continued talking, which was fine with Marc since he was early, and had plenty of time to get through security and to his departure gate. He was glad to have someone to pass the time with.

A few minutes later, the woman came back. She looked at him and then to Jason with a look of expectation.

"Oh! I'm sorry, Chief, let me introduce my wife, Jaci. She'll be yelling at me all the way across town if I don't."

Marc's eyes settled on the good looking woman. Staring back at him were large, unusual, green eyes. *Beautiful eyes,* he thought. "Nice to meet you, Mrs. Gilmore," he said, extending his hand to her. "I had heard something about you all getting married a while back. My belated best wishes to you both."

"Thanks, Chief," they said in unison. Then Jaci said, "Chief, it's a real pleasure to meet you. You're doing an excellent job." She then turned back to her husband and said, "You know I never yell at you!" Causing them all to laugh.

"I appreciate that," Marc told her. "I need all the . . ." He stopped mid-sentence when another woman walked up, pulled Jaci aside, and started whispering something to her. She kept her face turned away from him, so Marc couldn't get a good look at her at first.

"C.J.!" Jason said. "Look who we found wandering around the place. Chief, I know you all alre—"

Jaci interrupted him and said, "C.J., here's your gum, and I got a couple of candy bars too, just in case you don't like what they serve on the plane."

The name C.J. rang a bell in Marc's excellent memory and his eyes focused on the woman they were calling C.J. Where had he heard that name before? Then he remembered it had been from Lena and the caterer—both in conjunction with Catherine. All kinds of dots started connecting in his mind when he got a better look at C.J.

He looked from one woman to the other, noticing how much alike they looked. "Are you two sisters?" he asked.

"Cousins," Jaci answered.

Marc was frowning and looking at C.J. with a puzzled look. He saw a woman with the same beautiful green eyes as her cousin, but with hair the color of a new copper penny, and a smooth honey complexion. But even without the large glasses, the different colored hair and eyes, and name that didn't fit, there was no doubt he knew her. This only added to the mystery of the woman he knew had something she wanted hidden; who even now had people digging into her life.

"Sweetheart!" Jason said to Jaci in an urgent tone. "We've got to go! Now!"

Jaci looked up at him, rolled her beautiful eyes and kept talking. "Now have you decided where you'll be staying? Just call me when you get settled and let me know how things are going, okay?"

Jason looked at Marc, drew an impatient breath and smilingly said, "Women! Can't do with them, and can't do without them . . . and don't want to try," he added as an afterthought.

Jaci leaned over and hugged C.J., took the baby from Jason and handed him to C.J. then turned to leave. She thought of something else to say but before she could speak, Jason grabbed her hand and pulled her away. "Call us, C.J. and keep the faith. We'll be praying. Nice to see you, Chief," he called over his shoulder.

C.J.

C.J.'s thoughts ran rampant. *I don't believe this! Of the millions of people in the city, she had to run into the Chief of Police, who knew her 'other' persona.* She looked around the room—anywhere but at him and shifted the baby in her arms. She had gone to such trouble to keep her job identity separate from her personal life. But all the extremes she had gone to were about to go down the tubes. She knew it as well as she knew the man standing there starring down at her with a puzzled look on his face knew who she was. He just didn't know all the pieces to the puzzle. Why hadn't she stuck with her plan and donned her disguise? That had been dumb, but she'd honestly thought she would be safe since she was headed out of town. She should have known better. *Help me, Lord!*

She saw recognition dawning on the Chief's face and knew questions were forming. It would be only a matter of seconds before he would expect some answers – answers she wasn't prepared to give.

Marc

When Jason Gilmore and his wife walked away without the baby he had assumed was theirs, Marc's puzzlement grew by leaps and bounds.

The woman standing in front of him was Catherine. The same woman he had been attracted to from the moment he'd first met her; the same woman whose name and appearance were different; the same woman whose life was now on the verge of disaster, because evidently Cleah had stumbled on to whatever was going on with her—case in point, according to Cleah, this woman had indicated on her application that she had no children. Cleah had picked up on the fact that something didn't add up and she was right, since there was a baby in Catherine's arms.

"Catherine, can you help me out here? What's with the subterfuge?"

"There's no subterfuge, Chief. I am Catherine Stroman." She bent down to pick up the baby bag, tried to get the strap of her purse on her shoulder and started walking off toward security.

He followed her. "You know the policeman in me loves to solve mysteries. And right now, I see a doozy," he said, with a smile.

She drew a deep breath and still not looking at him, said in a barely audible voice, "I can't discuss it now, Chief. It's a long story and I'm dealing with something else at the moment."

In his mind, he pulled up the Catherine he knew from work. Short black hair, (obviously a wig, although he hadn't noticed before) brown eyes (obviously contacts) hidden behind large framed glasses that covered most of her face, and always with a cordial smile.

As she rushed toward the line to go through security, Marc had no problem keeping pace with her. "Here, let me carry him. He looks like he's pretty heavy."

C.J. sighed heavily. "That's not necessary. Thanks anyway."

She stopped and adjusted her load, obviously waiting for him to leave, then made sure she got in a different line to go through security.

After he cleared security, Marc heard her ask one of the workers for a courtesy cart.

"I'll have to call one for you, ma'am," the worker told her. "It'll probably take about ten minutes or so."

C.J. said, "Okay, that's fine, I'll wait."

Marc reluctantly walked away, but questions continued ringing in his mind..

Chapter Twenty-One
C.J.

C.J. DREW A SIGH OF RELIEF, CERTAIN SHE WAS OFF THE HOOK FOR now, because surely they were going to different airlines. She got to her gate, found a seat, glanced around and froze. Darn it, she just couldn't be that unlucky! The Chief was sitting across the room from her. He stood, walked over to where she was sitting and sat beside her.

"I didn't know you had a child. But as a matter of fact, I don't know much about you at all except you're a deer hunter, because you haven't given me the chance to find out."

"No, I haven't, Chief, but there's a reason for that," she answered.

"What's going on here, Catherine? Why the masquerade?"

"Chief, can you please just leave it alone for now?"

"You'll have to answer now or answer later. Why not now?"

"Because like I told you, I'm dealing with other issues right now. Please try to understand."

Geordi was getting fretful and C.J. knew it was because he was getting hungry. She had deliberately waited until now to feed him, hoping that by the time they boarded the plane, he would be sleepy. She ignored the Chief as she searched through the large bag and pulled out the sealed container of food she had prepared for Geordi. Another hunt into the bag produced a small spoon, a large bib and baby wipes. When the baby saw the food, he started smacking his lips. He was always ready to eat. All the while she was feeding him, she could feel the Chief's eyes on her.

She realized he wouldn't be satisfied until he got the whole story. He'd already told her he wouldn't leave it alone. A flash of inspiration hit. Why go back to the job? She could survive without it. But somehow she knew that even if she did quit, this man wouldn't let it go. He would still demand to know why she had been disguising her identity. He might even go so far as to have her investigated. She felt herself go hot all over at the thought of the press possibly getting wind of it. *Oh God, I'm so weary.*

She considered everything as she fed the baby, hard pressed to put each spoonful of food into his open mouth fast enough to satisfy him. What if she did quit this job? She'd planned to leave as soon as the divorce was final anyway. But stubbornness rose up within her. *Not until I'm ready!* She was tired of running.

Marc

Marc watched Catherine—or C.J.—intently as she fed the baby and felt a rush of intense emotion and longing. If he could have special ordered a family, he knew this would be it.

He took in the red hair, the beautiful green eyes that were large and slightly slanted, the nose, mouth, high cheekbones, full lips, and appreciated how it all worked together to spell gorgeous.

He liked the conversations they'd had —always brief and always leaving him wanting more. As he thought about it, he recalled that she had never gone to the extremes that others did to capture his attention. It had always been he who sought her out. She avoided sharing personal information that revealed much. She was friendly and cordial, took care of her job, and tried not to call attention to herself. Now, he knew why.

As he observed her with the baby, he questioned his judgment. Why did he feel so comfortable and drawn to a woman obviously living a lie? And more importantly, why was he presently sitting there almost salivating over that woman?

"Where are you going?" Marc asked C.J. in a quiet voice.

"D.C."

A shiver of excitement ran through him. "We're probably on the same flight. When are you returning?"

"I'll be at work Monday," she answered, not looking up from feeding the baby.

"That's not what I asked you," he said, agitatedly. "When are you traveling back to Houston?"

"Look, I honestly don't know. I left my return flight open. I'm hoping I'll be able to come back tomorrow, but like I said, I can't give you a definite answer."

"I had no idea you were so testy and antagonistic. I've never seen this side of you before."

C.J. gave him a hard look. "Remember, I did ask you to leave me alone. Of course I have to conduct myself in a cordial way at work. But I'm on my own time now and I've made it clear that I'm in no mood for conversation. I think I have that right."

He couldn't argue that point. But there was also such a thing as courtesy and respect. Things he had come to expect from just about everyone he came into contact with, whether it was real or fake, he got it.

"Look, I apologize if I'm invading your personal space. I don't mean any harm. I just thought that if we happen to be traveling back at the same time, we could coordinate getting to the airport together because I urgently need to talk to you about something. Where are you staying?" He regretted it the minute the question was out of his mouth. "Forget it! Forget I asked, okay?" He held up a hand to ward off the tart answer he saw reflected in her face.

"Wait a minute!" she said. "According to my co-workers you are married, and I really don't appreciate a married man always trying to come on to me."

He shook his head. "I've been divorced for years. If I were married, I wouldn't be trying to come on to you."

She finished feeding the baby and gathered up her things. "Excuse me, we're going to visit the ladies room before we board."

She had a load, with the heavy baby, the heavy baby bag, and her large purse, but he didn't dare offer help. He knew she would say no.

He watched her walk across the room, enjoying the perfectly fitting slacks that hugged a beautiful body, and knowing he wouldn't rest until he found out what was going on with her.

Chapter Twenty-Two

C.J.

C.J. KNEW SHE WAS BEING RUDE, BUT WITH THE SITUATIONS SHE WAS in—somewhere between married and unmarried, and deviations in her appearance and personal information, which he might have already checked out in her personnel file—rudeness was the only way she could think of to keep him at arm's length for now. The man was obviously attracted to her, and disturbingly, she was also attracted to him. But at this point, anything between them that went beyond friendship was a no-no.

She deliberately dawdled in the restroom, killing time until she heard the call for her flight and for those traveling with small children. She gratefully hurried to the gate and down the ramp to the plane.

She was traveling first class. Since Chuck and Tara were paying, she insisted on traveling in comfort. They could easily afford it. She got herself and the baby settled in her window seat and watched the orchestrated activities taking place on the ground as they readied the plane for take-off.

She jumped in surprise when a voice said, "Now see. After all that rudeness, you're still stuck with me."

The Chief stood beside her seat, grinning.

"Darn!" she said, before she could stop herself.

"Oh my goodness. I've learned more about you today than I have since I met you, C.J."

Her mouth fell open when he calmly asked the person about to take the seat beside her if they could switch seats. When he sat down, she said, "My name is Catherine. C.J. is what my family and friends call me."

"What does the "J" stand for?"

She turned her head without answering to look out the window again, hoping she would wake up from what had to be a nightmare.

Geordi started struggling to get out of the seatbelt, and she searched through the bag and pulled out his bottle.

"He looks just like you. Can't be much of his father in the way he looks," Marc commented, watching as the baby grabbed the bottle, and start sucking greedily, snuggling against her chest for a comfortable spot.

"Yep, there is," was all she said.

"What's his name?"

"Geordan, but we call him Geordi, after a character on Star Trek that his dad loves.

The plane finally took off and as soon as Geordi fell asleep, she pulled a blanket out of her bag and covered him, found a comfortable position for herself and closed her eyes. Hopefully, the Chief would get the message and leave her alone.

Not surprisingly, she slept deeply. She was tired. The day before had been hectic. After working all day, she'd gone to a group counseling session at the church, then had been up most of the night packing and getting ready for the trip.

She woke up when she heard the request to fasten seat belts in preparation for landing. Thank God, Geordi had slept the entire flight.

It was her custom to wait until the mad rush to exit the plane was over. So she patiently remained in her seat as the scramble took place. She noticed the Chief wasn't moving either. "Oh heck!" she said to herself. She was hoping he would be on his merry way.

When the aisle cleared, she gathered her bags and prepared to get off.

Chief stood and reached for the baby. "I'll carry him and you get the bags," he said, handing her his leather briefcase.

"That's okay, I can handle it. I know you're probably in a hurry."

"Will you just give me the baby, C.J.? I'm simply trying to help you. Darn it, why are you so contrary?"

She sighed in frustration, placed the still sleeping baby in his arms, grabbed her things and his briefcase and without saying another word, led the way off the plane.

They walked through the terminal and down to the baggage claim area. She was praying Chuck and Tara would already be there to meet them. A quick search squashed those hopes, so after they gathered their luggage from the conveyor belt, she led the way to a section of chairs and turned to take the baby from him.

"Don't be in such a hurry," he said, carefully sitting down with the baby. "I'm enjoying this, and I'm in no hurry. Is someone meeting you?"

"Yes, supposed to be, anyway."

"I think I see my transportation headed this way and I'm sure he won't mind giving you a ride to wherever you're going."

She looked around and saw a man in a police uniform hurrying toward them. *Come on, Chuck and Tara,* she pleaded silently.

The man walked up to Marc. "Chief Carrington?" An inquiring look covered his face. "I thought I recognized you," he said, when the Chief nodded. "I'm here to take you to your hotel." He started gathering up all the bags. "They didn't tell me you were bringing your family with you. How are you, Mrs. Carrington? The little one is knocked out from the flight, I see."

Chuck and Tara walked up just in time to hear the officer's remarks. Puzzled expressions were beginning to form on their faces and she spoke up. "Oh no, we're just acquaintances of the Chief. Hey, y'all," she said to her family.

"Chief Carrington, this is my brother, Chuck, and his wife, Tara. This is Police Chief, Marcus Carrington," she said by way of introduction. The Chief stood up, juggling the baby on his shoulder, while reaching to shake hands with all three of the arrivals.

"I was just about to take them with me if you hadn't gotten here," he told Chuck.

Tara reached out her hands for Geordi. "Oh my goodness, he's really big."

As soon as she was holding the baby, he woke up and started crying. Sounds came from his bottom indicating a diaper change was probably needed.

C.J. held out the diaper bag to Tara. "He needs to be changed before we leave. Everything you need is in this bag, and there's a ladies room right up the walkway."

Tara was holding the baby away from her body like he was something foul. "Oh no! I don't change diapers, and certainly not nasty, stinky ones. You should have changed him as soon as you got off the plane anyway. And we're not having that screaming either, young man, so shut up. She almost threw him into C.J.'s arms."

"Be a little patient, Tara," C.J. said softly. "He's just a baby, and he doesn't know you, so give him a little time. I'll be right back," she said, before walking toward the bathroom. She was livid. But what could she expect from a woman who had walked off and left her six week old baby, and hadn't even cared enough to check on him in several months. She was tempted to grab her bags and get on a flight back to Houston with the baby.

She fully expected the Chief to be gone when she got back, but he was still standing there talking to Chuck.

"Well, are we ready?" Chuck asked, impatiently.

"I guess so, but what's the temperature?" C.J. asked. It had been chilly when they left Houston but she had checked the weather and found out it was much colder in D.C. She had dressed herself and the baby in layers but they might need something heavier.

"Oh, it's already below freezing." Chuck answered.

"I need to get some things out of that bag," she said, pointing to the larger piece of luggage. She opened the bag and pulled out her coat, and a hat and heavy blanket for Geordi. She handed her coat to Chuck to hold for her, then with the Chief's help, slid the wiggling baby into the zip up blanket and pulled the hat down on his head, tying it under his chin. Then she slid into her own coat and took the baby from him. "Thanks, Chief," she said quietly.

Tara and Chuck started arguing as soon as they left the airport. "How could you refuse to change your own baby?" He asked angrily.

"You know why, so don't ask stupid questions. And you were standing there, why didn't you take him and change him?"

Back and forth it went until C.J. said, "Look, just turn around and take us back to the airport. Apparently, you don't want or need this baby here."

"No, he needs to spend some time with my family, so he's staying," Tara responded hotly.

C.J.'s mouth dropped, and surely Tara felt the hole burning through the back of her head from the fiery look she was sending. She wanted to take one of her boots off and beat the woman over the head, but instead asked, "What family, Tara? And where has that family been for the six months of this baby's life?"

"Uh, my mother, for one, and the rest of my family too," Tara answered.

"Strange, that it was only after I threatened to contact the authorities about him being abandoned that you decided that."

Marc

Marc's curiosity was peaked as he watched the interchange between Catherine and her family. From the red spots on her face and the fire shooting from her emerald eyes, it was apparent she was angry and upset about something.

He had watched as they gathered up the bags to leave and inexplicably, had been reluctant to see them leave. He had pulled a card from his pocket and handed it to her. "Call me when you know what flight you're taking back. And I would feel a lot better if you would give me your number so I can call and check on you."

She'd grudgingly rattled off a number, which he'd immediately entered into his phone and said, "I'll check on you later, ok?" He'd watched uneasily as they left the terminal. Only then, did he start making small talk with the officer sent to pick him up, who stood to the side with Marc's own bag. But in addition to being extremely curious about what was going on with her in Houston, he now felt a strange protectiveness toward her and the baby here in D.C. because something definitely wasn't right about this situation.

His instincts told him Catherine might have deeper issues than those Cleah was already digging into. It wasn't just the fact that she was a city employee who had reason for subterfuge; it was also the fact that he wanted to pursue his personal interest in her, but couldn't afford to make any more stupid mistakes.

Chapter Twenty-Three
C.J.

IT WAS HARD TO LEAVE THE BABY WITH PEOPLE WHO WERE STRANGERS— although his mother and grandmother, and C.J. cried and worried about the baby all night, and then all the way home the next day.

She ignored the calls from the Chief and couldn't resist calling Tara's mother to check on the baby several times. On Monday, she threw herself into planning the anniversary party for her boss' parents. She and Nita had already found and booked the perfect venue, mailed the invitations, and worked with the caterer to plan the menu. Now, it was just a matter of putting together the decorations and the program, and tying up loose ends. Of course, it required working closely with her department director, which she knew stirred curiosity among her nosey coworkers.

The Chief and their D.C. encounter hung over her like a dark cloud. She knew to expect a call from him and it finally came at the end of the week. *Darn it! Why did she give him her number?*

"C.J.? And yes, I prefer to call you C.J.," he said, as he opened the conversation. "Look, we really need to talk."

"I know, Chief. You want an explanation and like I told you, it's a long story, but trust me, I haven't done anything criminal. I just have some things going on in my personal life that I feel demand this type of extreme action."

"I know there has to be a good reason, but there's something else going on that I believe ties into that. Can we talk personally?"

Dread filled her, but she said, "Do you want me to come to your office? I prefer not to do so in mine because there's no privacy."

"No, I prefer to do it away from work, because of the privacy issue. Would you mind if I came to your place?"

Yes, I would! She thought. But unfortunately, she saw that it made sense. Where could they meet in public without the possibility of running into people who knew them? And she certainly didn't want to go to his place. She sighed. "I suppose that's the best option if we have to do it."

"Is there anyone—husband, significant other—that would object to that? We need to do this pretty quickly, like today."

"No, there's no one, but is tomorrow okay? I know it's the weekend, but I'm tied up with a church function tonight." At his okay, she rattled off her address. She was disturbed about the comment Chief had made about there being another issue. Could the media or someone at work have discovered who she was?

That, plus her worry and concern over Geordi, contributed to a restless night. The next morning, still worried about the 'urgent' issue the Chief wanted to talk to her about, she decided to clean her house. Cleaning was always therapeutic for her. She vacuumed, dusted, cleaned mirrors, and mopped the floors. She was tired, but still unsettled, and decided to treat herself to a long, calming bubble bath. She ran her bath, pouring a generous portion of scented oil into the water and lit a candle of the same scent. Sinking into the hot aromatic suds was pure luxury. She laid her head back and closed her eyes, just wanting to simply enjoy. But her mind went back to the Chief and she started praying. "Lord, I'm trying to grow into the woman You want me to be. I know I blow it a lot, but the desire is in my heart. Please help me, Lord."

After getting out of the tub, she rubbed her entire body down with scented lotion. If she hadn't been expecting the Chief she would have slipped into a silk lounging outfit and relaxed with a good book. Instead, she slid on some comfortable pants and a top.

Her hair, which she had shampooed before her bath, was twisted and pinned up on the top of her head. She took the pins out, and started vigorously brushing it to speed the drying time. She really needed to get it cut, since the length was starting to interfere with the way her wig fit.

It was almost dry, falling in thick, red-hued waves around her face and she was getting ready to pull it back into a ponytail when she heard the doorbell ringing and smiled, knowing it was too early for the Chief, so it had to be Ms. Maggie from next door, who was missing Geordi almost as much as she was. She hurried down the stairs in bare feet and without looking through the peephole, pulled the door open.

Her smile quickly faded, and aggravation flashed across her face. Leaning against the doorjamb was none other than the Chief.

"You're early!"

Marc

Marc wanted to respond with a witty comeback to C.J.'s words, but he was too busy trying to catch his breath. He felt as if someone had punched him in the gut, knocking the wind out of him. Darn, she was beautiful! Her large green eyes pierced him like needles, and copper-toned hair spilled over her shoulders in wavy abundance, making him want to run his hands through it. She wore casual pants and a top that hugged her body snugly, showing off her full breasts, small waist and round curvy hips. How in the world did she manage to hide all this at work? He finally managed to say, "I realize I'm a little early, but may I come in?"

"I guess so, since you're here." She said resignedly, and motioned him through the door.

"We really do need to talk and I have a feeling it might take a while," he said, as he stepped through the door, waited while she relocked it, then followed her through the foyer, turned left and took two steps down into a beautifully decorated living room. *How in the world could this woman afford all this?* He wondered as he took in the obviously expensive décor.

He took a seat on the snow white sofa that was adjacent to a matching love seat. She took the love seat.

"Well?" She gave him a hard look. "I'm anxious to hear what you so urgently need to talk to me about."

He couldn't take his eyes off of her. He hated he was there to talk about unpleasantness, but he wouldn't trade this moment for anything. He struggled to control his haywire emotions and said, "You first. I need to know who you are and what's going on."

"I'm Catherine Joy Stroman. That's the truth."

He gestured impatiently. "You know what I mean. Explain why you come to the job looking like a totally different person than you do now. Why does your personnel file indicate you are divorced with no children, and why is there an investigation being conducted about deceptive information in your file?"

Her mouth fell open. "Oh no! Not again!"

"What do you mean, not again? I have to know what's going on, C.J." He spoke the last words forcefully and compellingly.

"Will it help if I resign? Personnel will have my resignation Monday morning. Will that resolve everything?"

He sat forward on the sofa, hands clasped between his knees. "No, resigning won't help anything at this point."

"What? Why?" she asked.

He explained about the situation with Cleah and what she was doing. "So you see, she has a deeper agenda, but you will be caught up in the middle of it, and whatever you've been hiding will all come out. And by the way, it's only a matter of time before I know anyway, because I'm conducting my own investigation. I just want to hear it from you."

106

Chapter Twenty-Four

C.J.

WHEN WOULD IT ALL END? C.J. GROANED IN FRUSTRATION AS she covered her face with both hands. "Oh, God! I really thought I was going to be okay this time."

"Well, maybe I can help if you'll tell me what you're dealing with."

"Chief, I can assure you that I've committed no crime. You know they did a thorough background investigation before I was hired, including being fingerprinted. If I were a criminal, don't you think it would have been discovered?"

"Tell me, C.J.," he insisted.

She sat there with her head down a few minutes, before she started talking. "Do you know who Randy Singleton is?"

"The basketball player? Of course I know who he is. Why?"

"He's my husband."

The shocked expression on his face would have been comical if she hadn't been so stressed out.

"Randy and I are separated and in the middle of a divorce. I need a job because Randy cut me off from our finances—credit cards and everything except some small, personal accounts. And because of Randy's constant brushes with the law, I've ended up losing jobs because the media's hunger for sensationalism always seeks to draw me into it without a thought to the effect it will have on my life."

Understanding was dawning on his face. "So that's why you asked Personnel and the Director of Legal to keep your marriage to him confidential?"

"Yes. I know it may seem extreme, but you have to understand that I was desperate and just trying to hide my identity from the press and hold on to a job."

"So, where do things stand between you and Randy now?" He had to ask that question for professional as well as personal reasons.

"Well, you know with all the trouble he's in lately, he's trying to get me to put everything behind us and go back to the way we were."

"Are you going to do it?"

"No! I have no intentions of doing that?"

"So what finally brought your marriage to the breaking point?" He asked. "I sense you're not telling me everything."

She looked at him and rolled her eyes. "You are certainly a cop, aren't you?"

He grinned. "Yes, twenty-four-seven, and as such, I always have to get the full story."

She described the dreadful day that marked the end of her marriage, ending with, "I could have killed both of them if I'd wanted to, but God was just with me and Randy knows he's very lucky." It dawned on her that she was sharing things with him that only certain people knew.

Marc laughed. "I'm sorry, I know it's not funny, but I wish I could have seen the looks on their faces when those bullets started flying." When he finally stopped laughing, he said, "So that's when he beat you up and threw you out?"

"Well, let me tell you, laughter was the last thing on any of our minds. The woman ran out of the house with most of her clothes in her hand, and the truth is, Randy and I beat each other up. I mean, I wasn't going to just stand there and let him beat on me without fighting back. So we both ended up with battle scars."

Marc went into another round of laughter. "I believe you. You don't have that red hair for nothing. So where does Geordi fit into the picture? Is Randy Geordi's father?"

"No, he's not, and that's a whole other reason why I need the j…'"
She was almost relieved when the telephone interrupted her, prompting
her to run toward the back of the house.

Marc

After C.J. ran to answer the phone, Marc looked around apprecia-
tively, again admiring the décor. The central colors in the living room
and what he could see of the formal dining room were black and
white, with splashes of vivid color thrown in. Even the framed art on
the walls was black and white. The effect was dramatic, but beautiful.

Eventually, a flash of irritation shot through him when he realized she
had been gone quite a while, and he took exception to her leaving him
sitting there alone while she talked on the phone. There was such a thing
as good manners. He stood and followed the sound of her voice coming
from the back of the house and ended up in a large family room.

The vibrant color that was missing in the front of the house
was abundantly evident in this room. The first thing that caught his
attention was the wall of windows that provided a breathtaking view
of a lake. The room itself boasted vivid colors of mauve, navy and
light blues. A mauve leather sectional sofa, with adjacent matching
recliners faced the fireplace that sat diagonally in one corner of the
room, with a big screen television above it. A navy blue area rug,
framed with wide insets of mauve and light blue covered the hard-
wood floor, colorful framed art and pillows of varying sizes echoing
the color scheme were scattered around the room. To the left was a
breakfast counter with barstools that separated the family room from
the kitchen, a door that led to what he guessed was the garage, and
French doors that led to a plant-filled sunroom and a covered deck
that overlooked the lake. His immediate response to the room was
soothing relaxation and comfort to his senses. He knew he could
spend a lot of time there and enjoy every second.

A toy box sat in another corner of the room, and several articles of baby clothes had been folded and left in one of the recliners.

C.J.'s voice rose and penetrated his preoccupation with the attractive room. She was perched on one of the bar stools and it sounded like she was arguing with someone.

Marc sat down and listened unashamedly, trying to piece together what was going on from her end of the conversation.

"How many times do I have to tell you? I can't do that." She listened a while to the person on the other end. "Look, I don't know what else I can tell you. As much as I would like to, I can't come and get him because his parents left him in your care. I just wish I could kick their behinds."

She swiveled around on the barstool and gave Marc a dirty look before turning her back to him. "I'll call you if I hear from them and you do the same for me, okay?" She slowly placed the cordless phone back into the stand and rubbed her hands over her face in frustration before saying, "Look, I'm sure you've realized I'm in the midst of some family business, and I really would appreciate it if you would leave now."

He nodded. "Yeah, so I gathered. But I can't leave without asking, is Geordi your child, and not Randy's? Is that the other story?"

She shook her head. "Geordi is my nephew, my brother, Chuck and his wife's baby, but I've had him almost from birth."

He looked perplexed. "Why? They looked pretty healthy to me."

"They are, but neither one is ready to be a parent."

He stood to leave, but said, "I could tell she's not exactly maternal. So how did you end up with him?"

She walked ahead of him toward the door. "Chuck dropped him off one day and never came back to get him."

"What?" He definitely wanted to hear that story, but he followed her back through the house, where she unlocked the door and stood aside as he stepped out.

"Is there anything I can do to help you?"

"No." She shook her head.

"I'll check on you later," he promised. "And let me know if you think of anything. I do want to help."

110

Chapter Twenty-Five

Cleah

FIRST THING MONDAY MORNING, CLEAH RECEIVED CALLS FROM THE heads of three departments—personnel, legal and police—all requesting that she back off and leave the Stroman woman alone. She gave a vague promise to think about it, but her curiosity only increased. Who was this woman? And why were they trying to protect her? The unknown answers made her more determined to find out. Another bit of information that further incited her was that someone had spotted Marc and a woman with red hair and a baby in the airport together and getting on the same plane. Her suspicious mind made her wonder if this could also be the Stroman woman and prompted her to find out. She looked up Catherine's extension and dialed it.

"This is Catherine. May I help you?"

"Yes, you can, Catherine. This is Councilwoman Cleah Fields, and you can tell me what's going on between you and my husband."

"Excuse me! I'm sorry, but I don't know what you're talking about. I don't even know your husband."

"Yes, you do. I'm looking at pictures of you two together right now. My husband is Marcus Carrington—Police Chief, Marcus Carrington."

"Ohhh! Chief Carrington. We're merely acquaintances."

"Lying won't help you! Where did you work before your employment with the city, Catherine? How did you meet my husband? Exactly why are you working here?"

"Wait just a minute! I have no reason to lie, and I don't see where any of that is your business. I met all qualifications for this job and I have no responsibility to you in any way."

Cleah didn't like the woman's attitude. She didn't sound intimidated at all as most employees would have been. "I have a right to question the background of any person employed by the city."

"Well, I can assure you there's nothing earth shattering there. I'm just a person trying to make a living. Is there anything else, Ms. Fields?"

"Yes. You'd better start looking for another job because your employment with the city is over. And in the meantime, you'd better stay out of my husband's face."

"You didn't hire me, Ms. Fields, and you can't fire me. Also, I suggest you take any other issue up with the Chief."

Cleah's temper rose. "Who do you think you're talking to? You're nothing but a dumb little clerk trying to get your claws into a prominent man. I know exactly what I need to do and that is to get your behind away from this job and away from my husband. And I will do just that."

"And why is that so important to you, Ms. Fields?" Catherine asked boldly.

Cleah hung up with an ugly expression covering her face. "I'll show that cow who she's messing with," she mumbled, picking up the pictures again and noticing the wide smile covering Marc's face as he looked at Catherine. This was unusual. Marc was always careful not to stir speculation, even though there was always something stirring about him.

She winced inwardly, as the painful reality that it had been she who had destroyed their marriage hit her. She had learned a valuable lesson about being careless —not about ceasing with the behavior.

They had now been divorced longer than they were married, and that was unacceptable at this point. She was about to lose her council position due to term limitations, but that seat in the senate was nearly in the bag if she played it right. She needed a husband to validate her stance on family issues. And who better than Marcus, who, if things went as planned, was a future mayor of Houston. Getting her husband back was paramount, and she would use every trick in the book to do that. That meant she had to keep Catherine Stroman—and any other woman—away from him.

Chapter Twenty-Six

Randy

RANDY HAD LOST COUNT OF HOW MANY TIMES HE'D WANTED TO KICK himself for his stupidity. He was miserable as he roamed around his condo, which was too small for the roaming he needed to do. But he was reluctant to leave unless it was absolutely necessary because of the ugly, disapproving looks he received from those who recognized him. He was tempted to get drunk again, but was trying hard to cut back on the stuff because he was headed to being an alcoholic.

He could barely stand to think about how much his life had changed since he'd acted crazy and put his wife out. He wasn't a crying man but he actually wanted to cry because C.J. refused to even talk about them getting back together so there was little hope of that happening, even though he was far from giving up.

He was hungry, and tired of pizza and other fast foods he could get delivered. How he wished for one of his wife's home cooked meals.

As he was agonizing over the mess he'd made of his life and thinking things couldn't get any worse, his phone rang and he groaned when he saw it was his parents' number. Although he wasn't in the mood to talk to them, he answered, since it could be news about the health tests his dad had been going through.

"Son?" His mother said, then continued without giving him a chance to respond. "Son, we got some bad news about your dad today. The doctors confirmed that he has cancer. They are recommending that he go to that M.D. Anderson hospital in Houston, and are making arrangements to get him in there as soon as possible. I guess that's a good thing since you're there. I wish you could fly up here and drive us there."

Randy sat in stunned silence. Things had just gotten worse, and the tears he'd been holding slid down his face. His dad was his hero, mentor and leaning post. He couldn't bear to think about life without him. "Mom, you know I can't leave the city because of the trouble I'm in," he choked out.

"Well, get C.J. to come. Surely she'll do that regardless of the situation."

"No, she won't. She won't even talk to me. I've really torn things with her."

"Now, see, if y'all had some kids she wouldn't be acting so crazy. I told you after that baby died that y'all should have had another child as soon as you could. And you certainly should have had some more over the years. You should have insisted on that, but now with her being footloose like she is, no telling what she's getting ready to do. She was always too independent for my taste, even though my appreciation for her has increased since we've had to deal with you and all your mess."

Randy stayed quiet. No way would he admit he was at fault for them not having any children. "Why don't y'all just catch a flight here, mom? It'll be much faster."

"I guess you're right. But I'm telling you right now that I don't intend to stay in a hotel. We'll either stay with you, or with C.J. Surely she won't refuse that. Where is she staying anyway?"

"I think she got a house but I don't know where or how big it is."

"Well, why don't you ask her? Or I'll ask her myself. What's her number?"

"She still has the same number, but she won't even answer the phone most of the time when I call, and she might not say no to you like she will with me."

"Well, I'm going to call and ask her. I just don't think we'll be comfortable at your place, especially with you gone half the time."

"Okay, mom. Just keep me posted." He hung up and slumped in his chair. As he thought more about it, he decided it was probably a good thing if his parents stayed with C.J. It would give him a chance to convince her they needed to get back together. Not only did he need her, but now his parents did too.

Chapter Twenty-Seven
C.J.

C.J.'S MIND RACED FROM ONE THING TO ANOTHER AS SHE TOOK care of last minute items for the anniversary party. The threatening telephone call from Cleah Fields, the visit from the Chief and his troubling news that the woman was digging into her life then the call from Tara's mother, Lois, to tell her that Geordi had been left in her care by Chuck and Tara, who were now unreachable, all had her stressed out. There had been no discussion about when——or if——Geordi would be coming back and that caused distress as well.

"I can't take care of this child," Lois had whined. "I wish I could, 'cause I do love my grandbaby but I thought Tara was going to be here to help take care of him. My blood pressure was already too high and trying to care of this baby alone is too much for me. I tried to get one of my other daughters to take him, but they're already struggling trying to take care of their own children. You have to come get him, C.J. that's all there is to it."

Despite C.J.'s efforts to reach Chuck and Tara, they were not responding to her messages, and legally, she had no authority to retrieve him from the place they had left him. Chuck was a commercial pilot, and Tara was a marketing and P/R specialist with an international company. Both of their jobs required extensive time away from home which they both enjoyed, but was unfortunately not conducive to raising a child.

Chuck finally called after she left one of her not so nice messages. She learned that Tara had left on one of her marketing trips without a second thought to the disruption she was causing to her mother and her baby. And Chuck, unwilling to take on responsibility for the baby alone, had also disappeared. But with C.J. and Tara's mother pushing him, he had to make a decision. He asked C.J. to go get the baby as soon as possible.

She explained that she wouldn't be able to go until the next weekend, because she had the anniversary party coming up that weekend, and then only if he provided written permission.

Marc

Marc had promised to check on C.J. and was disappointed because although he'd tried, he hadn't been able to reach her. He knew she was busy with work and the anniversary party, but why couldn't she take a minute to return his call?

He'd also been busy checking out his friend, Harry Breckman's findings from his investigations on Cleah, as well as C.J. and her ex, Randy Singleton. He couldn't help but wonder how he and C.J. had ended up marrying people who apparently had such totally different values from themselves.

After going through the frustration of leaving messages, he finally connected with her. "C.J., how are you doing? I'm just checking on you like I promised. How are things? I know you were in the middle of some kind of family issue and I'm wondering how that turned out."

"Things are okay, Chief Carrington. Thanks for asking."

"Look, my name is Marc, and I'd appreciate if you would call me that."

"Oh. I really don't know if I would feel comfortable doing that. After all, you are a very prominent person in this city, and I am still married to someone else."

"I'm asking you to call me Marc. Isn't that reason enough?"

After a long pause, she said, "Okay, we'll see."

"Well, is there anything I can do to help you at the party? Since I plan to attend, I may as well make myself useful."

"No, I'm fine."

"You probably wouldn't tell me anyway. I'll see you soon," he said, before hanging up. He understood she was still legally married and understood her reluctance to respond to his obvious attraction. But when her divorce was final— as he hoped it would be soon—he planned to have his foot firmly planted in the door of her life. In the back of his mind, he wondered if he was wrong to hope for the end of a marriage, but he rationalized that it was over long before he met her. He was already visualizing them going deer hunting together.

C.J.

Saturday morning, C.J. was up early working on the anniversary party with Jaci and Nita's help. They went to the venue early to decorate, using gold as the dominant color with black and red accents. They checked the sound system and the couple's music selections, made sure the caterer was set, and the programs and mementoes were ready, then went home to get dressed. She debated if she should dress as her "other" persona since there would be people there from the job, and decided against that. Everything was falling apart anyway—might as well be real.

She was glad she was back at the venue early since many guests arrived early. She got them seated, and invited them to help themselves to hors d'oeuvres from the artfully arranged tables filled with appetizing selections.

Thank God she was aware that the Chief . . . uh, Marc would be there.

She smiled when she recalled him asking if she needed any help. What would she look like asking the Chief of Police to help her with a party?

She was blown away when he stepped in wearing a black suit with a stark white shirt and bowtie. The man looked good, and it took a quick adjustment to calm her beating heart and not appear flustered—although she definitely was. *Remember, girl, you're still married!*

Everything went beautifully, from the prayer of thanksgiving and blessing of the food to the quick and expedient serving of it, thanks to the catering staff with extra help from servers, Jaci and Nita, their husbands, Lena, and Jaci's daughter and her husband. Most of the speeches were short and sweet—okay, some ran a little long—but all one hundred plus guests seemed to enjoy everything.

By the time the dancing rolled around, C.J. was exhausted and her head, feet, and all points in between ached painfully.

She was definitely not in the mood when Marc insisted on dancing with her.

"So," he said, as he pulled her into his arms, "How is Geordi?"

"I hope he's okay. He's still in D.C. I have to go get him next weekend."

He went still, as bafflement filled his face. "You left him there? With those people?"

"Yes, and it's not like I had much choice since they are his parents."

"Oh, boy. I'm not liking the thought of that, but can't they bring him back? Maybe forcing them to take on their responsibility might put them on the right track."

"I don't think so. Geordi's parents are not just irresponsible, they just don't want him."

"Wow. That complicates things. So when are you leaving?"

"Not until next weekend, since I don't want to take time off from work."

"I can take you to the airport and pick you up."

"No, I know you're a busy man, but thanks. One of my cousins will do it, or I'll just drive myself and park in long-term parking."

"You don't have to do that. I wouldn't have offered if I couldn't fit it into my schedule."

"No. I just don't think that's a good idea." Keeping him at arm's length was critical and she didn't know why he didn't understand that.

"Why won't you let me help you?"

She gave him a "DUH" look. "Like you can't figure that out for yourself. Number one, I'm still married, and number two, you are too, unless you and your crazy ex have different takes on your marital status. Do you know she called me? It wasn't a nice conversation."

He groaned. "No, I didn't know that. Trust me, Cleah and I are divorced. And hopefully, it's just technicalities tying you to Randy. We're both free."

"Not in the eyes of the law—at least as far as I'm concerned. And until you and that crazy woman get on the same page, the same applies to you."

"Can't we be friends in the meantime?"

"Honestly, I would like to, but I don't know if it's wise since not everyone will understand."

"Well, wise or not, we're friends. And as your friend, I want to do what I can to help you, including taking you to the airport."

She shook her head. "I don't want to have this conversation right now. I'm tired. My head aches, my feet are numb, and I want to go home and sleep for a week."

"Well, can't you leave? I mean it's basically over. And my compliments, by the way. You did a great job, so you'll probably get more business from this. Are you passing out cards?"

"No, as a matter of fact, I don't have any cards. I've had so much going on that it just didn't cross my mind to have any printed."

"Hmmm. Don't worry about it. Word of mouth is the best form of advertisement anyway. And you'll get plenty from what I've heard. Come on," he said, leading her off the dance floor. "Sit down and rest for a while. When it comes to advertising, the Bradshaws are the ones to know." He led her to the table where he had been sitting with the Bradshaws.

She spoke to everyone and gratefully sank into the chair he pulled out for her. "I hope everyone is having a good time."

"Of course. What's not to like," Mrs. Bradshaw said with a smile. "Do you do this often? And by the way, I've finally realized why you look so familiar. I want you to know you have my support."

C.J. smiled. "Thanks. And although I've planned lots of parties over the years, nothing on this level."

"Well, if you're ever interested in doing it on a regular basis, call me. I've mentioned before that we're always looking for good people, and from what we've seen tonight, you're good."

"Hopefully, I'll be able to start my own event planning business soon —nothing too big, but manageable for me. I'm not in a position to do so yet, but I'll get there."

"That's wonderful. And we prefer to use sub-contractors when it's possible. We need to talk. You're being under-utilized working for the city."

"Thanks, I appreciate that. I, uh, might be calling you a lot sooner than you think." *If Cleah Fileds has her way,* she thought. "I don't know how much longer I'll be with the city, for a lot of reasons."

Mrs. Bradshaw sent a subtle look to the Chief, which caused C.J. to suspect they had already been talking. "I wouldn't worry too much about it. A woman with your talent and willingness to work hard will always land on her feet."

"Well, thanks again, and now it's back to work for me," she said, struggling to get to her feet.

Marc stood and walked with her across the room. "What do you have to do? I can help."

"I have to put the place in order after everyone leaves." She looked around the room. "And right now, nobody seems ready to leave." She groaned.

"Just go to the mic and thank everyone, say goodnight and wish everyone a safe drive home. That will get the message across."

"I like that suggestion, but my boss and his parents don't look ready to go yet. And they're the ones paying me."

"Well, it can't be too much longer or the management will start blinking the lights." They laughed together at the vision of that.

122

"Hmmm, maybe I can make that suggestion."

"I'll stick around and help you guys wrap things up. And then I'll follow you home. I don't like the thought of you going in the house alone, uh, friend!"

"Marc, I really don't need you to do that. I go in the house alone all the time."

"Not tonight. And please don't argue with me."

Chapter Twenty-Eight
Marc

MARC WAS BLOWN AWAY WHEN HE STEPPED INTO THE RECEPTION hall and saw C.J. looking beautiful in a long red fitted v-neck dress with splits on each side, exposing beautiful legs. He'd had to battle and command control against the lust-filled feelings that engulfed him.

He was surprised to see Jason Gilmore and his wife, as well as Jason's brother, Ron Gilmore, with a beautiful woman who resembled C.J. and Jaci, and was introduced as Ron's wife, Anita, who was a cousin to the other two women.

He hung out with them until the event started, all the while watching the interaction between them and yearned to be a part of the close knit connection and comradery that flowed between them.

After the crowd finally left, he helped them clean-up, then followed her home and laughed when, as soon as they stepped in the house, she kicked her shoes off and walked on obviously hurting feet to the family room. "I don't know why you wear those high heels anyway if they hurt your feet that bad." He laughed again at the dirty look she gave him.

"Look, I don't mean to be rude, but I did tell you how exhausted I am," she said, trying to hide a yawn.

"I know, and I'm not going to stay long. But I want you to know that I completed my investigation."

"And . . ."

"Basically, your husband has lost his mind since the team let him go. He's . . . well, I hope you are through with him. You do know he has a rape charge pending against him?"

"How could I not know? It's been all over the news. But what I want to know is, what's up with your wife? Why is she threatening my job and trying to stir up trouble for me?"

"Ex-wife," he stressed, forcefully. "And unfortunately, I've discovered that she's done that to every woman I shown an interest in. If it's something or someone she wants or believes will benefit her, she goes after it and she's very dangerous and not to be underestimated."

"Then that's easily fixed. Just let her know that there's nothing between us."

He gave her a searching look. "I can't do that because I wouldn't be telling the truth. The fact is, I *am* interested in you. But don't worry about Cleah, I'll handle her."

He couldn't believe how nervous he was about what he was about to ask. It was just that important to him. He wrung his hands and finally said, "Look, I know you've realized I'm attracted to you. I meant what I said about us becoming friends. I'd like to spend some time with you, get to know you better—— just as friends. Is that possible?"

She smiled. "Of course I've noticed that you're attracted to me, although I've tried to discourage and ignore it. You need to understand and accept my position. All I want and need from you at this point is for you to handle Cleah Fields and keep her away from me because I don't need any more problems."

He looked disappointed. "Am I being too aggressive in asking how things stand between you and Randy?"

"All that's important is that you understand we're still married. Not because I choose to be, but because Randy refuses to cooperate in an equitable divorce settlement, so we're at a stalemate. But even if I were free to do so, I'm not ready to jump into another relationship."

"But that doesn't mean you won't ever be ready, does it?"

"I stayed in a miserable, twenty-year marriage with a selfish, immature man who didn't love me and cheated constantly. He didn't really want to be married, but found it convenient. I was just his security blanket. So I have to figure out why I stayed in that kind of marriage. Was it that I didn't want to be alone? Was it that I got my self-worth from being married to him—even though I was miserable? Was it that I was mercenary, willing to settle for anything in exchange for money and a comfortable lifestyle? Was it that I didn't think I deserved a loving husband, children, and the God-centered life I've always wanted? These are questions I need to answer before I even think about another relationship."

"Maybe it was because you love him."

She gave him a disgusted look. "Any love I had for him died a long time ago."

Chuckling, Marc said, "I don't know, but I suspect you were just too stubborn to give up on your husband and your marriage. So what are you doing to find out the answers to those questions?"

"I'm in a divorce support and counseling group. I need to be whole and able to be a blessing to someone, including myself. I'm not there and I can't offer splinters to anyone. "

"Well, I'm not sure I agree with all of that. I've seen the love you show Geordi and others. So what are you doing beside the counseling group?"

She dropped her head before admitting, "For various reasons, I wasn't as close to the Lord as I should have been during my marriage. So I'm drawing closer to Him through prayer, study in the word, attending regular worship services and reading books by people who have gone through divorce."

"So are these things working?"

"Absolutely! I've accepted my part in the failure and know that it takes two to make a good marriage and two to make a bad one."

"Yeah, I get that. I had to reach the point of accepting that I was in a marriage that never should have happened. Even though I knew it long before I got out, I was just too stubborn to give up on it until I realized that staying would be detrimental."

This time it was her chuckling. "Well, you have a problem. Your ex hasn't reached that point and has no intention of letting you move on."

"I'm working to fix that. But back to my original question, I would like to get to know you better, as nothing more than just friends for now. Is that possible?"

"Dang, you're persistent! There's a lot more to consider since we're both connected to high profile people. The media would love to make a news story about us."

"But what's wrong with us being friends?"

She gave him a 'be for real' look. "Everything! The media can take a grain of sand and make a whole beach out of it."

"I know, but are we going to let them dictate who we can have as friends?"

"I just don't want that hassle right now. I'm weary of dealing with them."

"Isn't having a good friendship worth it?"

With an exhausted sigh, she said, "Let's be honest. You and I both know very well that you want more than friendship." She looked at him with regret. "We have to deal with things as they are, and not as we would like them to be. Anyway, I'm not talking about this anymore. I'm tired and you need to get out so I can get to sleep."

"Okay." He grabbed her hand and led her to the door. Before he opened it to leave, he leaned over and kissed her, then said, "I heard what you said, but I've wanted to do that all night — truthfully, since the moment I met you."

C.J.

"Oh, God!" C.J. closed and locked the door, set the alarm system and walked up the stairs, automatically turning out lights as she went. Her mind was still on that kiss. She really wished it hadn't felt so good. *Help me, Lord!*

127

She undressed, stepped in the shower and let the hot water run over her body as she replayed the evening in her mind and prayed that the event was enjoyed by everyone, but especially the honorees. Before she closed the prayer she added, ". . . and Lord, forgive me for stepping outside the bounds of my marriage—and enjoying that kiss so much."

Although she badly needed a word from the Lord, attending church the next morning was questionable, and she fell into bed and welcomed the kind of sleep that comes from exhaustion and relief.

Buzzing! What was that doggone buzzing? She had been sleeping so deeply that it took her a few minutes to realize that it was her cell phone, still in her purse sitting on the dresser across the room. She was tempted to let it buzz, but decided to answer in case someone was calling about the baby.

"Hello!" she croaked sleepily, after stumbling across the room and digging the phone out of the bottom of her purse.

"C.J., what kind of coffee do you like?"

"What?"

"I said, what's your favorite flavor of coffee? I'm at the coffee shop."

She finally figured out that the idiot who had dared to wake her up so early was Marc. "What the heck do you mean calling my house at the crack of dawn when you know how tired I was last night? I don't want any coffee!" She punched the disconnect button in frustration.

Of course, it started ringing again immediately. "What!"

"Do you know what time it is? Ten o'clock is not the crack of dawn. Now, what kind of coffee do you like? Or should I just choose?"

"I told you I don't want any coffee! Now leave me alone."

"Okay, I'll be there in thirty or forty minutes because I'm going to stop at the bakery. Can you get yourself together by then?"

"Don't. Do. That. Can't you understand I just want to rest?"

"You can rest later. I'm on my way."

She flopped back on the bed with a huff, and stayed there a few minutes before she struggled into the bathroom to wash her face and brush her teeth. Then, just as slowly, walked into the closet and threw on some comfortable jeans and a tee shirt, all the time grumbling about how she was going to throw that coffee in Marc's face.

Thirty minutes later, she was answering the door with a scowl on her face, which deepened when he started laughing.

"Where I come from, people are grateful when someone does something nice for them," he said, taking in her frown.

"Don't mess with me!" she said, in an angry tone. "I'm tired, sleepy and in no mood. I had every intention of throwing this coffee in your face. But I guess I'll drink it instead."

"Whew! I'm glad about that," he said with a chuckle. "It's a beautiful day, so I thought you'd like to get out of the house. There's a jazz concert on the boardwalk in Kemah, and we could drive down there."

"What are you up to, Marc?" she looked at him in frustration. "Don't you remember our talk last night? I'm married, and so are you."

"Yes, I remember but I thought we agreed to be friends, and I just want to take my friend to an innocent jazz concert. That's it. Now, let's eat and then you can get ready."

"Don't tell me what to do," she grumbled, while opening the lid and taking a cautious drink of the hot coffee.

He gave her a flustered look. "Are you always this grumpy in the morning?"

"When I'm disturbed out of deep sleep, yes, I am."

"Well get over it. Now drink your coffee and eat your pastry." He followed suit by taking a bite out of a large roll and taking a sip of his coffee.

An hour later, she had dressed in a casual, but dressy outfit, made up her face and combed her hair, and they were on the way to their destination which he said was about an hour away.

After parking, they strolled around the boardwalk enjoying the amusements, then hopped on a boat for a tour of the island, and later found a comfortable place in front of the stage to enjoy the jazz band.

Afterwards, they had dinner in a nearby seafood restaurant where they traded hunting stories and basically talked about their lives growing up on farms. It turned out they had similar childhood experiences, and wanted to carry values of God, love, and family into their adult lives. They agreed that both of them had blown it.

On the way home, C.J. tried to remember the last time she'd had such a good, relaxing time—she couldn't. *Lord, I'm in trouble. I'm still married to Randy, but I could really fall for Marc in a big way. Help me, Lord! I don't want to sin against you,* she prayed silently.

As soon as they stepped in the house, Marc hugged and kissed her—again! And yes, she enjoyed it, although it went against everything she had prayed about all the way home.

When she was finally able to break the kiss, she said, "Marc, we can't do this. You have to understand that I'm still married to Randy. Any kind of involvement with you just confuses the issues and causes all kinds of conflicting feelings. I really did enjoy today, and thank you for it, but I, uh . . . I don't think we should see each other again. And I definitely don't think we should be . . . you know."

Marc looked at her a long time and said, "Is there a chance you and Randy will get back together? If there is, I'll back off and leave you alone. But if you tell me it's over between you, then I'm going to keep coming after you. We both know there's something between us. I know we need to resolve the issues with our respective spouses one way or another. If it's over between you and Randy, then end it and move on, and I'm going to clear up things with Cleah so we can pursue whatever is between us."

She bit her lip as she struggled with what to say. "As things stand with Randy now, it's very hard to do that. And I don't want or need any pressure from you or anyone else. The quality and plans for the rest of my life are weighing in the balance. I'm trying to do this according to God's will."

"I want to be in God's will too. I just feel like you're it for me." He kissed her gently on the forehead, then went to the door, gave her a long look and walked out.

"Oh, God, I really should have gone to church today!" She moaned as she was getting ready for bed. She pushed Marc to the back of her mind and forced thoughts about the job to the forefront.

Dread shot through her when she thought of Cleah and wondered what the next week would bring. A song came to her mind, "Where Is Your Faith in God?" She groaned in self-disgust. "Yes, Father, thank You for reminding me I have to trust You to see me through all these situations I'm faced with. And Lord, I don't know if it's appropriate or not, but I do thank You for the enjoyment of this day, and I sure need Your wisdom and guidance regarding Marc. Give me the strength to obey Your will, Father."

Chapter Twenty-Nine
Cleah

CLEAH'S WEEK STARTED OFF BADLY. ONE OF HER SPIES REPORTED seeing Marc and a woman in Kemah together over the weekend. It sounded like it could be the same woman with him in the airport. The fact that Marc and this woman were being seen together coincided with Catherine's appearance as a city employee, and fed her suspicions that this woman and Catherine were one and the same.

"Umph! He never took me to Kemah or anyplace else, although we seldom spent any time together doing anything," she mumbled.

"But that woman has to go! I really need the scoop on her before I can decide how I'm going to handle things." She picked up the phone and called her assistant.

"Carl, will you come in here?" Carl arrived immediately with pad and pen and a large tan envelope in hand and sat down in the plush chair across from Cleah's desk.

"What have you dug up on Catherine Stroman? You know I've been waiting on a report."

Carl hesitated before answering. "I don't know, Cleah. Maybe you're letting your personal feelings interfere with rational thinking. I don't relish messing with these department heads. They asked you to leave that woman alone and they must have good reasons for doing so."

But Cleah was so lost in her vindictive thoughts that she didn't hear him. "I'm sick of that woman. Every time I turn around, someone is telling me about seeing them together and I need her out of the picture once and for all."

"You're not even sure it's the same person. I really wish you'd forget about this and move on. I just don't have a good feeling about this since I found out some things about Catherine."

Cleah frowned and sighed impatiently. "You're not going soft on me are you, Carl? I need someone with backbone and this is not the time to wimp out on me. "

"I'm not wimping out. But it's also my job to keep you out of trouble. Like Oliver told you, there is no indication of falsification in her personnel file. She hasn't done anything wrong and your only reason for going after her is because you think Marc is interested in her."

"Just tell me what you've found out. I don't need a lecture."

Carl shrugged. "Well, according to my media contacts, she was married to Randy Singleton, the basketball pro who's been in the news lately. Here's a picture of them together." He laid a picture from the envelope in front of her. "They broke up a while ago and she needed a job because her husband threw her out and cut off all her finances. That was in the news as well. She probably couldn't keep a job because of all the negative media attention surrounding them. That's probably the reason she's using her maiden name."

Cleah looked at the picture and compared it feature by feature with those she already had. The only thing different was the hair, and the big frame glasses. "Does Catherine have red hair?"

"Yes, she does, but apparently she's been wearing a wig since she started working for the city."

Cleah slammed the desk with her hand. "I knew this was the same woman! Maybe she didn't technically lie, but she is misleading and misrepresenting who she is by withholding the truth and disguising her appearance. Trust me, I can gain some press by pointing out how department heads are helping undeserving people take jobs from those who really need them."

"But Cleah! The woman did need a job. I told you her husband cut her off from any financial help and I also heard something about her having a child that may not be her husband's. I don't know how true that is. My sources weren't sure."

Anger vibrated in Cleah's voice when she spoke again. "What do you mean it's not her husband's? How old is it? Is it Marc's? If I find out she and Marc...," she huffed furiously, unable to complete the sentence.

"See! That's what I'm talking about. Why should you care if the woman has a baby, or if it's Marc's? You haven't been married to that man for years."

"But you of all people know that I fully plan for us to re-marry. I won't let another woman and her brat get in the way of that. You better decide who you're working for and if you're with me one hundred percent; otherwise, I suggest you find another job."

"Cleah, I'm only suggesting that you not let personal feelings get in the way of common sense, that's all. The entire city council is still under scrutiny after Sullivan and his staff got caught last year in that bid-fixing scandal. This is the time for us to lay low, not stir up the anger of people who can hurt us. I just don't want us to go down because of something crazy like this."

"You let me worry about that. I can shut all of them down."

"How?"

"I can use the media to expose how a rich woman managed to take a city job away from someone who really needed one, and how she falsified her employment application to get that job with the help of these department directors. It could stir up all kinds of mess about the city's hiring practices and make me look like the good guy—the person looking out for the little people."

"That's dangerous stuff, Cleah. Like I said, we need to tread carefully. People who live in glass houses shouldn't be throwing rocks at anybody."

Cleah acted as if she didn't hear his warning. "If Catherine is the woman Marc is seeing and if that's Marc's child, that could be the reason her husband threw her out."

"No, that's not true," Carl replied. "I heard he's refusing to divorce her because he wants her back. Why would he want her back if that were the case? You're off track on this, Cleah, and I think you should drop the whole thing. Need I remind you, we're not in the position to make anyone angry? And you know you don't want to make Marc angry."

Cleah thought for a minute, then said, "Maybe you're right. My issue is with the woman, not Marc. She's the one I need to get rid of—her and that child. Marc has always wanted children, but I didn't think he would go this far. I definitely miscalculated things by not giving him a child."

"No, that's not what I meant. I'm saying you should leave both of them alone. That chapter in your life is closed, Cleah. "

"I guess you didn't hear me. I told you what I want to do. Now, do you want your job or not? "

"All right, you're the boss," Carl answered, resignedly, then said, "but you're way off-track on this."

As soon as Carl left her office, Cleah picked up the phone and dialed Catherine's extension.

"Catherine Stroman, may I help you?"

"Yes, you can, Mrs. Randy Singleton. This is Cleah Fields Carrington and I'm calling because evidently you were too dumb to heed my previous warnings. Well, I know all about you and your husband. Now, either you resign immediately or you and all the people who helped you get a position with the city through falsification of information, misrepresentation and other illegal actions, will be in deep trouble. I'm going to call the media and reveal your true identity and how you have used deception to get this job, to get close to, and carry on a relationship with the Chief and possibly have his child."

Cleah gleefully boasted her plans to ruin the lives of others, not realizing she had serious, life changing trouble headed her way.

Marc

C.J. reminded Marc in some undefined way of his school teacher mother and grandmother—strong women who had shaped his life and values. If he had been true to those values, Cleah would never have had a chance. He could honestly conclude that marrying her was the biggest mistake of his life, and his prayer now was, "Father, I ask that You would be gracious to me and give me another chance with the right woman. Help me find my wife, Lord." Of course, in his mind, C.J. was that woman.

But first there were obstacles to overcome. Cleah's meddling, and C.J.'s marital status needed to be resolved. "Help us, Father. We both want to be in Your will for our lives."

That led him to the issue at hand. He looked down at the documents he had received from his friend, Harry Breckman. Regret filled him but he trusted Harry's judgment which had never steered him wrong.

Harry, who had been a lieutenant in the department when Marc graduated from the police academy, had recognized Marc's talent for assessing crime scenes and solving crimes. He took Marc under his wing and mentored him up through the ranks of the department. Of course, Harry had selfish motives since Marc's ability in solving crime had also propelled his own upward mobility.

After his retirement from the force, Harry had started his own corporate security and private investigation company. He had more business than he could handle and boasted to Marc over their regular lunches about how much money he was making.

When Marc expressed discontentment with his job a few weeks ago, Harry encouraged him to leave, saying, "Marc, as an attorney and a criminologist, you can basically write your own ticket. You can not only consult with Fortune 500 companies regarding security issues, but can also act as their legal counsel in such issues. But that fanatical ex-wife of yours can destroy your future if you stay where she has any influence. Just something to think about."

"Yeah, I know," Marc said. "My plan has always been to practice law when I leave the department."

"Well, don't throw your law enforcement experience in the trash can. With all the issues and problems we're seeing with police these days, you can make a killing as a consultant and lecturer in educational and law enforcement institutions all over the world. Might not be a bad idea to accept that position as an instructor to the F.B.I. and consultant to the Justice Department, if for no other reason than to build on your credentials."

Now, as Marc studied the results of the investigation Harry had done on Cleah, he had a sinking feeling in the pit of his stomach. Bluntly put, life as Cleah knew it was over.

He dialed Harry's number. "Hey, I'm going through the stuff you sent on Cleah. It's bad, man; much worse than anything I could've imagined. I kind of regret I asked you to dig into this. You know if the political powers get their hands on this, her career in politics is over, and if the District Attorney gets it, she's probably going to jail. I don't condone the things she's done, but is there any way we can keep this from going any further?"

"Forget it, Marc," Harry answered. "The political powers already have it. They're just letting her live in utopia, thinking she really has a chance at that senate seat, and waiting for the most opportune time to let it all blow up in her face. In fact, it's probably a good thing you found out so you can give her a heads up. I can handle that in a way that she'll never know who it came from. Her best bet is to get a jump on it and disappear. And I'm hoping for that more for your benefit than hers."

"What do you mean?" Marc's heart took a nosedive as he realized how the repercussions of this could affect him.

"Marc, you could catch some serious heat from this. After all, you were married to this woman."

Marc groaned in agony as he realized everything he'd worked for could go down the toilet along with Cleah's mess. "Okay, Harry, go ahead and handle it."

Chapter Thirty

C.J.

CLEAH FIELDS HUNG UP BEFORE C.J. HAD A CHANCE TO RESPOND TO her hateful words, but she was shaken—more in anger than in fear. She had hoped the woman would leave her alone and had in fact, hoped that Marc would handle the situation as he had promised. That evidently hadn't happened, and it left her with a big decision.

While she was trying to decide how to deal with Cleah's mess, her cell phone rang.

"C.J., this is Randy. Look, my trial is coming up soon and my attorney keeps telling me how important it is for you to be with me in court. Now, I know we're not on the best of terms, but you are still my wife and I really need your help. I just need to know if I can depend on you."

"I'm at work and I'll have to talk to you about that later," she whispered, always concerned about listening ears.

He ignored what she said, pressing on nerves already at a breaking point. "C.J., you know what Willa is about and you can tell that to the judge."

"I said I can't discuss it now. I have to get back to work."

"Well, listen. Has my mother called you yet? They want to stay with you when dad . . ."

"I have to go." She hung up before he could dump anything else on her. Besides, she had to handle the Cleah issue.

Tears filled her eyes and she quickly escaped to the stairwell, which was hardly used by anyone, to pray and get herself together. She took her cellphone with her and called Marc, but had to leave a message when he didn't answer.

"Marc, Cleah just called me again and told me to resign or she would call the media and make trouble for me and everyone who helped me get this job. I really need your help."

C.J. agonized all day and when she got home from work, she was so emotionally drained that all she could do was fall to her knees beside her bed and start praying. The job issue added to the stress she was already dealing with about having to go get Geordi over the weekend, not knowing what to expect when she got there. Chuck and Lois said it was okay to come get him, but was Tara in agreement? Unfortunately, she and Tara hadn't parted on good terms and of course, Tara wouldn't return her calls, as usual.

"Father God, I know You are faithful, that You promised to never leave or forsake me, but Lord, I have trouble on every side, and I need Your wisdom and guidance. So Father, show me what to do about Cleah's threats. I don't want to be the cause of any trouble for those who have been kind enough to help me get this position. But is leaving the answer? And will that keep her from going ahead with her plans anyway?"

She cried tears of helplessness and indecision for a few minutes as she thought about Lena and Jaci, and the directors of the Personnel and Legal Departments who had been willing to help her after hearing about her plight.

"Lord, please intervene, and block this woman's evil plans from succeeding. And then, there's Randy and his issues, and Geordi and the problems surrounding him. Father, all these battles are Yours, and I trust that You are at work even now, fighting them for me. I thank You, and stand still as I wait to see Your salvation and victory coming forth. In Jesus' name. Amen."

She stood up and drew a deep breath of relief, knowing she had cast her cares upon the Lord, and that He was in control. She decided it was a good night for pampering. She went into the bathroom, turned on the water and poured her favorite bath oil into the tub. She lit scented candles and decided to go downstairs for a cup of calming tea to sip on while she enjoyed her bath. But before she could get out of the bedroom, a flash of wisdom suddenly dropped into her spirit. It was so strong she almost fell to her knees; so simple, she wondered why she'd been stressing about Cleah's threats. She sank down on the bed, shaking her head and saying, "thank You, God, my Father. You are truly an all wise, loving God."

She could only conclude that it was her lack of faith that had made it so complicated in her mind. Her natural inclination was to find Cleah and kick her behind for causing her agony until she reminded herself again to trust in God—not Cleah's actions. She groaned in repentance. "Lord, forgive me," she uttered. She was about to continue her trip downstairs to get a cup of tea, but the phone rang, interrupting her again.

"Hey, C.J.! It's Nita, girl. How are things going with you?"

"Oh God, Nita. Believe me, you don't want to hear all the stuff that's going on. So, how are you? And let me thank you again for all your help with the anniversary party. I think things went very well and that they were pleased."

"Oh, I do too. And I was glad to do it. But what's going on? I have time to give an ear. Lord knows you've listened to enough of my troubles."

C.J. turned her bath water off and sat down to tell Nita all that was happening, including the answer she believed God had just given her about Cleah and the job.

"Well, we didn't miss how much attention the Chief was showering on you at the party. I think the man is already in love with you," Nita said, chuckling, then added, "so maybe that witch knows what she's talking about."

"That witch is not Marc's wife anymore, but unfortunately, Randy

140

is still my husband. So nothing can happen with Marc, although he would like for it to be, and truthfully, maybe I would too, if I had a right to."

"Doggonit! We have to get Randy's behind out of your life, Cij. He's blocking and keeping you from something that could be a blessing."

"He won't cooperate. Just keeps demanding more and more from me, but won't agree to do the one thing I need for him to do."

"Well, I'd love to see him get a taste of his own medicine, but, like you said, God is in control, and he can handle it a lot better than we can."

C.J. sighed. "Yeah, He can, although sometimes it takes longer than I'd like. It's so hard to remember that His timing is perfect."

"It's coming, cuz. It was a long time coming for me, but it came, and now it's like it was just a bad dream. I still have occasional nightmares about Frank, but the good thing is, I wake up and realize that's all it was, and I run and hug Ron and thank God for him."

"So, how is Destiny? Did she ever get over that ear infection?"

"Yes, she did. She's going to spend a few days with her grandparents while I go with Ron on an out of town job. I am really looking forward to that. I'm going to relax and shop while he's in meetings. I'll have to deal with a very spoiled brat when I get back, but it'll be worth it."

C.J. moaned in delight. "Sounds wonderful to me. I used to travel with Randy, but it was an entirely different scenario, and I definitely didn't look forward to it."

"Well, just don't give up. You don't know what God has in His plan for you."

"Thanks, Nita. You know I was talking to Gina and she said something I had forgotten. She reminded me of the prayers Grammy prayed for God to give us godly husbands and the gift of children to raise into godly people. She believes those prayers are still out there in the spirit realm, waiting on us to get to a place where God can answer them."

"Whoo! I believe that too. It's happened for me and Jaci, and that tells me it can happen for you. You just hang in there, keep praying, keep holding on to your dream, and watch God bring it to pass. I think Saturday night was a good indication that you're on the right track with the business."

"I appreciate that, girl. And yes, I will definitely keep praying and holding on."

"Good," Nita said, "Now, I have to go take care of Ron before he starts pouting. I'll talk to you later."

"Bye, Nita, and thanks for calling," C.J. said, before hanging up. She felt better after talking to her cousin, and went to continue her night of pampering as she reflected on her cousins.

Admittedly, she'd had to fight the spirit of jealousy when her cousins, Jaci and Nita both fell in love with men who loved them and got married. But when she put everything into perspective, she concluded that while she'd been in a somewhat tolerable situation, Jaci had been struggling through single parenting and barely surviving. And even after meeting Jason, there had been a long rough journey to marriage that included being stalked, persecuted on the job and even a close brush with being murdered.

And Nita had been in a horrific domestic violence situation that had caused the lost of an unborn child, and kept her fearful for her life and her other children's safety until God had said enough and delivered her. Now she had adopted Ron's child by an evil, conniving woman who ended up getting killed in a drug raid, and not only had a loving husband, but had the baby girl she'd always wanted.

Sadly, people had always assumed that because C.J. had plenty of money and was married to a famous man, she was happy with no worries, but that couldn't have been further from the truth.

As she dealt with her failed marriage, lack of children and the possibility that she might be alone for the rest of her life, she knew there was no perfect life in this world, even if she was successful in getting what was rightfully hers from her hellish marriage to Randy.

But at least it would provide a level of comfort and security, even though she realized it would come at a cost. It wouldn't alleviate loneliness or her desire for a husband and family and honestly, she would probably always wonder if a man was interested in her or her money.

While she was in the tub, she heard the phone ringing, but refused to interrupt her soothing bath to answer it. However, she wished she had when she discovered it was Marc calling to tell her not to worry about Cleah, and strangely, asking her to pray for him.

Chapter Thirty-One

Randy

RANDY, EVERYTHING IS ABOUT TO COME TO A HEAD," THE ATTORNEY said, as soon as Randy answered the phone. "The court date for your trial is set, and C.J.'s attorney is adamant. Either you agree to a settlement and finalize the divorce, or C.J. is not going to help you. So you have to decide what you want—take a chance on going to jail, or comply with your wife's demands. She could have forced the issue a long time ago, but for some reason she hasn't. I can't make it any plainer than that. So what's it going to be?"

Large drops of sweat poured from Randy's face and dripped down his neck. He gulped, trying to swallow the ball of fear in his throat. "I'ma have to call you back," he croaked.

He hung up and sat there trying to figure out what to do. He finally hit on what he considered was the perfect answer—call Willa and get her to admit she lied if he paid her enough money. That way, he wouldn't need C.J. and wouldn't have to give her any more of his money.

He called the number and luckily she answered. "Hey, Willa, I need to talk to you about—"

"This is not Willa, this is her sister. Her attorney told her not to talk to you because when they find you guilty, she's going to sue you for all the damage you done caused her, and get every cent you and your crazy wife have."

Randy could still hear the woman's laughter echoing in his mind even after she hung up. He dropped the phone and sat there in agony.

Thirty minutes later, his phone rang and it was his attorney again.

"Randy, why did you call Willa? You've been told not to do that, darn it! Now, she's going to add harassment to the charges already against you. You just made matters worse. She's probably going to come into court with a mental health professional pleading emotional trauma in addition to everything else."

"Oh, God!" Randy said, then hung up. He needed C.J. even more than he'd thought. He called her but of course she didn't answer. The one thing he knew he couldn't take a chance on was going to jail, and letting that greedy woman take everything he had, including what he had withheld from C.J., who he admitted had been a good wife to him and stuck with him when he didn't deserve it. Just the thought of that woman taking what was rightfully C.J.'s was more than he could stand. He reached for the phone again, and called his attorney back.

"Hey, listen, I need you to get in touch with C.J.'s attorney and let her know I'm ready to settle and sign the divorce papers. Whatever C.J. wants, okay? And can we get this done before the trial date?"

"I think so, since you're agreeing not to contest it and give her what she wants. So is she going to help you out at the trial?"

"I don't know, but I can't take a chance on Willa possibly getting money that should go to C.J."

"Well, I doubt she could, since that money is already tied up in your divorce case. But who knows what a judge will do."

Randy sighed. "I should have done this a long time ago. Maybe if I had, I might have my wife back."

After he hung up and thought about the mess his life was in—his marriage ending, being on trial for rape, his dad's illness—he did the only thing he thought would bring relief. He got stinking drunk out of his mind.

Chapter Thirty-Two
C.J.

UNLIKE THE PREVIOUS NIGHT, C.J. HAD A PEACEFUL NIGHT OF SLEEP and rest. Tuesday morning, she arrived at the office without her disguise, causing her coworkers to do a double-take when she walked through the office on the way to her cubicle.

She quickly gathered the few personal belongings she had there, and then went to the director's office and handed him the resignation letter she had already prepared. She explained why she had made it effective immediately, and apologized for any trouble she might have caused him for trying to help her. A similar letter would be delivered to the Personnel Director.

She picked up her belongings and walked out of the office without a word. But she figured Betty would be on the phone to Cleah before she was out of the building.

C.J. didn't know until much later when she got a call from Lena, who told her that soon after C.J. left, and probably before Betty could make her victory call to Cleah that she was gone, the Director called her into his office, and said, "Betty, this has nothing to do with Ms. Stroman's decision to leave—and trust me, it was her decision. But this is a good time to tell you that I need people with integrity and loyalty in this office. I don't think I have that in you and Agnes, so I've put in a request for you both to be moved out of this department. This is effective immediately and you are free to leave now, so you can look into other positions, perhaps in Councilmember Fields' office." Lena was laughing hilariously and ended her call with a loud 'woo-hoo, God reigns'!

C.J. went home and called Tara's mother. "Hi, Lois, this is C.J. I'm unexpectedly free for the rest of this week so I'm coming to get Geordi as soon as I can arrange a flight today. Is that okay?"

"Oh thank God!" Lois responded. "I didn't know how I was going to make it another day with this baby. You want us to meet you at the airport?"

"Yes, please do that and I'd appreciate it if you would pack some diapers and food in his baby bag because I plan to get a return flight back home today so I won't have to worry about a hotel."

"I'll do that, and I thank you so much. I can't wait to get a good night of sleep without that baby screaming."

"I'll call you back as soon as I know when I'll arrive," she promised. She had already called Chuck, who surprisingly answered, and asked for his help in getting flights. While she was waiting for Chuck to call her back, she packed a small overnight bag just in case.

She called Jaci and Nita to let them know what was going on, and was comforted by their promise to be in prayer.

Then she called her mother to bring her up to date. "If all goes well, I might bring the baby to Riverwood to see you all next week." Again, she was comforted when her mother said, "I'll be praying!"

Just as she was hanging up with her mother, a call beeped in from her attorney with the news she'd been waiting so long to hear—Randy had agreed to a settlement and would sign the divorce papers. She jumped around the room in jubilation, yelling, "Thank You, Lord! Thank You God, my Heavenly Father!"

Her jubilant outburst rendered the attorney speechless and it took her several minutes to react. "Well, don't rejoice too much until we have the papers signed and the money in hand," she cautioned.

"God is in control, not Randy, and God is not going to let him renege."

"Well, let's hope you're right," the attorney answered.

Chuck called with her flight information shortly after she hung up with the attorney. When she saw how close the flights were, she knew she would definitely need God's favor. She looked at the clock, saw she had three hours before her flight, and realizing she was hungry, decided to make a sandwich. She called Ms. Maggie, while she was eating. "Ms. Maggie, I just wanted to tell you that I'm getting ready to go get Geordi. I'm leaving shortly, and hopefully will be back tomorrow, so we'll see you then."

"Oh, baby! I'm so glad. I know you've been so worried about that baby, and I have too. I'll be praying that things go well with the flights."

Again, she was comforted in knowing people were praying for her. She drove to the airport, parked in terminal parking and made it to her gate in plenty of time. She called Lois while waiting to board and gave her the arrival time. "Please try to be there because I have a turn-around flight back home that I need to catch."

God answered the prayers. Lois and a friend were waiting for her when the plane landed, and the switch was quickly made. Geordi's joy in seeing her brought tears to her eyes. She checked in for the return flight, and got to her gate in time to feed and change him before boarding the plane. It wasn't an easy flight for the baby. He slept fitfully and kept jumping awake and screaming until he saw her. She only hoped her fellow passengers were tolerant.

It was the wee hours of the next morning when the plane landed in Houston, and she was so tired she felt as though she had been run over by the plane instead of on it. She struggled to get the baby and assortment of bags to her truck, and thankfully, the freeway was clear and she made it home without any traffic congestion. All the way home, she was thanking God for His goodness, grace and mercy. Nobody but God!

It was only after she was at home that she checked her phone and noticed that Marc had called her several times and left messages. Unaware of what he had been doing, she issued a disgruntled grumble. "He's late!"

Marc

Marc's phone started blowing up Tuesday morning—the Legal Department, the Personnel Department, Lena—all leaving messages regarding C.J.'s resignation.

He called Ryan in the Legal Department. "I got your message. What happened?"

"I just wanted to let you know that Catherine resigned this morning, effective immediately. She said Cleah is threatening to call the media and stir up all kinds of trouble for her and everyone who helped her get the job. So Catherine thought if she went ahead and resigned, it might stop her from doing that. Frankly, I don't think it will."

"No, it won't, but don't worry about it, my friend. I promise everything will be okay."

He pulled a copy of the document Harry had prepared on Cleah out of his briefcase, fought the regret stirring in him and actually felt sorry for Cleah. He bowed his head and prayed. "Father, if what I'm about to do is not Your will, then please don't let it happen. But I'm trusting that this is Your way of not only stopping Cleah from hurting a lot of people, but also pointing my life—and hers—in the direction You want us to go."

After praying, he called his boss, the Mayor of the city, and asked for a meeting right away. He pulled the letter of resignation out of his briefcase and read it again. He was glad he had mentioned this possibility to the Mayor a few weeks ago when he told him he had been offered another position, which he was seriously considering. This wouldn't come as a complete surprise.

A couple of hours later, all he felt was relief. His meeting with the Mayor had gone well. The Mayor asked him to stay another three months, which was reasonable. He also took the opportunity to give the Mayor a heads up on what was about to happen with Cleah.

Back in his office, he called his contact at the F.B.I. Academy in Quantico, Virginia, and accepted the job he had been offered. The job was perfect. He'd only be in Virginia a few times a year to teach courses, plus occasionally provide input on cases. He explained what was happening with his ex-wife to make sure that would not affect things and was blown away when he was informed that they were already aware of Cleah's activities and had cleared him of any wrongdoing. But he agreed it was best for Marc to leave his position as Chief of Police because of the shadow of doubt Cleah's actions would cast on him.

That was the same thing Harry had told him. They had planned out Marc's strategy down to what he would say at the press conference when he announced his resignation. As Harry explained, he was on top now, but that could change in the blink of an eye. A wise person knew when to make a change.

Chapter Thirty-Three
C.J.

C.J. spent Wednesday and Thursday resting and making plans to move on with her life. Strangely, with so much going on in her life, she hadn't had a lot of time to dwell on how much she had missed the baby, but with Geordi's return, she was back in her "Mommy" role, and happy she didn't have to worry about getting him into the nursery right away since she didn't have a job.

She went into preparation for the divorce hearing. Her attorney already had copies of everything—the financial records C.J. had taken with her the day she left Randy, the journal she had written of their years together, the video of Randy and Willa together in her bed, the pictures of her after the fight and the difficulties she'd had since the break-up. Everything had been turned over to the judge.

She prayed. "Father, You are an Awesome and Mighty God! I am so grateful, not just for what You've done in past years, but for what You've done just this week, and for what You're going to do tomorrow. Thank You for fighting this battle on my behalf. Thank You for Your faithfulness. Thank You for causing all things to work together for my good. Thank You for perfecting all things concerning me. Father, I just thank You!" She reflected on what was to come—on her life beyond the final break with Randy. "Father, I commit my way to You for the future. Please go before me and make every crooked place straight. Cover me with Your wisdom, favor, grace and peace."

As she was praising God, the phone rang. Without checking the caller I.D., she answered.

"C.J.? Is that you?"

C.J. dropped her head into her hand, thinking, *"This is the last person I want to talk to today!"* after hearing her mother-in-law's voice. "Yes, it's me. How are you?"

"I'm doing pretty good, but dad's not doing very well. He's been diagnosed with cancer, and his doctor is sending him to M.D. Anderson hospital for treatment. So I need to get him there as soon as possible."

"I'm so sorry, I hate to hear that." The baby started squirming, trying to rouse himself from his nap. C.J. moved out of the family room and into the kitchen, hoping her voice wouldn't disturb him, but it was too late. He started whimpering.

"Well, Randy's not much help. He told me to call you." She paused, then asked, "Is that a baby I hear? Musta been the television. Randy told me about the divorce hearing tomorrow. It's a shame, you and Randy divorcing after all these years. A crying shame, I tell you! You know, used to be when two people got married, they stayed married. Everything might not have been perfect, but they worked through it. Divorce wasn't an option."

C.J. felt her praise slipping away and the start of a headache replacing it. "Those days are gone, Mrs. Singleton. It's best that both Randy and I move on separately."

"No! It's not too late to stop all this foolishness and get back together. Nothing's gone right for Randy since y'all separated. He's ripping and running all over the world, getting into all sorts of trouble, and you . . . well, what are you doing? You used to come see about us even when Randy didn't. Now we need you, and you're not here."

Okay, with the guilt trip! "Well, since Randy threw me out of our home and froze me out of all our accounts, I've been working, trying to survive and there hasn't been much time for anything else."

"I'm sorry, Randy shouldn't have done that, but you've been a part of this family all these years and you can't go abandoning us now. You're still our daughter-in-law! I know we haven't been as close as we could have been, but that's not to say we don't love you. Anyway, I was wondering if we could stay with you when we come down there to that hospital. Randy said he'd put us up in a nice hotel, but I know we'll be more comfortable with you because with Dad being sick, I have to make sure he's getting the right food and rest, and that he's comfortable. I can't do that in a hotel. I know y'all sold that big house, but I know you've got an extra room wherever you are."

C.J. couldn't believe the nerve of the woman. She had criticized everything about C.J. for twenty years, even when C.J. had gone to Little Rock numerous times to help them, the woman hadn't been pleased with her, and now, knowing how badly Randy had treated her, she had no qualms about asking C.J. for help.

"Well, to be honest, I have a lot going on and I also have a baby to take care of. It's just not a good time for me to have houseguests. I'm sure Randy has plenty of room and a well equipped kitchen."

"So that *was* a baby I heard! When did you have a baby, and why didn't you tell us we have a grandchild? Just because you and Randy are not together doesn't mean we shouldn't have been told. How old is this baby?"

"No, no, you've got it wrong. It's not your grandchild. Anyway, I think you should call Randy back and tell him you need to stay with him."

"Is that why you and Randy can't get back together? 'Cause you went and had a baby by some other man?"

C.J. fought to hold on to her temper. *Help me, Lord!* Just leave it to the woman to think the worse of her. "Well, since it's not Randy's child or your grandchild, I don't see that it's any of your business. And you know what? The way your family has treated me, even if it *was* your grandchild, I don't have to tell you a doggone thing. Now, I really have to go." She was about to hang up when the woman yelled . . .

"C.J., wait a minute! Okay, you're right, we haven't treated you very well, but I just find it strange that you come up with a baby right after you and Randy separated. I—"

C.J. interrupted her. "I don't give a hoot what you find strange. Now, I'm going to hang up before I say something I shouldn't. I'm sorry about your trouble, but I can't help you."

"Please! I'm sorry, C.J., but don't hang up. We really need your help. Randy's trial is about to come up and we don't know what the outcome of that will be. And you know we can't depend on Randy. We've been in Houston since y'all broke up and it just wasn't the same. Randy wasn't even around most of the time. He just left us sitting in that condo by ourselves. Baby, we need your help. We can't get around in that big city by ourselves. If you don't help us, we can't come, and Dad really needs to come to M.D. Anderson."

It had to be God who moved C.J. to say, "I don't mean any harm by what I'm about to say, but the only way I'll think about agreeing is that you promise not to get in my business. You have to understand that it's over between me and Randy, and there's not even a remote chance of us ever getting back together, and just so you know, it's nothing but God's love that's working in me to help you."

There was a long silence. "Okay, C.J. We really appreciate that, and you have our promise."

"Alright, then. So when are you planning to come?"

"As soon as we can get his appointment with the hospital set up. I'm hoping it'll be next week because I want to be there for the trial too."

Wishing she could get her foot up high enough to kick her own behind, C.J. said, "Well, call me as soon as you know something so I can make arrangements."

"Yes, I'll do that. And baby, I sure do appreciate this. We're looking forward to seeing you."

"Talk to you later." C.J. hung up, still wanting that self-kick. There was no way it would turn out well, not with all the hostility that existed between her and Randy and his parents. "Father, give me the grace I need for this."

Chapter Thirty-Four

Marc

MARC WAS BUSY TYING UP LOOSE ENDS, AND HE KNEW C.J. HAD A lot going on too. He respected the reason she had kept him at arm's length, but he really wanted to see her and the baby. He called her.

"C.J., I would really like to come by to see you and Geordi tonight. I have a lot to tell you about."

She was quiet for a few seconds, then said, "Okay. I have some things to tell you too. What time will you be here?"

"Around seven. Is that okay?"

"Yes, that's fine. Geordi should still be awake then."

"See you soon."

Later that evening, he started right in on her. "I'm still upset with you for not calling me and letting me help you. There was no reason I couldn't have taken you to the airport and picked you up."

"We've been through that, Marc. It's all water under the bridge now anyway."

He sighed and said, "I just want you to understand that I want to help you. You don't have to handle everything alone."

"I have to do things the way I feel is right, Marc, but I do appreciate your desire to help—more than you know. But Marc . . . you need to understand that I'm just not a good basket to be putting your eggs in right now. I have issues coming from every direction."

He didn't like the sound of that. "Why don't you let me worry about that?"

She didn't answer, just shook her head. He then went on to tell her what was happening. "I've submitted my resignation. Some things are about to happen with Cleah that could cast negative shadows on me, so I've been advised to leave before it happens. Remember when we went to D.C.?"

She gave him a sarcastic look. "Of course I remember. How could I forget?"

"Well, one of the reasons for that trip was to talk to a high ranking federal official who wanted to offer me a position."

"Oh my God! So you've decided to accept? You're leaving?" She looked crushed.

"Yes. I'll be doing some training with new agents several times a year, as well as consulting on some cases. But some of my time will be here. I plan to work with a friend in his corporate security and consulting business. And I would like to work a law case every now and then.

"I'm assisting the Mayor with selecting my replacement before I set the date for leaving. And afterwards, I plan to take some time off to rest and relax a little before starting my new ventures." He looked at her with a question in his gaze. "So, what's happening with you and Randy?"

He could tell she was trying to grasp all he was telling her. She'd had no idea he was thinking of leaving his post as Chief of Police.

She finally said, "Well, if all goes like I'm praying it will, we'll be signing the final papers tomorrow."

A glimmer of hope ignited in his heart. "And if things don't go as you hope, will you still settle?"

"I'm praying that won't be an issue. I'm counting on a fair settlement so I can do some things I'd like to do. Hopefully, Randy won't renege on his agreement to settle."

"Well, C.J., I don't think it would be a bad thing if you don't get everything you want. Your next husband can help you and take care of you too. I wish you would keep that in mind."

She looked him in the eye and said, "I don't know if I should expect another man to do that."

"You don't think I would help you?"

"I honestly don't know, Marc. We really haven't known each other very long, and frankly, it's too soon for me to answer that. You could be a greedy, abusive, opportunist with your eye on a chance to make a big score, and God forbid, a cheater, for all I know."

He nodded. "Yes, I could, but if you'll give me a chance, I'll prove that I'm not any of those things. What I am is a man who wants a good wife, a family and a happy home to come to after I work my tail off to make a living for us. Nothing would make me happier than for you to tell Randy to take all his money and take a hike out of your life."

She gave him a hard look. "Well, let me tell you—I'm not going to do that. I hope what you're saying is true, but I have to be careful, and find out for myself. And for all you know, I might not be the kind of wife you're looking for."

"Well, I hope to remedy the issue of us not knowing each other. I'd like to spend more time with you and Geordi. In fact, I'd like to take you to meet my family in the very near future. Will you go?"

"Darn it, Marc! Please don't push me. I'm just trying to get out of a bad marriage at this point. Try to understand that I can't jump into another relationship—not this soon."

Marc fought to keep that glimmer of hope burning, but it was getting dimmer. "I just want to be there when you decided to do it."

She didn't say anything for a minute, then said, "F.Y.I., Randy's dad is sick and he's coming to Houston for treatment. They're going to stay here with me while they're here."

Marc frowned. "Why with you? That means Randy will be hanging around here too, and no telling what that will lead to."

She chuckled. "Let me assure you, it's not going to lead to anything. Randy and I are history. But a breakup doesn't necessarily mean you can leave that part of your life totally behind. These people have been a part of my life over twenty years. I can't turn my back on them now."

He grabbed her hand, caressing it softly. "But I don't want you to forget that they're your past, and you and Geordi register big in my future."

"Don't rush things, Marc," she admonished. "Just friends, remember?"

His hold on her hand tightened. "That 'just friends' thing is out the window after tomorrow. There are limits to being just friends. I don't want to mess around and lose you."

She looked uncertain about a response, and tried to dodge the issue by changing the subject. "Hey, would you like something to drink? And I made some brownies today. Would you like one?"

He decided not to push it. "Yes, to both," he said, as he got down on the floor to play with Geordi.

Before he left, she surprised him by asking if they could pray together. They did, with each lifting their personal concerns and issues, as well as the other person's up before the Lord, and praying for His will. That sealed it for Marc. C.J. was the wife he had been looking for and praying for, no matter what, or how long it would take.

Chapter Thirty-Five

C.J.

FRIDAY MORNING, AFTER LEAVING GEORDI WITH MS. MAGGIE, C.J. found the courtroom and took a seat beside her attorney. She really didn't know what to expect, but her silent prayer was, "Father, I trust You whatever the outcome of this may be—Your will be done."

The judge came in and took his seat. "Mr. and Mrs. Singleton, I want you to know that I've reviewed this case closely. Are you ready to finalize this divorce?"

"Yes, Your Honor," they both answered.

"Good, because one way or another, it is going to be resolved today. Mrs. Singleton, is there any desire on your part to work toward restoration?"

"No, Your Honor."

"And you've petitioned this court for half of all the community property and for transitional support?"

"Yes, Your Honor."

"Mr. Singleton, I've considered all the evidence submitted, and it seems you took possession of everything—the home, all of the assets, even your wife's ability to earn an income because of negative media attention due to your ongoing exploits. Do you have any desire to contest her petition, or to restore this marriage?"

Randy's answer was slow in coming as he looked over at C.J., but he finally said, "No, Your Honor."

"Well, in light of everything, I'm ordering that you pay her the support she should have had from the time you forced her out of your home. She will get half of all assets—and I do mean everything acquired during your marriage, and because you have purposely delayed the settlement of this decree, you will also give her the half you took from the sale of your home, and pay all of her legal expenses. You pay to play, Mr. Singleton, especially when you do it foolishly."

Randy, who looked to be in shock, shouted, "What!"

His attorney quickly grabbed his shoulder to quiet him.

C.J. sat quietly, but inside she was rejoicing and screaming praises to God at the top of her lungs. God had been faithful! After nearly two years of waiting, He'd given her a "suddenly" victory. So what if Randy was shooting daggers through her with his eyes?

Randy

Randy was furious. Yes, he'd been prepared to divide half of the money, investments and possessions, but to have to give her his half of the money from the sale of the house—money he'd already spent—pay all of her living expenses, and then pay her legal expenses plus his own would leave him . . . not broke, but with a lot less than he'd expected. He angrily expressed this to his attorney.

"But let me remind you that Willa could very well end up with what you have left. You need your wife's help with your upcoming trial, Randy. That's why I couldn't let you blow it with her."

As soon as Randy got home, he called C.J. but didn't get an answer. "Probably out celebrating taking over half of everything I have," he grumbled.

He called his parents to let them know the outcome and ranted his anger at C.J., her attorney, his attorney, and the judge. "They all sat there and took over half of everything I have!" he raged.

"Son," his dad said in a quiet voice, "maybe it's for the best. I'd rather see C.J. get it than that other woman, or to see you waste it. At least C.J. will do something useful with it. Your only objective now should be to get out that mess with that other woman. You gon' have to let this go."

"I'm still going to tell C.J. about herself. Why should I have to pay her legal expenses?"

"Your foolishness has cost you a lot. Let it be a lesson that you learn from."

"Why are you changing? All my life, you've been with me in everything—even wrongdoing. Why are you all of a sudden changing?"

"Son, it's because I'm staring death in the face, and realizing what's important. You and your mother and I haven't treated that woman right. You beat her and threw her out of her home without any support, and we didn't lift a finger to help her. I regret that, and I don't want you to come face to face with the end of your life and see nothing but a string of regrets behind you."

"Twenty years of playing pro ball is not exactly wasting my life."

"No, but you've managed to send those years down the drain in just a few months."

Randy was seething. "Now, you're sounding like C.J. That's the kind of talk she was doing before we split."

"I just hate you didn't listen to her, Son. Maybe things would have turned out different, and you wouldn't be on trial for rape."

Chapter Thirty-Six

C.J.

C.J. TOOK OFF FRIDAY AFTERNOON FOR RIVERWOOD, WHERE SHE and Geordi spent the weekend with her parents. She returned Sunday night, so she could get ready for Randy's parents, who would arrive Tuesday. No rest for the weary.

Monday morning, C.J. was up early, preparing for her houseguests. She cleaned the house, went to the grocery store, and was in her yard working by noon.

She finished potting some plants she had bought for the front porch, then pulled aggressively at some weeds she had spotted in her flower bed, while keeping a close eye on Geordi, who was busy trying to maneuver his walker through the grass.

Tired, sweaty and ready for a shower, and knowing Geordi would be ready for a nap soon, she was gathering up her tools and supplies to place them in the garage, paying little attention to a car cruising slowly down the street. She spoke to Ms. Maggie and her husband, Bert, who had come out of their house and were playing with Geordi.

The cruising car had turned around and was now stopping along the curb in front of her house. C.J. looked curiously as a pretty, well-groomed woman got out and walked toward her.

"Well, well! Guess who's coming to visit?" the woman said. "Let me introduce myself. I'm Cleah Fields Carrington, and I wanted to tell you personally that I don't take kindly to you coming between me and my husband. I run things in this city and I'm telling you to get your behind out of Houston, or I will personally see to it that you're run out."

C.J. stared at Cleah in amazement and said, "You must have lost every bit of sense you ever had to come to my home making threats. Go away! Get off my property." She waved her hands like she was swatting at a worrisome insect.

Cleah chuckled. "I am City Councilwoman Cleah Fields Carrington. I can go anywhere I please in this city, including this property." Her eyes roamed over the house and finally wandered to Geordi, who was still trying to run through the grass in his walker. Her face tightened with anger. "If you think having this little . . ." She called the baby a vile name, "for my husband is going to get you anywhere, then let me assure you, you're wrong. You and that brat are out of here."

C.J. dropped the tools she was holding and started walking toward Cleah. She was seeing the same red haze that came over her when she'd snapped and ended up shooting at Randy and Willa. "Lord, I promised not to lose it like that again, but there comes a time . . ." She started speaking the Word of God.

Cleah looked puzzled, but kept talking mess and throwing out threats.

C.J. kept walking toward her, speaking quietly, but with steel in her voice. "You will not come on my property, threaten me and call my child out of his name, Cleah. You think that because I have let you talk to me like I'm a dog that you're dealing with a weak person, but trust me, you are wrong. You probably also think that I left my job because of your threats, but be assured, I left for my own reasons. Now, if you don't get off my property, you're going to be eating a mouthful of my land, and then you're going to jail because you are trespassing. I'm telling you again, get off my property!"

"I knew it!" Cleah yelled, although she was starting to look nervous. "You're nothing but a low-life, street thug."

"I'm at my own house, and minding my own business, which is more than I can say for you. I'm a lady, but I do know how to fight, and I'm telling you one more time, to get off my property!"

Cleah took an aggressive step toward C.J., yelling, "You don't tell me what to do. I leave when I'm good and ready." She stopped when she realized C.J. was still slowly walking toward her, saying something.

"You come on my property with threats and harsh words, calling my child vile names. But I'm speaking to you in the name of the Lord, Jesus Christ. The Lord is my light and my salvation, whom shall I fear? The Lord is the strength of my life, of whom shall I be afraid. When the wicked, even my enemy and my foe come upon me to destroy me, she shall stumble and she shall fall."

Cleah looked around fearfully as though to see who C.J. was talking to, but C.J. continued walking toward her, still talking.

"If God be for me, who or what can be against me? I am more than a conqueror through Christ who strengthens me and gives me the power to do what I need to do. Greater is He that is in me than he—or she—that is in the world."

Cleah was stumbling backward. "Wh-what are you talking about? What are you . . ." That was as far as she got. She looked surprised and shocked when she was suddenly on the ground, her face buried in the ground and C.J.'s foot was on her neck. She managed to scream, "Call the police, this woman is trying to kill me."

"That's not the way we saw it," Ms. Maggie huffed. "She asked you several times to get off her property. We heard you threatening her and her baby and saw you getting ready to attack her, so what else was she supposed to do? "

C.J. leaned over and asked, "Are you going to leave or do you want to eat more of my dirt?"

"You're going to jail for this. As soon as I get back to my office, I'm filing assault charges and sending the police after you," Cleah said, struggling to get herself up from the ground.

C.J. took a step toward her, threw her hands in the air and yelled, "No weapon formed against me shall prosper and every tongue raised against me in judgment I will show to be in the wrong, halle-lujah, thank you, Jesus!"

Cleah screamed and tried to run, but stumbled over the curb and fell again before getting to her car and driving off.

Ms. Maggie was bent over laughing, and Mr. Bert was on the ground holding his stomach he was laughing so hard.

Cleah

A shaken Cleah managed to drive herself downtown to her office, with plans running through her mind of what she was going to do to Catherine Stroman. How dare that woman attack her! She was Councilmember Cleah Fields Carrington! The person soon to be elected to a state senate seat! Marc was going to hear about this immediately.

She should have known something was amiss when she saw her staff gathered around the television. Normally she would have said something to them, but she was so angry and disheveled from that woman's attack that she knew she needed to calm down, tidy herself, and take care of that Catherine Stroman.

A large envelope lay in the middle of her desk, and was marked confidential. There was nothing out of the ordinary about that, since she was always getting confidential mail.

She grabbed her letter opener and slit it open, curious to see what it was—Hopefully, a campaign contribution.

Her eyes widened in shock when alarming words jumped out at her—*Bid Fixing, Election Improprieties, Misappropriation of Funds, Illegal Actions to Influence City Policies* . . . With her heart beating double time, she started reading the document from the top. "You are hereby advised to leave your council position immediately, to withdraw your bid for a state senate seat, and to never seek to hold a public office in the city, county or state of Texas again. If you do, charges will be filed against you, and you will be vigorously prosecuted and sent to prison for these documented infractions.

If you choose to fight these charges, you may do so by turning yourself in to the District Attorney and advising of your intent to dispute them. Failure to act promptly will result in your immediate arrest and prosecution.

Cleah's mouth fell open, and her hands were shaking so badly she could no longer hold the document. "Marc! I have to call Marc! He can help me with this."

She managed to dial Marc's private number and was surprised when his secretary answered. "Where is the Chief?" she asked rudely.

"I don't know, Councilwoman. He hasn't made it back from the press conference yet. I'm sure he's probably still answering questions about his resignation."

"His what!"

"The Chief submitted his resignation today. Didn't you know?"

Cleah threw the phone down and started throwing papers into her briefcase . . . picturing herself being led away in handcuffs at any moment. She had to get out of there—fast! "Carl!" she screamed. "Come in here—now!"

Carl rushed in to see what Cleah wanted, and she gestured to the document on her desk.

"Help me! I've got to get out of here."

Carl picked the document up and started reading. When he got to the part about going to jail, he grabbed his head as though in pain. "Oh, God, I'm thinking about all the illegal acts I've done for you." He dropped the document like it was on fire.

Cleah looked at him and screamed, "Didn't you hear what I said? Help me!"

Carl ran to the door, then stopped and said, "I'm getting out of here as fast as I can. I've done a lot for you but I'm not going to jail for you. I told you not to mess with Marc and that woman, because you know he doesn't play!"

He grabbed some things from his own office and was gone without saying another word to Cleah, who was still yelling for his help.

166

Chapter Thirty-Seven

Randy

RANDY PICKED HIS PARENTS UP FROM THE AIRPORT AND DROVE them to C.J.'s house. It hit him like an avalanche the moment he walked into the house—home sickness! He peeked into the formal living and dining rooms on the way to the family room.

The familiar furnishings and decorations, his wife's presence, the aroma of home cooking—all made it feel like home. The house was not as large as their other houses, but plenty spacious enough to live in comfortably and he was filled with longing to come home.

After they relaxed, C.J. offered to show them around. Randy was handling his longing okay until he heard a baby crying and saw C.J. pick a baby up from a playpen. His heart stopped cold.

"Whose baby is this, C.J.?" he asked, while trying to calculate the baby's age. When she didn't answer, he ran and got in her face. "I said, whose baby is this? And you better not say it's yours!"

"That's not your business, Randy. But just so you know, it's my brother, Chuck's baby."

Randy grabbed and started shaking her. "I don't believe you! He looks just like you. How are you going to be having a baby by some other dude while you're taking over half of what I own? I ought to beat the hell out of you, and throw both of y'all out of this house you bought with my money."

"Randy! Stop that!" his dad yelled. "What's wrong with you?"

"I don't care if you believe it or not," C.J. said, angrily. "This is my nephew, but he might as well be mine since I've had him for most of his life."

"Come on, C.J. and show us around." Randy's mother said, giving her son a disapproving look. "Then I'm going to get comfortable and eat some of whatever that is that's smells so good."

Still fuming, Randy followed them up the stairway that opened into a large open space that held a pool table—his pool table—and comfortable chairs grouped around a television set on one of the walls. C.J. led them across the room and into a corner bedroom.

"This room is connected to another one by a Jack and Jill bathroom." She led them through the bathroom and into another bedroom. "You can have either one of them."

Then she led them back through the pool table and TV room to the other side of the house. "This is my bedroom," she said, leading them into a spacious bedroom with a king-sized bed and a baby bed in the corner. Double doors led to a bathroom that was just as fabulous as the bedroom.

Out of C.J.'s bedroom, to the other end of the house was another room which had a queen-sized bed and French doors that opened onto a small deck that looked out over the lake. "This room has its own full bath, but it's not as large as the other two you saw with the Jack and Jill bathroom. I think I'm going to eventually turn it into a sitting room."

They followed her back downstairs where they saw a nice size office next to the family room, the large kitchen area, and a sunroom that led out to a covered deck and back yard that overlooked the lake.

"I'm going to love sitting out here," Randy's father said, with a smile. "I love your house, C.J., and sure do thank you for sharing it with us."

"You're welcome," she said. "Now, why don't y'all eat some

homemade soup, salad and cornbread, then you can rest. I know y'all must be worn out, and you have a busy day ahead tomorrow."

"Thank you, C.J.," Randy's mother said. "I feel right at home. Randy, you need to go to the grocery store for me, but first, take our bags to that first bedroom we looked at."

"I'm not doing anything until after I eat. I'm hungry," he said, as he headed to the kitchen. He left after he ate the delicious food C.J. had cooked, and again felt intense homesickness. Randy didn't like going to the grocery store because he never knew where to look for things, but he managed to find everything on his mother's list with help from store employees. After he returned with most of the things on his mother's list, he was reluctant to leave because truthfully, he felt like he was at home already. He was tempted to ask C.J. if he could stay but just couldn't figure out how to ask.

He finally went home and got drunk so he could forget what he had lost, and what his bleak looking future might hold.

Chapter Thirty-Eight
C.J.

C.J. MADE SURE THE SINGLETONS WERE SETTLED FOR THE NIGHT before she took Geordi and went to her bedroom, where she prayed for Mr. Singleton, who didn't look well at all; for Mrs. Singleton, who looked tired and worried; and for Randy, facing trial and possible prison time for rape.

The next morning they ate breakfast and waited on Randy who was supposed to pick his parents up and take them to the hospital. Randy didn't show up, and didn't answer his phone, so C.J. ended up taking them. She asked Ms. Maggie to keep Geordi because she didn't know how long they would be at the hospital. She was so glad she did—they were there for hours.

Finally, Mrs. Singleton came home with her, but Mr. Singleton stayed the night to undergo more tests and treatments.

Thursday morning, C.J. and Mrs. Singleton got to the courthouse early for Randy's trial, and sat behind him, along with Randy's friend, Kyle, and his wife, Willa's ex-husband, and a woman who looked familiar but C.J. couldn't place her.

C.J. had asked several people to be in prayer for the truth to be revealed and justice to prevail. She had turned the video of Randy and Willa together in her bed—the same one used to prove his infidelity in the divorce proceedings—over to Randy's attorney and submitted a written statement (leaving out the shooting part of course) The attorney said she still might have to testify though.

As soon as the judge entered the courtroom, Randy's attorney requested a conference in the Judge's chambers. Both attorneys followed the judge out of the courtroom.

Thirty minutes, then an hour passed. Everyone in the courtroom became antsy, wondering what was going on. When they finally came out, C.J. knew it was okay. Randy's attorney was smiling, and Willa's attorney had an angry, sour look on his face.

The Judge settled in his chair, then said, "I have reviewed the evidence in this case, including a very explicit video involving the plaintiff in another incident in the defendant's home, and statements from several witnesses, including the plaintiff's ex-husband and the defendant's ex-wife, all of which have been reviewed by the District Attorney. We are in agreement that the plaintiff's case is flawed and is therefore discredited, and was filed for the sole purpose of extorting money from Mr. Singleton. I am therefore dismissing the charges against Mr. Singleton, and instructing the D. A.'s office to take appropriate action against the plaintiff and all those involved."

When they heard the Judge's verdict, most of Willa's supporters made quick exits. Two women, who C.J. assumed were Willa's sisters because of their resemblance to each other, jumped up and ran out of the courtroom, and another woman who Willa called Courtney and kept telling to shut up, started yelling that Willa blackmailed her to do everything including helping her set Randy up, drug him, and accuse him of rape, which never took place. She screamed out the information as she was on her way out. A nervous looking man who was supposed to testify on Willa's behalf about the emotional damage the rape had done to Willa, didn't run, but hurried out.

It turned out that in addition to what C.J. had provided, Willa's ex-husband had provided testimony that Willa had tried to do something similar to him, and the woman C.J. didn't recognize was a woman who worked in C.J.'s beauty salon, who had informed Willa of C.J.'s appointment times. That was how Willa had known C.J. wouldn't be home on that disastrous day. The woman felt guilty and provided a statement that she had inadvertently helped Willa destroy Randy's marriage and didn't want to be a part of what could be a false accusation of rape.

Randy turned and hugged C.J. close, saying, "Thank you, babe, thank you!" He then went to the others and thanked each one, before going to his mother, hugging her and thanking her for always being there for him.

C.J. and Mrs. Singleton left to go to the hospital to pick up Mr. Singleton, who was being released that evening and Randy disappeared.

On Friday, Mr. Singleton had to go back for a final treatment and consultation. C.J. sat with him and Mrs. Singleton as they received instructions from the patient care counselor. He was advised to rest before he traveled back home. His file would be sent to his doctor in Little Rock, where his treatments would continue, but he would come back to M.D. Anderson in three months for a follow-up evaluation.

Mr. Singleton was weak from all the tests and treatments, but was in good spirits. "Thank you, C.J.," he said, in a weak voice. "I don't know what we'd do without you."

"That's for sure!" Mrs. Singleton said. "And thank you for helping Randy get out of that rape mess too."

"C.J.," Mr. Singleton said, "Will you take me to church Sunday?"

Her heart swelled in praise to God. "Of course I will, Mr. Singleton. I'd be happy to take you to church."

Randy

Randy went home after the trial and celebrated by getting drunk. He wanted to go to C.J.'s house, but he knew they were at the hospital, and he didn't want to go there.

At some point during the day, his mind cleared up enough for him to remember how much C.J.'s house felt like home, and a thought hit him. If C.J. bought that house before the divorce was final, it was community property, and half his. He gleefully called his attorney.

The attorney called him back the next morning. "Sorry, Randy but your wife hasn't purchased the house—probably on the advice of her attorney. She's leasing with the option to buy."

Randy's next thought was to buy the house. She couldn't refuse to let him move into his own house. But ironically, the owner of record was Gilmore Enterprises—Jason Gilmore to be precise—the guy married to C.J.'s cousin, Jaci. That caused him to groan, but he decided to make an offer for the house anyway; *after all, Jason is a businessman*, he thought.

The next day he walked into Jason's stylish office, and immediately noticed the numerous pictures of Jason's wife scattered around the office. The dude was obviously crazy about the woman.

He noticed that Jason didn't try to hide his dislike for him. "What's up, Randy? What can I do for you today?" Jason asked, coldly.

"Well, it's like this. You own a particular piece of property that I'm interested in buying. I'd like to get the ball rolling on that today," he answered.

"What property is that?" Jason asked, although Randy was sure he already knew.

"It's the house that C.J. is leasing. I want to buy it from you."

Jason shook his head. "I can't do that, Randy. C.J. has a lease/purchase agreement on that property and has already started the process to buy it."

"I'm willing to pay above the asking price. You name it."

Jason shook his head. "Like I said, that house is not available, but I can find you one that I'm sure you'll like as much."

"Uh, uh. I want that house for personal reasons."

Jason's eyes narrowed. "Why, Randy? Because C.J. has it? You put the woman out of one house, now you want to put her out of another one? What has she done to you that makes you so vindictive toward her? She's trying to get her life back on track and move forward. Why don't you leave her alone?"

"Not that it's any of your business, but I want to buy the house for her. I'm trying every way I know to make up for what I've done to her. To be honest, I'm trying to put my marriage back together. I want my wife back."

"Well, I don't think buying that house out from under her is the way to get her back. And as long as I have anything to do with it, you won't be doing that. I suggest you reconcile with your wife, if you can, then I'll sell it to both of you, but as of now, C.J. has first dibs on it."

"Look! I came to you man-to-man, asking for your help. Can't you cut a brother some slack?"

"No, I can't. Even if I wanted to, ethically, I would be unable to do what you're asking. And since C.J. is part of my family now, I certainly wouldn't even think about it. My advice to you is to leave her alone so both of you can move on. Now unless you want to commission me to look for another house, I think that concludes our business today." He stood and extended his hand to Randy.

"Keep your advice," Randy said, nastily, and walked out of the office.

Chapter Thirty-Nine

Marc

MARC CALLED C.J. FRIDAY NIGHT. "I HEARD ABOUT RANDY'S acquittal. How are things going with his parents?"

C.J. told him briefly about Randy's dad's treatment, and that he would have to come back in three months for evaluation and any needed treatment.

"And they're staying with you again?" He groaned in frustration at her answer. "I still don't like it, but I know you couldn't say no to them because it sounds like Randy hasn't risen to the occasion. So when are they leaving?"

"No, I couldn't say no, Marc," she said quietly. "I was hoping they'd leave Saturday or Sunday, but Mr. Singleton is enjoying sitting out on my deck and playing with Geordi so much that he's not ready to leave. He wants to go to church with me Sunday, so hopefully they'll leave Monday."

"Is Randy driving them, or are they flying back?"

"I don't know, Marc. I gotta tell you though, I'm ready to have my house back again."

"And I'm ready for you to have it back. I have a lot to tell you."

"About what? Your new job?"

"Yes, and about what's happening with Cleah."

"Oh. I didn't tell you what happened. Cleah came to my house and threatened to run me out of town."

Marc laughed. "She told me. Said you attacked her and was yelling something about God and how He was going to get her. I don't know what you said, but trust me, Cleah is scared of you. She's in deep trouble so you won't have any more problems with her."

"I did not attack her! She was the one trying to come on like gang-busters. I merely spoke the Word of God to her."

"Well, she had no business coming to your house anyway. But what-ever you did, it rattled her badly. Anyway, she's gone. Cleaned out her office and disappeared without a word to anybody. But she really had no choice because of the trouble she's in. I'll tell you about it later."

C.J. was amazed at how completely God had answered her prayer to stop Cleah's evil plan to harm her and others. "Thank You, Father, for another victory!"

"Amen to that!" Marc said. "Now, all I want to know is when you'll go out with me."

"Don't push! I'm praying about it, and I suggest you do the same."

"I am praying, C.J., but there comes a time for action." He was getting impatient, although he knew she was right.

Marc called Jason Gilmore the next day, and followed up with a meeting at Jason's office. When he arrived, Jason's brother, Ron was there. After they got the small talk out of the way, Marc got down to why he was there.

"I know it's no secret that I'm interested in C.J. Have been ever since I met her even though I didn't know about all the baggage she has. Anyway, I'm very interested, and I was wondering if you guys could tell me a little about her. I mean, you're married to her cousins, and from talking to C.J. I know they all grew up together."

Ron was the first to respond. "Look, Marc, C.J.'s good people, as long as you don't make her mad. If you do, she might grab her rifle and start shooting. Ask Randy." They all laughed uproariously before Ron continued.

"Seriously though, C.J. will do anything to help you, but she's not going to take a lot of mess. How she stayed with that jerk, Randy for so long is beyond me."

Marc said, "Yeah, I know about the shooting. She did say she missed them on purpose, that she could have hit them if she'd wanted to."

"Yep," Jason said. "Those cousins are nothing to play with. Ron and I both have found that out, but I tell you what, I wouldn't trade my wife for anything."

"Me neither," Ron said. "And it hasn't been that long ago that I thought I would never settle down with one woman. But when I fell for Nita, it was all over. She put me through hell but that's because she was in an abusive marriage for years."

"Yeah, Jaci had trust issues and it took me a long time to convince her I really love her," Jason added. "But let me tell you, those cousins don't play. There are some more of them too, so you'd better come right with C.J. or you gon' have to answer to a lot of people," he warned, with a hard look at Marc.

Ron chuckled. "Man, I saw my wife whip a big dude's behind, and make him crawl away from her crying for mercy."

Jason laughed, then said, "And Ron had to pull Jaci off a crazy woman who was messing with her about me. That woman got up running too."

Marc was cracking up at the stories they told about their wives. "That's why I'm trying to find out more about C.J. before I'm too far in—which I might be already," he admitted. "But I don't want my strong attraction to her to lead me into another mistake."

"Let me tell you, Marc. You can come on like an eighteen wheeler, but until C.J. is ready, you're not getting anywhere," Jason said, with a chuckle.

"That's right!" Ron added. "You can't rush those cousins, or you'll lose them. Your best bet is to be patient and love her from a distance. If it's supposed to happen, she'll come around when she's ready and it'll be worth the wait."

"I just don't want to take a chance on losing her. Randy is still very much in the picture, and I wouldn't trust him as far as I can throw him."

"You'd better not!" Jason said, with a look of dislike. "That dude tried to buy C.J.'s house right out from under her. Claims he wanted to buy it for her, but this was coming from a man who threw her out of their house with no support. No, that dude is not to be trusted."

Marc looked disgusted. "That kind of makes me want to do some serious damage to him."

"Well, C.J. beat the hell out of him herself," Jason told him. "I was talking to Kyle Bingham, Randy's former teammate, and Kyle said Randy looked like he'd been in a gang fight with about five men. He was scratched up, had big knots on his head, and could hardly walk because of some well-placed blows to certain areas. C.J. did him in. I bet he won't try that again."

They all cracked up. "I hope she won't ever have to," Marc finally said.

Before he left, they invited him to come to their church ManPower meetings on Saturday mornings. "You'll learn a lot about how God wants us to live as godly men and husbands," Jason told him.

That night, he called C.J. and told her he was leaving for Virginia for a few days for meetings, and that hopefully when he returned, she would agree to go out with him.

"Marc, you're supposed to be praying about it and letting the Lord guide and direct this," she reminded.

He laughed, remembering the advice from Ron and Jason. "Okay, okay! But can I call you?"

"I don't think it'll do any good to tell you not to," she answered.

Chapter Forty

C.J.

S UNDAY MORNING, C.J. GOT READY TO GO TO CHURCH WITH THE Singletons, and was surprised when Randy showed up to go with them.

"What?" he asked snidely, after seeing her surprise. "I can't go to church?"

"No, it's fine," she said. "I'm just blown away by it since you've never shown any interest before."

They drove to the church with his parents in the back seat with Geordi, and Randy in the front passenger seat. She led them into the large worship center, but stopped short of going to the front of the church where she usually sat. She also kept Geordi with her instead of taking him to the nursery, in case Mr. Singleton started feeling bad and they had to leave.

The choir was great, as always, and when Pastor Robinson stood and gave his sermon topic, she silently thanked God. It sounded like it was right on time.

Randy's parents had lived their entire lives believing that everything they had accomplished was through their own efforts and without help from nothing and nobody else.

They proudly boasted about how they had worked hard, pushed themselves, and overcame all the obstacles that stood in the way. "Randy became a successful professional basketball player because we pushed him and taught him not to let anything stop him." Mr. Singleton said often. "When other kids were playing and goofing off, Randy was somewhere practicing to get that ball into that basket, and instead of sitting up in church, we were working to pay for basketball camps to help improve his skills."

Even though they belonged to a church and went occasionally, C.J. knew they didn't have a strong foundation in the Word of God. Obviously, Mr. Singleton's illness was having a serious effect on his spiritual condition. She silently prayed, "Lord, speak to their hearts and let Your light shine so brightly that they will all be drawn to You."

Pastor Robinson started the sermon by saying, "The Word of God tells us that in this world, we are going to have troubles, trials and tribulations, but we should not be afraid because God has overcome them all. So I want to stress today that we should never under estimate God."

He continued by reading a passage of Scripture from Second Corinthians, Chapter 4, verses 1 – 9. "I'm going to be focusing on the last two verses, which reads, *'We are troubled on every side, but not distressed; we are perplexed, but not in despair; we are persecuted, but not forsaken; we are cast down, but not destroyed'*. Sooner or later, we're all going to be confronted by troubles, distresses, perplexities, and persecutions. But notice there is a 'but promise' behind each of these conditions which tells us that because we have the treasure—which is the presence and power of Almighty God—in us, with us, and for us, it's going to be alright. So I would like to leave just two words with you today and they are: BUT GOD. If we can just remember these two little words, we will have the victory over the troubles, perplexities, persecutions and being cast down. Whatever trouble you may be dealing with today, (and like I said, in this world we are going to have trouble) don't be distressed, don't be in despair, don't feel forsaken, and don't be destroyed. God has promised to never leave or forsake us and we can trust that He will help us through it. However, I have to ask—have you invited the Lord, Jesus Christ into your heart? He is the only way to that powerful treasure. So let me tell you about Jesus, and all He has done for us, then you will have the opportunity to invite Him into your own heart if you haven't done so."

C.J. noticed both Mr. and Mrs. Singleton crying as Pastor Robinson continued the sermon, and when he extended the invitation to come to Jesus, they both stood and went forward. Randy, again surprisingly, stood, looked at C.J. and said, "Will you go with me?" Without hesitation, she stood with the baby, and led the way down front to a counselor, who escorted them out the door.

When they got home from church, a large floral arrangement was sitting at her front door. Randy picked it up and brought it inside since C.J.'s arms were full carrying Geordi and his bag.

"Who's sending you flowers?" he demanded curiously, and was about to open the card when she snatched it out of his hand.

"None of your business, Randy," she snapped, and turned away from his hard stare.

Mrs. Singleton went to change clothes, while Mr. Singleton went to his favorite spot on the deck, taking the baby with him. When C.J. got back downstairs after changing clothes, Mrs. Singleton was in the kitchen and Randy had joined his dad on the deck.

"I thought I would make a salad and put the rolls in the oven. That roast you have in the oven smells wonderful," Mrs. Singleton complimented.

C.J. smiled. "Great," she said, as she checked the roast which was nestled in onions, potatoes and carrots. "We'll be eating soon. By the way, when do you think you'll be leaving?"

"Tomorrow. Randy promised to drive us back, which I'm happy about. We've just about gotten to the place where we hate the hassle of flying. I know it's going to be a long ride, but we'll stop if we need to."

"Hopefully, it'll be okay," C.J. answered. "They worked together to get the meal finished, then called Randy and his dad in to eat. C.J.

was anxious to look at that card, although she knew who the flowers were from.

They ate, and enjoyed some of the cake C.J. had baked earlier, then the Singletons went upstairs to nap and Randy left. Finally, she was able to open the card. She smiled when she read, *Thinking of you, and hope to see you soon. Love, Marc.*

Unfortunately, it would be longer than either of them expected.

Marc

Marc was ready to blow a gasket!

He'd had a great trip to Virginia to discuss his position and pinpoint expectations regarding his duties, and was pleased at the outcome. He was working to assure a smooth transition on his current job, and was happy that several very promising candidates had been interviewed to replace him as Police Chief, and although he would have input he wouldn't be the one to make the final selection.

He was working with Harry to learn the ropes of the security consulting business and had also been offered a visiting professor position on the staff of a local university, and was trying to see how he could fit it in. But as C.J. had cautioned, he had to be careful not to spread himself too thin.

Why couldn't things go as well in his personal pursuits? He had been trying to give C.J. the space and time she requested and he'd thought things were moving toward that, in spite of Randy and his parents' demands on her. He'd been going to the ManPower meetings on Saturday with Jason and Ron, and had decided to join their church, especially since C.J. was also there. So he almost lost it when he saw her at church, not only with the in-laws, but with Randy too. He'd stopped on the way to church and sent flowers to her, and had been envisioning her joy at receiving them. But when he saw her with Randy, that vision turned to something else, and other than a brief conversation when she called to thank him for the flowers, he hadn't talked to her at all Sunday. He was anxious for the Singletons to leave.

But when he called her Monday, they were still there, waiting for Randy who, according to C.J., could not be contacted. Randy's dad wasn't feeling well, and his mother had vetoed C.J.'s suggestion that they fly home, so they had settled in to stay another day or two with her.

Marc wanted to cuss, and was tempted to put out an all-points-bulletin for Randy's arrest, although he didn't have a legal reason to do so. He ranted to C.J. about letting them take advantage of her, and to say the least, that hadn't gone well.

"Marc, I'm stressed enough without you throwing your two-bits into it. Now, you need to back off. I have to go." She'd hung up before he could respond.

But she called him Wednesday morning with news he didn't want to hear.

"Hi, Marc, I'm at the grocery store to pick up a few things for my houseguests, and I just wanted to let you know that we still haven't heard from Randy, so I'm going to drive them to Little Rock."

"You're what! C.J., you don't owe these people anything, and you've already gone beyond what's reasonable. Put them on a plane and be done with it."

"I know you're right, Marc, and I would do that but Mr. Singleton is just not up to flying. At least if he's traveling in a car, we can stop if we need to."

"How long a trip is it?"

"It's nine or ten hours, but I know we'll have to stop at a hotel and spend the night on the way, so it'll be a two day trip."

He grunted in frustration and asked, "Why are you doing this, C.J.?"

She sighed. "Marc, I asked the Lord to help me forgive these people and to let me be a light in darkness, and a vessel of His love. Granted, I didn't have this in mind when I prayed, but I can only assume He did. They all prayed to receive Christ on Sunday, and I praise God for that, but now, I have to continue to be the light and the witness before them that He would like me to be. And there are some good things that can come from all this."

He grunted again because to his way of thinking, she was reading way too much in what she thought God was requiring of her. "And what would they be?"

"I'll be able to visit with my parents on the way back, and the main thing is if I don't do this, its no telling when they'll leave. Honestly, they don't seem to be in a hurry to get home, and of course, they're worried about Randy."

Marc chuckled in spite of being upset. "Well, that's because you've made them too comfortable. But I would honestly like to do some damage to that jerk Randy. So when are you leaving?"

"Tomorrow morning. I'll try to get to Marshall or Texarkana to spend the night, and then drive the rest of the way to Little Rock Friday morning."

"Well please stay in touch," he said before hanging up. He sat back in his comfortable desk chair to complain to God. "What's up with this, Father? Why did You send a woman into my life who's still tied to what she should be leaving behind her? I want a wife now, but the woman I want is in no hurry to become my wife. Haven't I waited long enough? What am I supposed to do? How long am I supposed to wait?"

He almost fell out of his chair when he immediately remembered what his grandfather used to say; *Be careful what you ask for because you just might get it.'* And right on the heels of that came thoughts that could've only come from God; *'You asked for a woman who loves the Lord and wants to serve Him. You asked for a woman who wants a family and who has the same family values you do. What did you expect? That she would only love who you want her to? That she would only serve who you think she should? That she would only value the families you want her to?'*

Marc sat up straight and was motionless for a while. He suddenly remembered all he had learned about C.J.——From Jason and Ron, that she would do anything to help anyone, but didn't take any mess. From Geordi's situation, that she was full of love and caring. From the anniversary party, that she was thoughtful and sought to make others happy. But he had also learned from Randy and Cleah, that

184

when pushed, she pushed back—— hard! He had to accept that C.J. was a strong, independent woman, and the question he needed to answer was if he was the man she was praying for.

He picked up the phone and ordered flowers for C.J. and asked the flower shop to write on the card that he loved and respected her.

He continued to work determinedly toward making his last days as Police Chief come to a successful end. Thankfully, there had been little fall-out for him from Cleah's disappearance, and although she had called him several times, he couldn't help her. He had warned her and others had warned her, but she'd believed she was invincible and had walked into a mess of her own making that no one could get her out of.

Chapter Forty-One
Randy

RANDY HUNG UP THE PHONE AFTER LISTENING TO SEVERAL MESSAGES from his parents that sounded like they were distressed and worried, followed by blistering messages from C.J. calling him all kinds of low-life jerks.

He knew they were calling because he had failed to show up to drive them back to Little Rock. He didn't have a good reason—— other than he was not only in the dumps, he was underneath them. He knew he was letting his parents down but couldn't seem to help himself. From the time he'd left C.J.'s house, he'd tried to drown himself in alcohol.

He was devastated by all he'd already lost, as well as all he was probably going to lose. His basketball career was over, his wife and home were gone, and his dad was on the way out. He honestly didn't know how to handle it all. He'd prayed for the Lord to come into his heart and take control of his life when he went to church with C.J., but nothing had changed—— in fact, things seemed to get worse. Both C.J. and the person who had counseled him and led him in the prayer had cautioned him that praying that prayer was only the beginning; that he needed to get in the Word of God and learn about the Savior he had prayed to receive. Instead, he was trying to lose himself in alcohol.

He was heartbroken over his dad's illness, jealous over the fact that his mother, who had always disliked his wife, now seemed to love her more than she loved him, and his wife didn't want anything to do with him and by all indications, had another man in her life, as well as the child she'd always wanted, while he had . . . nothing.

He wallowed deeper into self-pity. Who did he have? Who was going to take care of him? Who would love him? He had no adoring fans anymore, and he had run all his friends away. "I hate my life!"

He ignored the constantly ringing telephone as he staggered across the room and grabbed another bottle of scotch and guzzled it down, seeking to find solace, comfort and oblivion with alcohol. The last thing he remembered was repeating in a slurred voice, "I hate my life!"

C.J.

The Singletons were so worried about Randy that they asked C.J. to try to find out where he was and if he was okay.

C.J. called Kyle, told him what was going on, and asked him to go to Randy's place to check on him. Kyle called her back a couple of hours later. He'd had to get the maintenance man to open the door to Randy's place, and had found Randy unconscious on the floor. Kyle called an ambulance and was following it to the hospital.

There was no way Randy's parents were going to leave until they saw Randy through this crisis. It turned out that he was in an alcoholic coma, and would be in the hospital several days, then moved to a rehab facility. That meant C.J. would have houseguests indefinitely, which posed a problem with Mr. Singleton's treatments. She had to go through the hassle of arranging for him to get interim treatments at M.D. Anderson. She ran herself ragged taking Randy's dad to the hospital for his treatments; taking them to see Randy; and making sure they had everything they needed.

After Randy was moved to rehab, his parents decided they could finally go home. C.J. drove them to Little Rock, then visited with her parents on the way back home.

She was weary, and thankfully the next several weeks passed without incident. Life had been hectic for so long, she had to mentally shift gears and force herself to relax. Surprisingly, Marc spent a lot of time with her helping her take care of some things and just relax.

She and Marc also talked about the situation with Geordi, but he only said, "They're wrong and inconsiderate to leave this in limbo? I mean, this baby will be a year old pretty soon. You do realize they're taking advantage of you, huh?"

"I know it, but what can I do?" she answered in a sad voice.

Chapter Forty-Two

Marc

MARC TRIED NOT TO CRITICIZE C.J.'S ATTACHMENT TO RANDY AND HIS family, but it bothered him. So when she returned from taking them home, he started using his abundance of accrued vacation time and kept his promise about making sure they got to know each other better. He was at her house almost every day, helping her plant a small garden in a corner of the back yard, playing with Geordi, and even cooking what he called his specialty—which turned out to be spaghetti—and shooting pool and watching movies with her.

They spent a lot of time talking about their hopes for the future, their likes and dislikes, and yes, they did spend some time on the couch, exchanging some hot kisses and embraces, but she made sure she cooled things off before they went too far.

He finally brought up his desire for her to meet his family. "I've been talking about you so much to my sister that she wants to meet you. So she's invited us to a cookout this weekend. Just family, so will you go?"

"I don't know, Marc," C.J. answered. "Do they know I just got a divorce?"

"Yes, and they know how long you waited for that divorce. My sister thinks you're way overdue for another relationship."

"I'm not sure I agree with that, but okay, I'll go."

The following Saturday afternoon, Marc happily picked C.J. and Geordi up and drove them to his sister's home. His sister, Rosalind, who they called 'Roz' and her family welcomed her and the baby and made them feel right at home. C.J. complimented them on their beautiful home, then offered to help in the kitchen, which made Roz even happier.

Marc's teenage niece took over the care of Geordi, playing with him like she was his age, and Geordi loved it.

Throughout the evening, Marc watched C.J. to get a read on if she was enjoying herself, and as soon as they were in the car headed home, he asked, "So, did you enjoy yourself?"

"Yes, I did, very much. I admit I was a little nervous because I didn't know if they were going to be comparing me with Cleah or expecting someone like her."

"The answer to that is a resounding no. In fact, they couldn't stand her and were happy when the marriage ended."

By the time he got home that night, his mother was calling. "Son, Roz told us about meeting C.J. and Geordi, and sent us some of the pictures y'all took, and we feel slighted. She's lovely, Marc, and that baby is beautiful. We can't wait to meet them, so when are you going to bring them to see us?"

"Geez! My sister and her big mouth!" Marc exclaimed. "I don't know because C.J.'s just come through a pretty rough divorce, and she's very cautious about getting involved with anybody until she's sure she's ready. She's been reluctant to go out with me until now."

"Well, bringing her to see us will be a good thing. Do you want me to call and invite her? Give me her number."

"Mother, slow down!" He took a deep, frustrated breath. "No, I don't need you to call her. I can do my own talking. I'll see when she can get away."

"Well alright then, but I'm going to bug you until you bring her. We want to meet this woman who makes you happy. That's something we haven't seen before."

"I know that, Mother. I'll call you when I know something."

He called C.J. "Look, I started something. Roz called my parents and sent them some pictures, and now they're anxious to meet you."

"Oh, no, Marc. What did you tell them?"

"That I would ask you, and that was after my mother wanted to call you herself. They're not going to let up either. She said they feel slighted."

C.J. laughed. "Well, okay, I guess. But I hope we won't be giving them false hope."

"How about next weekend? And we'll make sure they understand that."

"Okay, I guess that'll be alright."

He had never enjoyed a road trip so much. C.J. was a lot of fun and she kept him laughing on the entire four hour drive to his parents' farm outside of Longview, Texas. When they arrived around noon on Saturday, a gang of people ran out of the house to greet them. Not only were his parents there, but two of his other siblings and their families, his grandparents, aunts, uncles and cousins—the whole clan. "Oh, we're so happy to finally meet you, C.J., and the baby too. My son's been wanting a family for years," his mother stated.

Everyone hugged C.J., then grabbed Geordi and smothered him with hugs and kisses. "He looks like you, Marc," his grandmother said.

He and C.J. looked at each other in amazement, and she spoke up. "Geordi's not my child, he's my nephew, but I've had him most of his life."

"Well, that's good, but this baby looks so much like y'all, he could belong to you and Marc," his mother said.

"Well, come on in," his dad said. "We've got dinner ready. Marc already told us y'all couldn't stay long."

Again, as soon as they were on the way home, he asked, "Well, did they scare you off?"

"Of course not, Marc. I'm used to big families and I really enjoyed meeting everyone. I don't know how they got the idea that Geordi is our child, though."

"Roz. I know you explained about him, but you know how families are. Wishful thinking will have them making things the way they want them to be."

"Oh, Lord! I hope I cleared that up."

"Maybe, but they love you and the baby so there's no way you're getting away from us now," he said with a grin.

Chapter Forty-Three
Randy

As soon as Randy got out of rehab, he acted on a decision he had made while there and headed to C.J.'s house. He pushed the doorbell, noting the large SUV parked in her driveway with more than a passing interest. He knew another dude was sniffing around, sending flowers and trying to get to his wife, but that was not going to happen if he had anything to say about it.

When C.J. opened the door, he stepped in without waiting for an invitation. "What took you so long?" he asked irritably.

"Randy, what are you doing here? You should have called first, because I have company," C.J. complained.

"I need to talk to you," he answered, as he moved further into the house where he saw a man sitting in the family room playing with the baby C.J. claimed was not hers. His eyes narrowed and his suspicions were aroused. Had she lied and was this the daddy? "Who is this?" he asked, rudely.

"This is a friend of mine. What do you want to talk to me about?"

The man stood and walked toward him. "I'm Marc Carrington," he said, extending his hand for a handshake.

"The Police Chief?" Randy asked, ignoring the hand and backing away. He hated cops. "What are you doing in my wife's house? Which my money paid for, I might add. Are you the dude who's been sending her flowers and trying to weasel your way in to help her spend my money?"

"She's a friend, and from what I understand, she's no longer your wife and I don't need your money."

Randy angrily retorted, "C.J. is always going to be my wife, mister. No divorce can change that, and I'm telling you now to step back off of her."

The cop crossed his arms and said, "As far as I'm concerned, she's a free woman, even if you've decided that your unfaithfulness, throwing her out of her home, the public humiliation you put her through and ultimate divorce was a mistake. You can't come back and play married until you get bored again. You need to grow up, man, and understand that this woman deserves better."

"Naw, dude! What you're not understanding is that C.J. has been my wife for over twenty years and will always be my wife. Now, we've had some problems, but that's the way it is. Now get out, or I will throw you out of my house if I have to."

"Randy!" C.J. yelled. "You have no right to come in here talking crazy. You're the one who needs to get out."

Randy shook his head. "No! You tell him to leave and never come back."

The cop looked at C.J. "Maybe I'd better leave, unless you need me to stay." He cut a warning eye to Randy.

"Okay, Marc, maybe that's best, and don't worry, I'll be okay." She walked with him to the door, where he kissed her, and said, "Call me if you need me," then tossed another hard look at Randy before walking out the door.

Randy was furious! That dude had the audacity to kiss his wife right in front of him. "I do not appreciate this, C.J.," he huffed angrily. "I came over here because I want to talk to you about us getting back together. I certainly didn't expect to find another dude here cooling his heels. What's up with that?"

He sat down and shook his head. It was costing a lot of effort to try and stay calm as he recalled all the reasons he wanted his wife back. She had taken care of him for so long and nothing had gone right in his life since she hadn't been there. He hated being alone. He wanted to have a place of comfort to come home to. He wanted his wife there to massage the aching muscles that still bothered him. Nothing was as soothing or as tender as her touch.

What had he been thinking to throw her away? She was a beautiful, faithful woman. He should have known another guy would waste no time swooping in on her.

C.J. had an angry, incredulous look on her face. "Randy, if you think I'm going to spend the rest of my life alone or living in misery with you, you're dead wrong. And understand this, I am not your wife anymore and you are the one who made that decision. And another thing you better understand is that this house and everything in it is legally mine. You have no say over who I invite into my house. I earned it the hard way—putting up with you for twenty years."

"That's why I'm here. I know I made a mistake. I want to come home, babe. I need you, we need each other. We've accumulated too much together to throw it away."

"If that's the only reason you want us together, you can forget it. There's more to life than money and material possessions."

"Like what?"

"Love, joy, peace, contentment, just to name a few things."

"Huh! You can't eat or live on none of that." Randy said, then realized he wasn't getting any closer to his goal. His whole life had been centered on reaching a goal and scoring. Now, C.J. was his goal and his biggest mistake had been to let her realize she could get along without him.

C.J. said, "And you can't buy it, and you can't buy me either, if that's what you're thinking."

"Okay, look! If you forget this divorce mess, I'll give you every-thing. I'll sign papers and it'll be in your bank account the next day. I just need you to let me come home. I'll even let you keep that baby.

My parents are crazy about both of y'all. But you have to let that other dude go . . . like yesterday. I don't want you seeing him ever again."

"You're crazy, Randy. You haven't heard a word I've said. There's not the remotest possibility I would ever go back to life with you. You want to live like an unmarried twenty year old, with no understanding of what it means to be a responsible, forty-year-old married man. I want a mature man; a man who appreciates having a good woman; a man who wants a family; a man who loves and serves God. That's not you, Randy, and sadly, you have no desire for it to be you. Now please leave. We don't have anything else to talk about!"

"And you think some policeman is going to be all that?"

"That's between God, me and Marc, and it's none of your business. I've prayed hard to forgive you because I know I must. Despite all that's happened I want us to get along. But the marriage is over and we both need to move on. "

"I'm not giving up, C.J. I know I made a huge mistake, and I want to correct it. I'll leave you alone for now. Just don't make any hasty' decisions about marrying someone you don't really know. Better the devil you know than the one you don't. Remember that."

"Just get out, Randy!"

Chapter Forty-Four

C.J.

C.J. CALLED MARC AS SOON AS RANDY LEFT. "MARC, HE'S GONE. I'm so sorry about that."

"I would be lying if I said I'm okay with your ex-husband coming to your house talking like you are still married to him," Marc answered. "I've been trying to be patient and give you some time, but you need to set him straight or tell me where I stand in this."

"I know . . . you're right, and I tried to do that, Marc. The thing is, Randy is having a hard time understanding our marriage is over. I just explained again that he and I are history."

"I hope you really mean that and that he got it this time. I'm on my way back right now."

"Okay." She hung up the phone and sat down to reflect on what had just happened. She had tried not to let things go beyond friendship with Marc until she was legally free to do so. But the question that still hung in her mind was where did God want her to go from here?

The doorbell rang. "Dang, he must have been around the corner," she mumbled as she ran to open the door, and as soon he came in, he grabbed her in a tight hug.

"I love you!" he said softly. "And let me make myself clear, I want you to be my wife. I know you don't want to jump into another marriage too soon, but I want you to understand that I want to marry you and have a family with you someday."

She side-stepped the proposal and said, "I'm so sorry Randy was rude to you."

"No problem, I would probably react the same way if I had destroyed my marriage and I knew someone was after my wife." He kissed her, hugging her tightly and C.J. thought she was going to melt.

She led him to the sofa. "Marc, I know you're ready for a serious relationship, but we're still a long way from that happening. We're still getting to know each other."

"Not in my mind. I know enough about you to want to marry you today. I've already profiled you, and you'd be surprised what I know about you."

She gasped! "Now that's scary! What? What do you know?"

He grinned and said, "I know you're argumentative, strong-willed, hot-tempered and stubborn. But you're also the most loving, caring, generous, dependable, sincere woman I've ever met. You love the Lord, you love and care for a baby that's not even yours, you'll go deer hunting and fishing with me, serve the Lord with me, and make a home that I'll love coming home to.

"I'm used to giving orders to thousands of people and fully expect them to be obeyed. But I know you will be hesitant to do as I ask unless it's what you want to do, and are more likely to have me obeying you, at least some of the time—in fact, I'm halfway intimidated by you. You're the woman I need to keep me on my toes, but more importantly, you are the woman I love and the one I want to spend the rest of my life with. You're likely to see a grown man cry if you say no.

"I know I can't offer you the kind of lifestyle you had with Randy, but I will make sure you are comfortable and secure. I'll be a loving husband, and one you can always depend on. I want to be the father of any children you have—in whatever way they arrive." He leaned over and planted another sweet kiss on her lips. "So will you marry me?"

She was blown away. "Wow, I have to admit I wasn't expecting all this."

"Well, what's your answer?"

"Marc, you know I can't say yes to your proposal now, huh?"

He gave her a disappointed look and said, "Well, you can't blame me for hoping, but I understand. We met each other at different seasons in our lives. My marriage was shorter, and has been over a long time. I've had time to adjust and get ready for a wife and family. You're just starting your adjustment process. And you're probably trying to decide if you even want to get married again, huh?"

She nodded. "I'm so glad you understand. I know you want a wife and a family, and I know you've wanted that for a long time now. And you're right about the fact that I haven't reached the point where I know I even want to get married again. But if I was ready, you would be the one."

He smiled and looked hurt all at the same time. "You know it won't be long before I'll be going to Virginia for six weeks. I was really hoping we would have some decisions made before I leave. So what are we going to do?"

"Needless to say, I am attracted to you, and I love being with you, love everything about you, but it's not fair for me to ask you to wait when you could easily find another woman who is ready right now."

"I don't want to find another woman, but any idea how long before you're ready? I don't want to wait indefinitely; after all, I'm not getting any younger, and I want children, but I was hoping to have some time alone with you for a while before we start a family, unless of course we still have Geordi."

"No, I have no idea how long it'll take, but I promise to think about it and pray," she said.

Marc looked disheartened and sighed. "Well, I'd better leave." He picked Geordi up who was playing with a toy Marc had brought for him. "See you later, big guy, he said hugging him."

C.J. walked with him to the door, hugged him, and watched as he backed out of her driveway.

She sat down to think. "Oh, Lord, two proposals within an hour.

What would You have me to do?" Three things they talked about in her counseling sessions when considering a new relationship came to her—Wisdom, watching and waiting. She just couldn't get away from the waiting, but at least she knew who she was waiting on—nobody but the Lord.

Randy didn't love her, and was only concerned about his own comfort and convenience. On the other hand, Marc said he loved her, wanted to marry her, be a godly husband, serve the Lord with her, and have a family with her. But was he God's will for her, and was it right to make a commitment when she was basically on the rebound?

A malicious demon sitting on her shoulder jabbed her with his pitchfork and whispered, "At least you know for sure what Randy's motives are, but Marc . . . can you be sure about who he is and why he really wants to marry you? Is it because you are a millionaire? Is it because he wants a family and you're his way of getting a ready-made family?"

BAM! She knocked that demon off her shoulder and told him to go to hell and stay there!

Chapter Forty-Five

Marc

MARC UNDERSTOOD C.J.'S HESITANCY, BUT HE WOULD'VE LIKED more assurance that he wasn't wasting his time. He recalled Jason and Ron's advice not to pressure her to make a decision, but he couldn't stay away from her.

After his resignation was effective, he was at C.J.'s house every morning, bringing her coffee and pastry. They'd drop Geordi off at the nursery or with Mrs. Maggie, and spend the day together. They worked in the yard and garden, he helped her paint a couple of rooms and kept her SUV washed and gassed up so she wouldn't have to do it with Geordi in the truck. They drove down to Galveston to visit Moody Gardens and walk on the beach, and spent a day at a fish farm where she caught more fish than he did.

They drove to her home town of Riverwood, Arkansas so he could meet her parents and had a delicious meal of buffalo fish, fries, hush puppies and salad. Marc ate until he couldn't get another mouthful in his stomach, and promised to come back and go deer hunting with C.J.'s dad. And while there, he met another cousin, Gina, who reminded him a lot of C.J., Jaci and Nita, and confirmed the validity of Jason and Ron's warning by threatening to hunt him down if he did anything to hurt her cousin.

Some days, they simply hung out at her house, walked around the lake in her neighborhood, and watched movies. He went to several counseling sessions with her and learned why she was so adamant about being cautious. They called it wisdom, watching and waiting. He also started attending church with her on a regular basis.

They shopped, and she helped him pick out some heavy clothes for when he would be in the much colder climate of Virginia. They prayed for God's guidance and direction for them, for God's keeping power over Marc and his new ventures, and for C.J.'s as well.

He needed to spend some time with his parents before he got too busy with his new job but he hated to leave C.J. No matter how hard he begged, she wouldn't agree to go with him.

"No, Marc, you need that time with your folks, and I need to get to work. I promised the Bradshaws I would start doing some work for them a while ago, and haven't been able to do it because of all that's been going on."

After spending several days with his family, he returned to Houston, spent a couple of days with C.J., then headed for Virginia. He left with a heavy heart, knowing he had some serious thinking to do. If C.J. couldn't—or wouldn't—accept his proposal soon, perhaps he should give up. But just the thought of doing that not only went against the grain, it also almost ripped his heart out.

C.J.

After Marc left, C.J started making plans for her event planning business. As a result of the anniversary party she had gotten several requests but had been unable to commit to them because of the hectic state of her life.

She missed Marc. But he was sending her flowers, calling her everyday, sometimes several times. During one of their conversations when he expressed his frustration about waiting, she shared that after all the life altering transitions she had recently gone through, she couldn't trust her emotions. "Marc, emotions are a powerful thing, and I made a mistake with Randy by not understanding that. Now, I'm too old to make any more stupid decisions. You do realize that statistics prove that the success rate of second marriages is less than that of first marriages, huh? We don't want to find ourselves in that predicament." He had to agree.

Marc told her his job assignment had already changed. In addition to teaching, the F.B.I. Academy was asking him to consult on more cases as a profiler, and the Justice department was calling on him more, which would mean more time there.

"Oh God, Marc. I'm starting to hate you took that job."

"Honestly, I didn't get the full scope of the job like I should have. But maybe it's for the best. At least I won't be close to you and pressuring you to make decisions you're not ready to make. That doesn't mean my feelings have changed though. I love you, and I plan to come home next week so don't make any plans."

The next week, she was so happy to see Marc that she let him convince her to go with him to visit his parents, and while there, Marc challenged her to demonstrate her shooting ability. C.J. tried to beg off, stating she was out of practice and she didn't have her own rifle with her.

But Marc insisted, went to get one of his dad's guns, and set up tin cans as targets for her to shoot at.

C.J. reluctantly agreed to do it. "Okay, let's do this. I can see I have to make a believer out of you." After she hit all the cans, which he kept moving further and further away, or throwing in the air, Marc was definitely a believer.

His dad laughingly said, "Give it up, Son. All I can say is, don't make her mad with a gun around."

Marc and C.J. looked at each other and laughed. She knew they were both thinking about Randy. "I told him I was out of practice. Otherwise I would've hit them all right in the middle," she said.

It seemed as though something or someone was just waiting for her to get back to Houston. Things started happening with a domino effect. A frantic call from Randy was the first domino to fall.

Chapter Forty-Six

Randy

RANDY WAS ALREADY AT A LOW PLACE WHEN HIS MOTHER'S CALL came with bad news about his dad. He hung the phone up and broke down in tears. His mother had just told him his dad's cancer had spread and the doctors didn't have a lot of hope for him. She wanted Randy to come home to Little Rock as soon as he could, and also wanted C.J. to come—something about a legal issue they wanted to discuss with her.

C.J.'s refusal to give their marriage another chance still had him steaming. Also, her involvement with that cop was driving him crazy. He knew as long as that other dude was in the picture, he had no hope of getting her back.

It made him want to get high, even after the last alcoholic fiasco. Now, he had to find a way to get over his anger and call her. He would beg her if he had to, because other than the fact that his dad was insistent that she come, Randy desperately needed her.

When he finally connected with C.J., he wanted to break down again when he heard her voice, but somehow held it together. "C.J., did my mother call you yet?"

"No, why? What's wrong?"

"My dad's not doing well. In fact the doctors don't have a lot of hope that he'll make it. And he's asking for you because he has a legal issue he wants to talk to you about. Now, I know that cop will probably tell you not to go, but please don't say no to this, C.J. Dad wouldn't ask if it wasn't important to him. I hope you can get past what happened with us, and go see him."

"I don't know about that, Randy. Are you doing okay?"

"No, I'm not, but ain't a darn thing I can do about it." He wiped at the tears on his face.

"Yes, there is, Randy. You can start by praying, and then you can get yourself to Little Rock to see about your parents."

"I'm going to do that. But will you go with me? I'm begging you, C.J. I need you!"

"I'm not going with you, but I'll think about going."

"Okay, babe. Thanks."

C.J.

C.J. sat down to process what Randy had told her. She really hated to get the news about Mr. Singleton, and was curious about what legal issue he could possibly have to discuss with her.

A big concern—*what would Marc say?* She knew he wouldn't be happy about her going to see Randy's dad because as he consistently told her, he didn't trust Randy or his parents.

The doorbell rang and she was surprised to see it was Marc—She didn't even know he was back in town.

"Marc! When did you get back? I was just thinking about you. I have something I need to . . ." She stopped when he grabbed her in a tight hug. The second domino was about to fall.

"My grandmother . . . had a stroke, and they don't think she's going to make it," he choked out.

"Oh my God, Marc!" She tightened her arms around him "We just saw her a couple of weeks ago and she seemed fine." She led the way into the family room, where they sat down.

"Well, she's had a couple of strokes before. She's almost ninety and the doctors warned us that she might not survive another one. She collapsed yesterday and she's still unconscious. So I caught the first flight I could get. She has a DNR order on file. She said if the Lord was calling her home, that we should let her go."

"So when are you planning to go see her? You probably should have gone straight there. I mean . . ."

He squeezed her hand. "I don't think it matters. She won't even know I'm there. I keep thinking I need to pray, but I don't even know what to pray for."

"You'll pray for God's will; can't go wrong asking for that." She pushed the dilemma with Randy's dad to the back of her mind. "Have you talked to Roz?"

"I talked to her last night right after I got the news. She decided to go ahead and leave. Whatever happens, Mother will need someone to support her."

"I'm so sorry, Marc. I know how much you love her. Is there anything I can do for you?"

"I'd really appreciate it if you'd go with me. This is a hard blow, honey. This woman helped raise me and helped to make me the man I am. I hate to think of life without her in it."

"Of course, I'll go with you." she said, pushing Randy's dad even further to the back of her mind.

Marc

Having C.J. to share his heartache and concern about his grandmother made all the difference. They left the next morning, and all the way there he was hoping to get a call that his grandmother had experienced a miraculous recovery and was her old self. That didn't happen. She passed away without regaining consciousness shortly after they arrived.

They left the hospital and returned to Houston for a few days, then went back for the services. His parents wanted them to stay at the house, but C.J. refused and insisted on a hotel room, stating there was already enough people there. Marc decided she was right, and got a room for himself as well.

They returned to his parents' house after the services, sat around with the family as they reflected on Granny's life, ate, and visited with family members Marc hadn't seen in a long time. Of course, the question of when he and C.J. planned to get married came up.

Marc's mother said, as she observed Geordi, who was sleeping in Marc's lap, "Well, I hope it's soon, because y'all don't need to be waiting around too long. If you love each other, and I know you do, you ought to go on and get married. This baby needs both of y'all. In fact, one of the things Mama said about y'all was that she wanted to see y'all get married."

Marc grunted loudly. "Doggonit, Mother, why don't you apply a little pressure?"

C.J. added, "We're both products of bad marriages—just recently for me, so we're trying not to make another mistake."

Marc squeezed her hand. "Right. Y'all just keep praying for us."

Marc's dad, who was always cracking jokes said, "This woman can shoot the tip off a pencil from fifty feet." He looked at C.J. and asked, "Do you want me to go get my gun? We still believe in shotgun weddings in these parts."

"Dad!" Marc yelled. "Don't plant any ideas in her head."

C.J., of course, was cracking up.

They spent another night at the hotel, had breakfast with his family the next morning, then headed back to Houston. Although still saddened by his grandmother's death, he had enjoyed his family. That made him even more determined to make C.J. and Geordi his family. Little did he know, things were about to happen that had the potential of keeping that from ever happening.

Chapter Forty-Seven
C.J.

WHILE SHE'D BEEN OUT OF TOWN WITH MARC, RANDY HAD called her several times about coming to Little Rock, and his parents had also left messages, asking her to call them. She put off calling them until she returned.

"C.J., Randy said he told you about what the doctors said about my prognosis. According to them there's not much hope, so I'm trying to tie up loose ends and get my affairs in order," Mr. Singleton told her. "So I really need you to come to Little Rock. I have an important legal issue to talk to you about. And we really want to see the baby."

"I'm so sorry to hear that, Mr. Singleton and I'll keep you in my prayers. But I can't imagine what legal issue you could have to talk to me about. Everything between your son and I has been resolved, and frankly, I don't have any desire to change that."

"I'm begging you, C.J., and it has nothing to do with your divorce from Randy, but it is important."

Her curiosity was peaked. "Is it something you can talk about over the phone? My life is pretty hectic right now, and it'll be hard for me to get away."

"No, it's kind of complicated, so I would rather not discuss this over the phone, and like I said, I really want to see you and Geordi."

She sighed. "I'm not promising anything, but I'll see what I can do," she reluctantly said.

"C.J. didn't want to go to Little Rock without telling Marc she was going, and she really wanted to get his thoughts about it before he left for Virginia. She had pushed it to the back of her mind until after the funeral because she hated to dump it on him, but now, it was time to deal with it.

"Marc, I have something to tell you, and I hope you can understand my dilemma."

He shot a look at her, filled with both dread and curiosity. "What? Have you decided you're not going to marry me?"

"Well, no, it's about Randy and his parents." She let that hang between them a few seconds before continuing, then told him what was happening with Mr. Singleton." I can't imagine what he wants to talk to me about but I'm thinking I should go."

Marc was silent a long time, then said, "Why can't you just call him?

"Because for some reason he doesn't want to discuss it over the phone."

"All the legal issues between you and Randy were settled, right?"

She nodded. "But he said it has nothing to do with the divorce."

"So, is Randy there?"

"Yes, of course he's there, but . . ."

"Has he called you?"

"Yes, he's called, but . . ."

"Then no, you're not going. Absolutely not. "

"What do you mean, no? Why?"

"Just that, C.J. I mean no! You asked and I'm telling you. You shouldn't go for obvious reasons. That part of your life is over and you should have said no without even considering it."

C.J. fought her aggravation. His attitude was like waving a red flag in front of her and she was like a bull ready to burst out of the pen. "Well, he's also asking to see Geordi and since I know how much he loves the baby, I don't think it's unreasonable for me to go and take the baby to see him."

Marc shook his head. "C.J., you know Randy is still hoping for y'all to get back together, and his parents probably are too, so why do you encourage that?"

"I don't do that. And they know it's over between me and Randy."

"When have you said no to them—or Randy? Every time they call, you try to please them. Personally, I think they just want you to come so they can finagle around to get you back with Randy. I suspect that's why they insisted on staying with you when they were here. There was no good reason they couldn't have stayed with Randy."

She was still trying to process his attitude and fight her temptation to get angry. "That's not true, Marc, but as I've said, I can't just wipe them out of my life like they've never been there."

"No, but you can and should put them in the past and leave them there. They know Randy is not responsible enough to take care of himself and they need you to do it like you've done his whole adult life." He drew a frustrated breath. "Will you at least wait until I can go with you? I have to go back to Virginia for a couple of weeks, but I'll be able to go with you when I get back."

"I'd rather not, Marc. The man is sick and it's never a good idea to delay when a sick person asks you to come see them. I need to go as soon as I can."

"So knowing how I feel, you'll go anyway?"

"Yes, because I don't think you're being reasonable and that you're over reacting."

Marc sighed agitatedly. "You're the one acting unreasonably, C.J. You know doggone well how I feel about you. I love you, and want to marry you. Doesn't that count for something? That should be all that matters for you not to go. I'm telling you in no uncertain terms not to go."

Temper rising, C.J. said, "Wait a minute! I don't like your attitude. I'm not one of your subordinates that you can issue orders to. You have no right to tell me what I can or cannot do!"

"I don't believe this, C.J." He stood, walked around the room, rubbed his hands through his close cropped hair, then said,

"Apparently you care more about what Randy and his parents want, than you do about what I want. Tell me I'm wrong about that, or I'm leaving. I'm out of here."

"This has nothing to do with us, and you're wrong to issue that kind of ultimatum." Her eyes blazed in anger. "I don't appreciate your attitude, and I don't do ultimatums, so if that's how you feel, this conversation is over and you know the way out."

"That's it then? You're ending things just like that?" When she didn't say anything, he walked out without another word.

What. Was. That? C.J. thought after Marc left. *Who did he think he was anyway? How did he fix his mouth to tell her what she could or couldn't do? He wasn't her husband. And where was the love, the trust?*

The wisdom of watching and waiting was proving to be valuable.

Marc

"Darn! When it rains it pours." Disturbing thoughts battered Marc's mind—but the main one was his fear that C.J. might be having second thoughts about her divorce and wanted to get back with Randy. Why was she so determined to stay connected to them? Was it because she still loved Randy? Or more to the point, because she didn't love him? That fear caused more hurt than he could bear.

This, following on the heels of his grandmother's death made his pain excruciating. He stopped to see his sister on his way to the airport and poured out his pain to her.

Roz was as bad as C.J. in blasting him for being domineering and controlling. "You can't order a woman around like she's one of your rank and file. You need to leave that at work."

Frowning, Marc said, "But I think I'm right. She doesn't need to be holding on to connections with her ex-husband and his family, especially when she knows he's trying to get her back—unless she wants him back too." He linked and unlinked his fingers in aggravation.

"It doesn't matter if you're right, you should have gone about it another way. I'd sure hate for you to mess things up with C.J., Marc. I like her."

"Well, she has to understand some things too. Like my feelings for her, and letting reason, rather than that hot temper of hers, dictate how she responds."

"I'm not saying she's right, but from what you said, it was you who provoked her by issuing ultimatums. There has to be a middle ground for y'all. And you have to find it, otherwise, you can forget about ever marrying C.J.," Roz strongly emphasized.

He looked stressed. "Roz, how am I supposed to change who I am? That's like asking me to cut off a part of my body."

Roz chuckled. "Well, how badly do you want C.J.?" She gave him a stern look. "Marc, everything has always come easy to you up until now, but by all indications, this is not going to be one of them. And you're right, you can't do this on your own. You need God's help. Start praying, and then get your behind back to C.J. and talk to her like a man instead of a policeman and beg her to take you back."

"But the fact is, I haven't changed my mind. I don't think she should go. What am I supposed to pray? Or how can I get her to understand that?"

"Well, that's what you need to pray about. God knows your heart, He also knows your need, and how you should express that to C.J. in the right way. See, this is why you need to know His Word. God honors His Word and uses it to guide us. You might start by asking God to help you walk in the Fruit of His Spirit, which is, 'Love, Joy, Peace, Patience, Kindness, Goodness, Faithfulness, Gentleness, and especially, Self-control. This is found in Galatians 5:22-23. Another good verse to meditate on is Philippians 4:13 that says, "I can do all things through Christ Who strengthens me and gives me the power to do it."

He sighed. "Okay, what else do you think I should do? I'm at a loss."

Roz laughed. "That's because you've never had to work to get a woman. You're used to them chasing you. I suggest you be patient and give C.J. the time and space she needs to disconnect with that family. That didn't happen when those divorce papers were signed. Things are different with a woman, and her divorce was different from yours."

On his plane back to Virginia, he thought about what had happened. So maybe C.J. and his sister were right and he did need to be reprogrammed. Maybe he did need to pray for direction, but for the time being, he hadn't changed his mind about C.J.'s plan to go to Arkansas and he was still angry.

The more he thought about it, the more he realized that as he and C.J. learned more about each other, the more issues came up that had to be dealt with and the more he was starting to understand her point about why using wisdom, watching and waiting were so important before jumping into a relationship with someone.

One thing this situation confirmed was that if things worked out between them, life would always be fiery, difficult, definitely not boring, and in need of a lot of help from God.

Chapter Forty-Eight
C.J.

WHEN MARC ANGRILY WALKED OUT OF HER HOUSE, C.J. WAS SO upset that she had to take a minute to calm down. After she did, she started to see Marc's point. But that didn't mean she appreciated him telling her what she couldn't do as if he was issuing orders for her to obey. "Lord, I am not ready," she moaned.

She struggled through the following days feeling miserable. She really expected him to call her, and when she didn't hear from him, disappointment, sadness and hurt were added to her misery. It didn't help that Mr. Singleton and Randy kept calling, begging her to come. But for some reason, she was still undecided about what she should do—until she had lunch with her cousins, who didn't mince words...

"C.J., have you lost your little hot-tempered mind?" Nita asked. "After all those years with a jerk like Randy, you now have a good man who loves you, and you're trying to dog him? Girl, you better wake up! Men like Marc don't come along often."

Jaci nodded. "You're definitely on point, Nita." She turned to C.J. and gave her a disbelieving look. "What's wrong with you, CiJ? Why are you trying to return to garbage when you have a steak being offered? I'm sorry, but that's how I see it. Listen, you don't owe Randy or his parents a darn thing. Did his parents ever support you when Randy was running around cheating on you? Did they offer you any help when he beat you and threw you out of your home? Girl, you better recognize, and get your priorities straight, or you're going to be by yourself. A real man is going to take his rightful place in your life, and if you don't let him, he's going to get away from you as fast as he can."

"But does that mean I'm supposed to let him boss me around? I didn't let Randy do that!"

Nita was shaking her head. "Cij, you can't compare them. They are two different men. Randy is still a little boy, who didn't care what you did as long as he could do whatever he wanted to do. Marc is already showing you that he's a man. He's not going to put up with what Randy put up with. I went through this with Ron. I had that 'I'm not going to be a victim anymore' mindset, but he got me straight early in the game by letting me know that if I wanted him, I had to leave Frank in the grave."

"Do you love Marc, C.J.? Do you want him in your life?" Jaci asked quietly.

C.J. nodded. "I think so, but I'm afraid of making another mistake."

Jaci grunted. "You know what? The devil always uses the same old tricks to bring confusion and destruction into what God is building. Remember when I was getting ready to marry Jason and afraid of taking a step into the unknown? Then out of the blue, Maxi showed up. Now, I hadn't seen or heard from that jerk in years. This was a man who hadn't bought his daughter a piece of bread during her entire twenty years, and suddenly there he was— broke, busted and broken down, making demands and trying to find a soft place to land."

"I remember," C.J. said, laughing. "Jason beat the stew out of him and threw him out."

"Yes, he did, but it did confuse things, and I had a decision—was I was going to let Maxie, who I knew meant me no good, destroy things with Jason? or trust Jason, the man who had shown me in every way that he loved me? See, when you put it in the right perspective and ask God for direction, it's really a no brainer. Now, when something I don't like comes up between me and Jason—and yes, it happens—but because we love each other, we both know to seek God about it and leave it in His hands."

C.J. struggled to capture the reasoning trying to break through. "Well, this confirms everything I've already told Marc. I can't marry him until I know I'm ready for him and he's ready for me, and this proves we're not ready."

Nita and Jaci gave each other knowing looks. Jaci said, "Well, a godly, whole man wants a godly, whole woman, and vice-versa. We went through that, and know about that battle, and so did Jason and Ron. So you'd better get to praying. Just understand that there's a cost you have to pay by doing what is needed for the other person through sacrifice and compromise. You can't always have it your way, C.J., and you only throw the good out the window with the bad when you try."

"Yeah, it's not easy, honey," Nita said. "Why do you think the divorce rate is over fifty percent?"

"Okay, we've given you some heavy stuff to think about so we'll get off your back for now," Jaci said, chuckling. "Have you talked to Gina? She's in the middle of a difficult situation now too."

C.J. frowned. "Yes, I've talked to her, but she didn't mention anything."

"Probably because she didn't want to add anymore to your already full plate, but she's got a lot going on too," Jaci said, with a concerned look.

C.J. tried to remember if she had even asked Gina how things were going with her. She didn't think she had, and made a mental note to call her cousin. It bothered her that she'd been so consumed with her own issues that she had failed to ask about Gina's.

Was it the same case with Marc? Had she been so busy with her ex-husband and his family that she failed to understand how it made Marc feel?

It amazed her how God worked. Her counseling session that night was about moving on, and the Scriptures used were, Isaiah 43:18-19 that says, *Remember not the former things, neither consider the things of old. Behold, I will do a new thing; now it shall spring forth; shall you not know it? I will even make a way in the wilderness, and rivers in the desert, to give drink to my people, my chosen;* and Philippians 3:13-14, *which states: Brethren, I count not myself to have apprehended; but this one thing I do, forgetting those things which are behind, and reaching forth unto those things which are before; I press toward the mark for the prize of the high calling of God in Christ Jesus.*

She didn't know if she and Marc had a destiny together, but she did know one thing—She needed to focus on reaching for what God had in front, and not behind her, or she was going to be alone for the rest of her life.

Chapter Forty-Nine
Marc

MARC WAS MISERABLE. WHAT HAD HE BEEN THINKING? HE'D learned to control his emotions and think rationally under pressure years ago. Why had he lost it with the woman he loved and wanted to marry? He knew she didn't have the temperament that would accept ultimatums.

He tried to lose himself in his work, but his fight with C.J. was always there, stalking him, stealing his peace and filling him with deep regret. He wanted to call her, but didn't dare. He couldn't take it if she didn't answer.

He definitely needed to hear some words of wisdom and guidance about how he should handle relationship issues, and he knew he would get that at ManPower Hour at his church. He made sure he was back in Houston Friday night and at the meeting Saturday morning.

Marc was not surprised that word had gotten to Jason Gilmore that he and C.J. had split, so when Jason invited him to go for coffee after the meeting, he knew what it was about.

After getting their coffee, Jason sat across from him with a serious but uncertain look on his face.

"What's going on, man? What's on your mind?" Marc asked with a grin to try to ease things.

Jason looked a little more comfortable and said, "Well, I won't beat around the bush. I know it's not my business but I heard about you and C.J. breaking up. I'm really sorry about that, Marc, because you are both good people who need good mates. I sure hope you guys can work things out. I acted like a fool and almost lost Jaci over some mess, but thankfully, I had people around me who spoke wisdom and reason to me and God was gracious enough to help me get her back."

Marc grimaced. "I don't know, man. I shot off my mouth and gave C.J. an ultimatum, and anybody who knows C.J. knows that didn't sit well. She showed me the door, and I've been miserable ever since."

"Well, have you called her? Tried to work things out?"

"No … afraid she'll tell me to take a flying leap," he said, with a long face. "And truthfully, it might be for the best. She's hard headed, hot tempered and strong-willed, and I'm stubborn and used to having things my way, so I don't know if things could ever work between us."

"Don't give up, Marc. Whether C.J. realizes it or not, she needs you."

Marc gave him a cynical look. "How? Why? She has more money than I have and can buy herself whatever she wants."

Jason shook his head. "Forget the money, Marc. The pastor was right on time this morning in his teaching on how to deal with women. Men and women think out of different sides of the brain, so we won't ever understand how they think, but we have to know our women well enough to trust that they have a reason for whatever they do, or be able to provide them with the wisdom why they shouldn't do it.

"Marc, C.J. needs a godly man who is strong but sensitive, cares for her and understands her, and has the spiritual and emotional substance in himself to be her balance. Like Pastor Robinson said, that's why women have such a hard time with us. Too many men fail to develop into godly men. But we both know you have to have all that to handle C.J. But on the other hand, she has a lot more than money to offer you too."

219

"Yeah, I know this. In fact, I was telling her not long ago, that she was the kind of woman who could keep me on my toes. But I lose sight of that when I let jealousy get in the way. I keep telling myself that I'm going to give her the space and time she needs to get beyond her marriage to Randy, but then, I keep blowing it."

"Hey, it happens when you're in love with a woman. I don't blame you, and I gotta tell you, you may have to deal with Randy man to man."

Marc looked at him sharply. "How so? I mean, they do have a lot of history together. I don't know if I can get in the middle of that."

"The operative word is history. You have to get C.J. to understand that, and if she can't, it may be up to you to make a believer out of Randy. I won't go into it now, but I had to do that with Jaci's old flame."

"That's something to think about. I appreciate this, Jason. I knew I was supposed to be at ManPower today, and I needed you to re-enforce that teaching from the Pastor. You've said a lot that I needed to hear."

"Well, the most important thing you can do is pray, of course, but I just hope I've said something that helps. I want to see y'all together."

Marc smiled. "I'm hoping we can work things out, although we have some battles to overcome. One, I'm ready to get married now, and she's not. I'll deal with that though. But there's another potential one on down the line if things work out between us, and that's going to be a tough one."

Jason looked concerned. "What?"

Marc hesitated. "Well, I'm just thinking about what you just said about dealing with Randy. My last altercation with him was at C.J.'s house and he ordered me out, and told me not to come back. I live in a condo now, so if or when, we get to the point of getting married, we're going to have to find another house."

Jason was puzzled. "Why, man? C.J. has a great house and Randy has no say over it. And if you're uncomfortable about living in a house she paid for, there are ways to handle that."

"I know that but Randy does not, and it will always be stuck in his mind that the house was bought with his money. He will take every opportunity to throw that in my face, and that can't happen."

Jason laughed, then said, "Uh oh! C.J. loves that house. You're right, that's going to be a battle."

"You better believe it. But I'm just putting you on notice that I might need your services."

"Yeah, I'll be happy to do it, but only after the battle is over and it's settled with C.J. No way am I getting in the middle of that." He raised his hands as if to shield himself. "Nope. No way!"

After talking to Jason, Marc decided it was time to talk to C.J. It had been two weeks since their argument, and Marc wanted to see her. They hadn't communicated at all, so he didn't know if she'd gone to Little Rock or not.

He had told himself he was letting her stew a while before confronting her again. *But who was he kidding?* It was his fear of rejection.

When he pulled into her driveway, he was hoping the element of surprise would give him an edge.

The door opened to reveal C.J. dressed in a pair of cut-off jeans and a tee-shirt. Her hair was pulled back in a ponytail, and her feet were bare. He had to restrain himself to keep from pulling her into a hug.

"Marc! What are you doing here? I thought—"

He interrupted, "Can I come in C.J.? We need to talk."

She stepped back without a word and let him walk past her through the door. "I was on the deck doing some re-potting," she said, on the way to the family room, where she slid her feet into some scuffed up shoes, and led the way out to the deck, leaving him no choice but to follow her. He stepped out and looked around the covered deck. She had added even more potted plants since the last time he'd been out there. A utility table on wheels was backed up against the outside wall of the house, which held planting tools, potting soil and other gardening supplies. She picked up the half full bag of soil and placed it in a compartment under the table then gathered up the tools, went to a hose and rinsed them off before laying them out to dry on a lower shelf of the table.

He quietly watched her before finally asking, "Need some help?"

"No, thanks. I'm done." She then led the way back into the house, and secured the door. She slipped her feet from the shoes and walked barefoot into the bathroom in the hallway and washed her hands.

"Would you like something to drink?" She asked in such a soft voice that he almost didn't hear her.

He walked over and took a seat on one of the barstools. "Yes. If you promise not to poison me," he said with a grin.

She gave him a hard look, with nothing remotely near a smile on her face. "Don't go putting thoughts in my head. What would you like? All I have is tea or water."

"Tea is fine. What are you cooking? Something smells really good."

"It's just something I threw together. Nothing special. Want some?"

"Well yes, if you have enough to share. I'm really hungry."

"Yes, I have enough."

He searched for a way to break the ice with her. "What's up, C.J.? Are you still angry because of our argument over you going to Little Rock? So we had a disagreement. Can't we agree to work through our disagreements?"

She looked at him and asked, "Can we?" Then said, "I'm not angry at just you, I'm also angry at myself for reacting like I did. That wasn't right because you do have a right to your opinion, so I'm sorry. But I still don't appreciate you issuing orders and ultimatums to me though. So why are you here?"

"To apologize to you for letting my jealousy get the best of me." He looked at her with a contrite smile, and said, "I'm so sorry. You're right, I shouldn't have been telling you what to do or issuing ultimatums. But I'm also here because I don't think we should throw what we have away. We both have baggage that needs to be sorted out, but in spite of all that, I love you and I want to marry you and I hope you'll eventually feel the same way. Maybe with some counseling, we can make it."

She sat down on a barstool beside him. "Well, that's something we agree on. I've been so focused on getting my marriage to Randy resolved, that I've failed to prepare for a future beyond life with him."

"I understand that. I thought about what you said about me treating you like a subordinate. I need to learn how to communicate with you without sounding like I'm issuing a command. I know enough about you to know that's never going to go over well."

"Well, actually, I decided not to go to Little Rock," she said, quietly.

"What?" He looked at her with confusion. "You mean you didn't go?"

She shook her head. "I did hear what you were trying to say, even though your delivery had me seeing red."

"Why didn't you call me and tell me that? I've been miserable, worried and imagining the worst."

"I didn't call you because I was angry, stubborn, and confused. But I did finally realize I didn't need to go to Little Rock. And why didn't you call me to find out if I went? I don't think I'm the only stubborn one."

He laughed. "No, you're not, even though it was more fear than stubbornness. But this proves that if we can just calmly talk to each other without blowing our tops, we'll probably reach the same conclusion."

"Yeah, I guess. But frankly, I don't know if I can deal with a strong, opinionated, domineering man like you without going off, because honestly, I know we are going to be who we are and it's going to happen."

"Well I know it is too, but I don't care, I'm not going anywhere. We know things will never be boring." He stood and pulled her off the barstool and into his arms. "I love you," he said before kissing her.

She hugged him tightly and said, "And they won't be easy either, but I love you too, and at least we're being realistic about it. But where do we go from here?"

"I know we need to get into some counseling for however long it takes. I'm willing to do it."

"I am too, but we'd better be praying too."

"I totally agree with that. By the way, where's Geordi?"

"Napping. I'll wake him up when we finish eating." She went into the kitchen and a little while later, they were sitting down to eat.

"Mmmm! This is so good!" Marc said, obviously enjoying the

lasagna, salad and garlic bread.

"Thanks, it's just my own variation of lasagna," she said.

After he finished eating, he said, "Now I'm ready to play with the baby. How long before you wake him up?"

"He'll be waking up on his own shortly, so let me show you the plans I've been working on for my business before he does."

They went into the office where it was obvious she had been hard at work. The desk was covered, and a large vision board leaned against the wall. "It's the same concept as those popular one-stop places you see along travel routes, where they have a gas station, convenience items, and gift shop attached to food places. I'll have a coffee and sandwich shop, a business center where people can come in and make copies, send faxes, or get a document prepared or notarized. In the bookstore, I'll have books on the shelf, as well as the option to order or download what we don't. The gift shop will have a nice selection of framed art, figurines, other unique gift items and greeting cards."

She pointed to each item on the vision board as she talked, where pictures and diagrams illustrated everything.

"On the second floor, I'll have meeting rooms that can be expanded to hold up to five hundred using round tables of ten, and more with auditorium seating. I plan to accommodate large and small receptions, weddings, conferences, conventions, children's reading hour and events, book club and community meetings, and of course event planning and catering will be offered."

Marc heard her out, then said, "That's not going to be too much for you, is it? I mean you'd have to have a pretty large staff to keep all that running."

"I'll build gradually, starting with the event planning, then gradually add other components as I can. Knowing and working with the Bradshaws will put me in the right arenas to make the kind of contacts that will be valuable later on. And I'm sure they'll help me with advertising and publicity."

"This is great, Sweetheart. I can help with the legal aspects, security and loss prevention. How soon are you planning to implement all this?"

"To be honest, my life has been so turbulent that I haven't been able to give a lot of thought to that, but my cousin, Nita, is researching vendors we can buy the inventory from, and we've both been taking on-line business and event planning courses."

"Well, I'm impressed. Would you consider letting me partner with you on this? I'd like to have an office there since I'll need an office for my consulting and legal services."

"Of course, I'll consider that, and there'll be a place for you," she said, with a smile. "But isn't your plate already pretty full?"

"Yes, but if I'm going to have a wife and family to take care of, I have to do what's necessary."

Her smile disappeared. "Marc, I know you don't understand, but my whole point of fighting Randy for a fair settlement was so I could do this."

"I understand that now. But I hope you'll seriously consider letting me invest in it. I don't want this to be just your endeavor; I want it to be our endeavor."

She smiled. "As we know, a lot will have to happen before that can take place. Anyway, it'll be a while before any of this will materialize. It's not like we won't have enough to do trying to see if we can learn how to live with each other."

He laughed. "You got that right for sure. Hey, I heard from Cleah's sister. She called and told me that Cleah is hiding in a backwoods town in Louisiana. She took a page out of your book and changed her name, and is working as a law clerk."

C.J. gave a distasteful smirk. "Why did she want you to know that? I can tell you right now that I don't like you being in contact with her. And why is she working as a clerk? Isn't she an attorney?"

"I don't know why the woman called me. To be honest, it's information I'd prefer not to have. And with the charges pending against her, Cleah will lose her license to practice law."

"I hope she's not trying to stay in touch with you in the hope that she's going to finagle her way back into your life."

"Hmmm. Is that jealousy coming out of those green eyes?" he asked with a mischievous grin.

"Well, your jaws were pretty stiff when you thought I was going to Little Rock to see Randy's parents," she quickly shot back.

"Okay, lets agree that we have some work to do on us." He hugged her tight and kissed her. "I love you. I can't say it enough. Is that the baby waking up?"

They would soon realize that the battles with their ex's were far from over.

Chapter Fifty
C.J.

C.J. WAS GLAD THEY'D SURVIVED THE FIGHT AND AGREED ON THE fact that they needed counseling, because realistically, she knew if they were together, there would be many more fights and disagreements.

Two weeks later, Marc was back from Virginia, and they went to Jaci and Jason's house for one of their famous fish fries. It had been a while since C.J. had been to one, and of course, Marc had never been, but he knew Jason, Ron and a couple of other guys there, including the caterer she'd used while working for the City. C.J. took a lemon pound cake, since the custom was that the guys did all the cooking, and the women supplied dessert. Marc joined right in with helping to fry the fish and hush puppies. He had a ball, and she almost had to pull him out of the house when it was time to leave.

"That was great!" he exclaimed excitedly. "I haven't had a chance to enjoy myself like that in a long time—except with family, of course. Either I had meetings, or I was interrupted by some kind of police action that I had to stay on top of, or I just didn't have the right group of people to hang out with. I enjoyed dinner with your parents but in a different way. I was nervous."

She laughed. "Wow, I never would have guessed that the former Chief of Police of the fourth largest city in America, and now an F.B.I. official, would be nervous about meeting and eating dinner with my country people."

"Well, I was, and will probably be the next time too. And don't try to act like you weren't a little nervous with my folks. I know better."

"No, I was, I admit it."

"Ready to go again? They've been asking when we're coming, and really pushing the marriage issue. I think they're afraid I'm going to blow it before we can get married."

She laughed. "Well, that almost happened, and realistically, still could. When do you want to go?"

"Whenever we can get our schedules coordinated, which won't be easy."

"Okay. When do you leave for Virginia again?"

"Monday. I have two more teaching weeks to do in this quarter, plus some consulting work they've asked me to do. I love the work, but I hate it takes me away from you and my family. Also, it's proving to be a challenge to work it around my security consulting business. That could really take off if I had more time to focus on it."

C.J. looked thoughtful. "Marc, I just had an idea. Have you considered recording your classes and doing a workbook to go along with them? That way you could be teaching in many different places at the same time. Maybe you could make one personal presentation to answer questions and things like that, but it would still free up a lot of your time for other things." She shrugged, when she realized he was looking at her with astonishment. "Just a thought. I don't know enough about what you do to understand if something like that is feasible. I know others are doing things like that and it's working."

He finally said, "No, I love the idea. I'm just shocked I hadn't thought about that myself. I don't know if I'll be able to do it at the academy, but I can certainly do it for other law enforcement agencies and schools."

"Why wouldn't the academy approve it? It'll be like you're there in person. You cover a chapter in the video, while students follow along in the workbook, and at the end of each chapter, you can review what was covered and have a pop quiz, and regular tests to evaluate each student. You can also have the answers in the back of the book. I was in a class not too long ago and that's exactly how the person did it. You can set up a website and teach the class from there, put it on You-tube, Amazon and other sites as well. Every student will have to purchase the workbook and each institution will have to purchase the video. That would also be another source of income."

Marc looked excited. "You don't have to convince me. I'm in, but will you help me?"

"Yes, as much as I can, but you'll really need a technologically astute person to help you with the video. You'll have to synchronize the video segments with the workbook but that should be easy for someone who knows how to do it."

"But you'll help me with setting the chapters up and everything, huh?"

"Of course. My only question is when either of us will find the time to do this."

"Oh, we'll find the time. I'm anxious to get started on the workbook covering the curriculum right away. I'm going to run it by the F.B.I. Academy training coordinators as soon as I get back to Virginia. But I'm thinking I can go ahead and get started working on those for other law enforcement agencies, as well as universities." He hugged her. "Wow, you are a blessing, sweetheart."

Shortly after Marc left, excited to begin working on his workbook, Randy's mother called her again, begging her to change her mind about coming to Little Rock. But this time, the answer was clear. The Singletons had cost her way beyond what should have been expected and she'd almost let it ruin things with Marc.

"Mrs. Singleton, I've moved on. I have new things and new people in my life that requires my time and attention. I'm sorry, but I won't be able to come."

Mr. Singleton got on the phone and said, "I hate to hear that you can't come, C.J. We really need you and want to see you and Geordi.

But I guess we'll have to accept that. Anyway, I have a proposition for you. I would like you to be the executor of my estate, with your agreement that you'll look after my wife after I'm gone. If you do, I will leave everything to you to do whatever you want with it. All I ask is that you will let her live her life out here in our house, and that you will help her maintain a good quality of life, and Randy too, of course."

"I don't understand, Mr. Singleton. Why can't Randy do this?"

"Randy just hasn't shown the responsibility that he needs to handle things. Frankly, I don't know where he'd be if it weren't for you. I just can't take a chance on him messing up his mother's assets and stability. That's why I want you to handle everything. You're the one I trust. I've explained it all to him."

"Mr. Singleton, I'm sorry, but my initial thought is that I have to say no. I'm trying to move on with my life and to do that I have to leave some things—and some people—behind me."

"Well, it shouldn't take a lot of time and I think you can handle most of it from where you are. I just need someone overseeing things."

"I'm not the one to do that, Mr. Singleton. Surely there's someone else who can handle this for you."

"No, no one I know I can trust. I know I'm asking a lot of you, but I have to try to leave my wife and son in capable hands and you've always been the one we could depend on."

"Not now, Mr. Singleton."

Mrs. Singleton got on the phone. "What do you mean, not now? You've been a part of this family for over twenty years. We may not be connected by blood but . . ." She hesitated before continuing. "on second thought, we may be connected by blood. When I think about how quick that baby bonded with me and my husband, especially my husband, I can't help but think that the story you gave us about Geordi being your brother's child is just not true. I don't understand why you told us that, possibly because you don't want him to be Randy's child, but I just feel in my heart that Geordi is our grandson. I can't believe you'd be so heartless as to take that baby away from us, C.J."

A flash of anger swept through C.J. and she was tempted to hang up without another word. But staying quiet to keep the peace was out the window. The woman had called her a liar, and that cut deep on several levels. She angrily said, "Let me clear up some things right now. I've tried to help and support you all in every way I could, even though I'm not obligated to do so. I didn't mind doing it, but be clear about this, Mrs. Singleton. That's the last time you will call me a lie. Understood? Is Randy there?"

"Yes, he is," she answered, huffily. "I don't know why he's letting you get away with this."

"Why don't we find out right now?" This wasn't the first time Randy's mother had insinuated that it was her fault that they hadn't had anymore children, and Randy, in his usual cowardly manner, had stood by and let her take the blame. But no more. That would be cleared up today. "Will you put the phone on speaker please?" She waited to give her time to do it, then said, "Randy, are you listening?"

"Yeah, I'm here. What's going on?"

"Randy, tell your parents the truth about why we never had any more children. Tell them there's no way Geordi can be their grandchild. Tell them what you snuck and did without telling me, and how long ago it was. If you don't, I'll send them the proof myself."

Long minutes passed before Randy finally said, "I had a vasectomy. Right after the baby died because I didn't want any more children."

Mrs. Singleton gasped. "Oh Lord have mercy! Randy, why would you do that?" She screamed at him. "All these years I've blamed C.J. for not having any more children and it was you. I wanted and needed that baby to be my grandson. My husband is about to leave me, and you're not around half the time. I need someone to love or I might as well go too."

C.J. felt sorry for the woman she'd been ready to fight minutes ago. "That's not true, Mrs. Singleton. First of all, you still have your husband. Those doctors don't know, it's up to God to say how long he has. And secondly, you still have your son, who needs you very much. You can't give up on him."

231

C.J. heard Mrs. Singleton sobbing, and then Mr. Singleton, who said, "I'm sorry about everything, C.J. I can understand why you don't want anything more to do with us."

"It's okay, Mr. Singleton. It's all water under the bridge. And don't worry, Mrs. Singleton, y'all can be Geordi's grandparents as long as I have him."

She hung up with emotions bouncing all over the place—compassion for Mr. and Mrs. Singleton and anger at Randy—again.

Chapter Fifty-One

Randy

IT STUNG RANDY THAT HIS PARENTS DIDN'T TRUST HIM ENOUGH TO TAKE care of business. They tried to explain, and it all came down to his irresponsible lifestyle. But heck, he had to live his life the way he saw fit. If they didn't like it, then so be it. His telephone rang and interrupted his silent rant.

"Well, what do you know? Just the person I need to talk to. Why are you trying to cause trouble between me and my parents? Haven't you done enough?"

"Randy, you are taking care of that very well yourself. You need to grow up and stop being a selfish immature jerk! You've been that way all your life, but now you don't have me to cover for you. You're going to have to do better because your parents need you."

"I'm around when they need me. And anyway, what difference does it make? They're putting you in charge of everything like I don't matter."

"No, you're not around when they need you, and that's why they want me to oversee things, but you can change all that, Randy. As it is, you're wasting your life when there are so many good things you could be doing."

"Like what?" he asked snidely.

"Settle down and do something worthwhile like showing your parents you're there for them; Volunteer at a school or youth center working with the teenagers. Go to your old high school and volunteer to work with the coaching staff, become a referee or game analyst. What about starting a basketball camp? You could get some of your old teammates to help you with that. If you don't want to work with kids, then go to a senior citizen facility. I'm just saying, there are any number of things you could do, if you would grow up and start acting responsibly."

They were good ideas—not necessarily what he wanted to do. "Not that I can't do all that you just said, but I'll do it only if you come back to me. I need you."

"No, Randy. Responsibility for your life does not rest on me. Get it through your head that we're over. It's time to seek a life beyond us, and beyond how you're used to living. In other words, it's time to grow up."

"Are you going to do what Dad wants?"

"No, but I wouldn't need to if you would straighten up and be a man."

That angered him. "I'm a man who wants to live my way. I've given my whole life doing everything I could to live up to their expectations. And then you took over where they left off, telling me all the things I should be doing. Then y'all get mad and accuse me of being irresponsible. Well, I'm tired of it. I don't need y'all telling me . . ."

"Grow up, Randy!" she said, and hung up.

He had already been upset with C.J. on several levels—Distressed that she wouldn't resume their marriage; disturbed that she had replaced him with another man; troubled that his parents wanted to put her and not him in charge of their business affairs; and now, he was angry that she had pushed the issue about his vasectomy and forced him to admit what he'd done; Now, his parents had even more reason to distrust him.

His mother tore into him as soon as he was off the phone, accusing him of depriving her of grandchildren, and contributing to his dad's health issues because of his irresponsible behavior.

Despite the fact that he knew it would probably make things worse, he walked out of the house, went to a bar and proceeded to get good and drunk.

Chapter Fifty-Two

C.J.

AFTER EATING, C.J. AND MARC, ALONG WITH GEORDI, DECIDED TO walk around the lake and enjoy the unusually mild temperature. Marc was flying in almost every weekend so they could work on his workbook and video, which were coming along nicely. She joked that even if they didn't become partners in marriage, by all indications, they would make great business partners.

"I see no reason why we can't be both," he responded, giving her a serious look.

She reluctantly told him about the legal issue Mr. Singleton wanted to discuss with her. "I don't know, Marc. I totally understand why he wants to do it, but I don't know if I'm the one to take on the responsibility."

"Well, I know," Marc said, with a frown. "You shouldn't. If you do, you'll always have them dependent on you, rather than finding a way to handle things themselves."

"I know, and I see your point. They cut themselves off from their families because they got tired of them begging for money. Now that they need someone, those people are not there for them. Admittedly, they are a part of the left over baggage from my marriage to Randy, but it's difficult for me to ignore their need for help."

Marc didn't look happy. "Things will never be perfect, but we have to learn to deal with all the issues that are necessary for us to get on with our own lives, and get rid of those that are not. To my way of thinking, the Singletons are unnecessary issues for you to have to deal with. So, what did you tell them?"

"Well, after I threatened Mrs. Singleton about calling me a liar, and exposed something Randy did and told him he needed to grow up and act like a man, I think they understand that my answer is no."

"Wait! Why did she call you a liar? What brought that on?"

She explained what happened, including forcing Randy to tell them the truth about his vasectomy.

"Wow! I can't believe he did that—I mean getting a vasectomy without telling you," Marc said. "That was lowdown on his part. I can relate because I know how I felt when Cleah aborted children when I didn't even know she was pregnant."

She nodded. "Apparently, the people we were married to didn't think there was anything wrong with what they did."

"Obviously not. Speaking of children, I've been meaning to ask you about Chuck and his wife. Have they made up their minds about Geordi?"

Her frustration was apparent when she answered, "I don't know what's going on with them. The last I heard, Tara was in Asia with plans to move on to Africa, Italy and only God knows. Chuck is involved with another woman and has started divorce proceedings. Now where Geordi fits into all that, or if he fits at all, is a mystery to me."

Marc's frown was back in place. "What are you going to do? You can't just leave it hanging indefinitely."

She sighed. "Marc, I'm tired of fighting. It's been one battle after the other for so long that I'm reluctant to take on another one, especially when the outcome may not be what I want."

His frown deepened—an indication that he didn't particularly like that approach. "So how are things going with your business?" he asked, changing the subject.

"Oh, things are going well. I've rented a storage unit and Nita and I are ordering unique gift items, as well as books and art. And I plan to ask Jason to start looking for a facility. I don't know whether to lease or purchase, and if a stand-alone building, or space in a shopping center is better. What about you? How are things going with the job?"

"They're still reviewing my proposal about the workbook and video, but at any rate, I plan to pursue it with other agencies and levels of law enforcement. However, something else has come up that I need to tell you about, but let's wait until we get back to the house."

Marc

When C.J. told him about the Singletons' request, he didn't like it, but tried to keep his cool. Then when he asked about the situation with Geordi, he didn't like her response to that either. All he saw was people taking advantage of her. She was hot tempered, true enough, but she was also soft hearted and loving and an easy prey for users, but there was only so much he could say since he wasn't her husband—a fact that was starting to weigh in heavier and heavier.

After they were back and relaxing in her family room, although he didn't want to do anything except hold and kiss her—and more, he scooted away from her, took a long breath, and said, "I've been reluctant to mention this, but I've been asked to take on an assignment with the Justice Department. It will require a lot more time there, unless I let everything else go, but there's a significant increase in pay and other benefits so I'm considering it."

"What kind of assignment?"

"The Justice Department has asked me to work on a Presidential Commission to establish guidelines for hiring, training and monitoring police officers, as well as police departments. With the increases in police shootings and conflicts between police and citizens coming to light nationwide, things are only going to get worse if something isn't done to curb it. The problem is that much of this starts at the top, and many don't even have policies in place to combat that kind of thing. The added benefit that comes with this is that I can take independent consulting jobs with police departments who need help promoting community policing and establishing positive interaction between police and citizens, and can basically set my own fee.

She hugged him. "Oh Marc, that's great. What a wonderful opportunity and I'm so proud of you, but what about your consulting business here? And what about us? Pretty soon, I won't see you at all."

"It is a great opportunity. I talked to Harry, and he thinks so too. I can put off working with him for a while, and well, frankly, I don't think it's a bad thing, honey. Do you realize how hard it is for me to see you, spend time with you, and then have to leave you? I know it's God's will for single people to live celibate lives, but honestly, it's hard for me to do so when I don't see an end in sight. I love you and want to express my love for you in every way. But since that's not possible, I have to do the next best thing and keep my distance."

She bristled, and said huffily, "Are you saying you're doing this because we're not sleeping together, but if we were, you would stay here?"

He caught her hand and pulled her back down beside him. "No, Sweetheart. I'm merely explaining one of the reasons why I'm considering doing this. I'm trying not to put pressure on you because I do understand where you are on things. But if I'm not here, close to you, maybe I won't be as frustrated."

She sighed. "There's no way you can say no to this kind of position, even though I'm going to miss you," she said in a resigned voice.

Before he could respond, he saw the tears running silently down her face and almost lost it. He hugged her close. "Don't cry! It's not like I'll never be back. You'll still see me often enough. I just think it's best to put some distance between us for now."

On the one hand, Marc hated to see her cry, but on the other, it made him happy since it was the first real light he'd seen at the end of a long, dark tunnel.

Chapter Fifty-Three
C.J.

S O...I HAVE SOME THINKING TO DO," C.J. SAID QUIETLY. "MARC has been patient, but how much longer can I expect that? And being asked to work on this commission is an honor and a privilege, and a very important undertaking."

Her cousin, Gina, started shaking her head. "You can't have it both ways, Cij. Men are different from women, and it is asking a lot to put him on hold indefinitely. Perhaps if you would give him some indication of when things can change—three months, six months, whenever. But to give him no hope, well, that's asking a bit much. I don't blame him, I would stay away from you too."

C.J. had driven to Riverwood, mainly to see Gina, and they were sitting in the kitchen at C.J.'s parents' house, drinking tea. Geordi was with her parents, who had taken him with them to Walmart. She knew they would be gone a while since in their small town, Walmart was the place to meet up with friends and catch up on news as well as do their shopping. And today, they had the added pleasure of showing their grandbaby off.

C.J. considered what Gina had said, and stated, "I know, and I'm afraid I'm going to lose him if I don't do something. I mean, there are some women out there who aggressively go after a man they want and Marc is a ripe target for someone like that. I just don't know what to do."

"Yes, you do know what to do. You have to stop waiting for bolts of lightning to shoot from the sky and for God to scream down from heaven in a deep James Earl Jones voice, "Alright, C.J., you've procrastinated and wallowed around in indecision long enough, now suck it up and marry that man!""

After they finished laughing, C.J. said, "I'm not *that* ridiculous. I just want to be sure I'm not making another mistake that I'll have to live with for years."

"There are no guarantees, girl! You pray, you step out, you do the best you can, you trust God to do the rest. That's what life is all about." Gina paused. "Wow, I don't know where all this is coming from, because I'd probably be doing the same thing you are. So it must be straight from the Lord."

"So what's going on with you, Gina? I've been meaning to call you, but decided to wait until I was here so we could talk in person."

Gina looked down, and sighed. "Cij, I just hated to burden you since you already had so much to deal with, but yeah, there's a lot going on and I don't know what I'm going to do."

"What is it, Gina? Surely, we can figure it out."

"It's okay, just so aggravating to deal with. I won't go into all the details, but my son has gotten into some serious trouble—not with the law, thank God— but trouble with long-term consequences that we have to deal with. I wish I could just leave him to deal with his mess on his own, but I just can't do it. I have to try to help him. There are some other things going on too that I don't even want to talk about."

"Oh, Lord, Gina! Is that why you're here in Riverwood so often?"

"Yes. At least I have some peace here, and in fact, I've decided to move back here as soon as I can get things straightened out. All things considered, it makes sense to do that."

C.J.'s mouth fell open in surprise, as she remembered how eager she and her cousins had been to get away from the small community.

"That's hard to believe, but I guess you have to do what you have to do."

"That about sums it up. I've learned to go the way of peace, and right now, this is my place of peace." Gina answered.

The way of peace sounded so good to C.J. that by the time she made it back to Houston, she had made up her mind to pursue peace of mind in the parts of her life that were causing stress— namely, the situation with Geordi, and Marc. It scared her to think about life without the baby, but it was time for another 'or else' talk with Chuck and Tara. She left messages for both of them, demanding that they talk in person.

Then, there was Marc . . . It was time to get off the fence of indecision, and when she thought of life without him, she knew that wasn't her place of peace.

C.J.'s messages to her brother and sister-in-law brought her brother out of hiding, although not surprisingly, not a peep out of Tara. Chuck arrived at her house a few days later, looking nervous and uncertain. C.J. didn't beat around the bush. "Chuck we have to settle the issue of Geordi."

Chuck sighed. "I knew we would have to talk about this at some point so I might as well lay it all on the table. I'm sure you know by now that Tara and I should have never gotten married. We weren't together six months before both of us were messing around with other people. Then she got pregnant, and she didn't know who the father was. The other guy wanted her to get rid of the baby, but with all her faults, Tara said that was something she couldn't do, even though she didn't want a child. So that dude disappeared and I was left holding the bag. Anyway, after the baby was born, and we found out he was mine, she packed up. Said she wanted to pursue her career and that she might or might not decide at some point if she wanted to be a mother. She actually left him alone in the apartment when she got a call about a job assignment she wanted, and I was out of town. I had suspected she was leaving him alone and had started calling and checking to make sure she was at home. Good I did, because that time, the baby had been alone for almost a whole day before I found out she was gone. I rushed home and got him and brought him to you."

"Chuck!" C.J. was blown away. "Oh, Lord! Anything could have happened to that baby. Why didn't you tell me all of this from the beginning?" she asked, angrily, and really wanting to kick Tara's behind.

"I know that," he answered in a frustrated tone. "Anyway, Tara's not even interested in talking to me about it and I couldn't figure out how to deal with it. I think the only reason she hasn't broken all ties with me is because of her mother's wish that she stay with me and the baby. But Tara's back with that other guy and they're running all over the world together. The truth is, I just don't know what to do about Geordi. So I've just stuck my head in the sand and left him with you, even though I know it's not fair to you."

"Right about that!" C.J. said, hotly. "And you should know that I'm not playing that game with y'all anymore. As much as I love that baby, I'm not getting in any deeper. You have to make a decision, Chuck. Or I will do it, and you and Tara are both going to jail for child abandonment."

"Oh God," Chuck whined. "We're back to that again?"

"Yes, and I mean it this time. That baby needs a mother and daddy, and a stable home that he's not subject to be snatched out of at anytime."

"What are you talking about? He has that here with you, Sis."

"Until when, Chuck? Until you or Tara decide to walk in here and take him? No, I refuse to be in such a vulnerable position any longer."

After a long pause, Chuck said, "Well, I have wondered if you would consider adopting him."

Without hesitating, C.J. said, "Yes, I would, but only if you and Tara are certain about it. I won't be accused of taking your child when, after a few years, one of you decide you want him back. If I adopt him, it will have to be with the understanding that he's legally and permanently mine."

"I don't have a problem with that, and I doubt Tara does either, but I'll get a lawyer to get in touch with her, otherwise, I doubt she'll respond to me about it."

"Okay, but I'm also going to put my own lawyer on it. You and Tara have to make a decision."

After Chuck left, C.J. called her cousin, Nita, and asked for the name of the attorney who had handled the adoption process for Ron's baby. That had been a messy situation also.

She felt a sense of satisfaction and relief that came from tying up the loose ends of her life. She had dealt with Randy and his parents, and had taken a timid step to get the ball rolling with the baby situation. Now on to Marc— the most difficult challenge of all.

She and Marc talked often, but she sensed that he was distancing himself from her. She had waited, watched and trusted God's wisdom to show her the way. She knew the time had come for her to get off the fence, and take some action steps toward the way of peace. So, unsure of what to expect, she made a decision that she felt she needed to tell him in person.

Marc

Marc was struggling to focus on his job because his mind was still in Houston with C.J. and Geordi. He was frustrated that C.J. couldn't make a decision one way or the other so they could move on together, or so he could move on without her, but he had been reluctant to force the issue. He knew C.J. was subject to go crazy and throw him out, because he had found out the hard way that she didn't deal with ultimatums, and he wasn't sure he was prepared for that.

"Lord, I've been praying about this a long time, and I know You've heard my prayers. But, maybe You're telling me it's time to face this head on and work this out myself." He spent a lot of time racking his brain for a creative way to force the issue so that it would lead to the outcome he wanted. The only answer he came up with was more prayer. He smiled at that, finally remembering his Pastor saying that too often we get weary of waiting and start trying to figure out a solution to our dilemma, when the only answer that ever matters is

243

the one that comes by prayer, and the time we spend agonizing over the answer until reaching the point of saying, 'I guess there's nothing to do but pray,' is always wasted time.

He started praying again . . . pouring out his heart's desire to God, thanking Him for bringing C.J. and Geordi into his life, for the blessing they were to him, that he wanted them to be a family, and asking that God's will for them all would be done. "For all I know, Father, You have worked it out and the answer is already on the way."

Perhaps if nothing else, they could be business partners like C.J. had suggested, and that was a viable option since she was definitely gifted in business matters, but would that work with him being in love with her?

He groaned in agony. "I have to trust God!"

C.J.

C.J. flew into Virginia, rented a car, and drove to the hotel near the F.B.I. Academy where she had booked a room.

After she got settled, she called Tara's mother and made arrangements to take Geordi to see her the next day. It would have been unkind to the woman for her grandson to be that close and not see him, afterall, it wasn't fair to blame her for her daughter's failures.

Then she called Marc to let him know she was there and where she was staying, hoping he would be able to come to her hotel, or at the least, meet her somewhere that evening.

Marc was surprised. "What! Why didn't you tell me you were coming? I could've met you at the airport. Is everything okay? Has something changed with Geordi's situation?"

"No, everything's fine. I just wanted to surprise you. So, is it possible for us to see each other this evening?"

"Just try to keep me away!"

When he knocked on the door to her hotel suite a couple of hours later, she took a deep, empowering breath before opening the door.

When she did, he quickly enfolded her in his arms, hugging her close, before kissing her.

"I don't know why you're here, but I'm so happy to see you." He turned and grabbed Geordi up from the floor and hugged him close. "Hey, big guy. How're you doing?"

Geordi returned the hug, smiling broadly.

Marc finally put the baby down and walked across the room to sit down, an expectant look on his face. "I know you didn't come all this way for nothing," he said, nervously.

C.J. went over and sat next to him. "Well, I won't beat around the bush . . ." She twisted her hands nervously, unsure how to say what she had come to say.

She could see both curiosity and fear chasing each other across his face, and something else—dread, and the effort to prepare himself for what she was about to say.

"Marc, I'm grateful for the friendship, the love and the patience you've shown me, and I'm sorry for putting you through so much uncertainty. You've asked me to marry you and I've put you off for too long. But now, that changes. I'm here to ask you humbly, and with much love, will you marry me?"

A huge smile of joy replaced the previous emotions on his face and he jumped up and grabbed her in a tight hug, swung her around and planted kisses all over her face before settling on her lips.

"Yes, I'll marry you! I can't think of anything I'd like to do more. Haven't I asked you enough times? Yes. Yes. Yes. My only question is when. You know I'm ready right now. Oh Honey, I love you and can't wait for you to be my wife."

When she could speak, she said, "I love you too, and that's why I couldn't make you wait anymore. I just hope you're ready for what life with me is going to bring you."

"I know what it's going to bring, and I'm ready for it. Honey, you have made me the happiest man in the world."

"I haven't thought about when though, Marc. I only thought about getting through this part. I don't know what I would have done if you'd said no."

245

He hugged her again. "There was no chance of that happening, but we have some things to do and talk about. How long are you going to be here?"

She told him about her plan to take Geordi to see his grandmother, and then, to hopefully spend some time with him—planning.

"That sounds great! I'll go with you to see her, and then we're going shopping for an engagement ring."

While visiting Lois, C.J. told her she wanted to adopt Geordi if she could work it out with Chuck and Tara. Lois agreed that it was the best thing for the baby and promised to encourage her daughter to agree if C.J. promised to let her be a part of the baby's life.

A few days later, she and Geordi were on a flight headed home. She felt giddy with excitement and couldn't help gazing at the beautiful engagement ring on her finger. Again, she felt the satisfaction and peace that came from the steps she was taking to get her life in order. She sighed with relief that Randy and his parents had finally gotten the message that she was out of their lives, that the situation with Geordi would be resolved soon, and that she and Marc were finally on the road to marriage.

But her excitement would be short-lived, and trouble beyond all she could imagine was about to invade her life again, knocking her hopes and plans so far off track that getting them back there was questionable.

Chapter Fifty-Four

Randy

DANG! HIS MOTHER WAS GETTING ON HIS NERVES AGAIN AND HE had to get away from the house. He grabbed his keys and headed out the door, with the intention of going to a bar. His mother ran behind him, begging him not to go.

"Randy, we're worried about you. It's just a miracle you haven't killed yourself, driving around drunk day after day. You need to stop this! Why don't you stay at home and spend some time with your dad? He needs you to do that, Son."

"I'll be back in a little while to watch the game with him," Randy blatantly lied, before getting into his SUV and driving off to drown his discontentment in alcohol again.

The events after then were just hazy, disconnected, dream like memories . . . him going to a bar and drinking until he was too drunk to see clearly . . . staggering to the parking lot . . . finally finding his vehicle and climbing in . . . fiddling around and getting it started . . .driving off and wondering why the street kept zigzagging.

It gradually occurred to him through his alcoholic haze that maybe he needed to slow down when he realized he was having a hard time staying on the highway. It took several attempts, but he finally stomped on what he thought was the brake pedal, pushing it all the way to the floor, but instead of slowing down, the truck surged forward at full speed. Too late, he realized he'd stomped on the gas pedal and before he could get that message from his brain to his foot to react, the truck was out of control. Seemingly from a distance, he heard a loud noise and everything went black.

As darkness and pain engulfed him, the only thoughts that came to Randy's mind was that he didn't want to die. He wanted to be back on the team, making his famous three point shots. He wanted to hear the cheers from the crowd, and see the admiration on the faces of the fans. He wanted to celebrate another big win with his teammates, enjoy the company of the women who always showed up to party with them, and then go home to his wife and demand that she give him a massage and nurse his aching, battered body into a level of comfort. He wanted the life he loved —the only thing that brought him recognition, admiration and praise. He wanted to play basketball.

He was vaguely aware of the sirens and flashing lights, of people trying to get him out of the truck and loaded into an ambulance, of his inability to answer their questions, and their efforts to find his emergency contact information. "My wife," he mumbled. "C.J."

C.J.

All day Monday, C.J. was still reveling in her excitement. She and Marc had been on the phone with each other several times, discussing—and yes, arguing—over everything from when they would get married to what would be happening in the meantime.

She groaned when both her cell phone and the house phone began ringing almost simultaneously, interrupting her pleasurable reflections. She answered the call on the cell phone first, simply because she was curious about why someone from the Little Rock Police Department would be calling her.

"Mrs. Randy Singleton?" a deep voice inquired.

"Well, yes, I used to be," she answered in a hesitant voice. "Who's calling?"

"This is Sergeant Chet Fuller with Little Rock Police Department. I'm calling to inform you that your husband, Randall Singleton, has been involved in a serious accident, and has been taken to an area hospital."

She reeled and sat down hurriedly. *Randy, accident and hospital* were the only words that penetrated her brain. She battled to focus and asked, "Uh, is he alright? Have you contacted his parents, who live in Little Rock? I'm his ex-wife, and I live in Houston, Texas."

"Yes, his parents have been notified, but you're listed as his first emergency contact, and he was asking for you. I'm really sorry, Mrs. Singleton. I'm a big fan of his and it looks pretty bad. That's why I called you as soon as I could, but I'm sure the hospital will be in touch."

"What's the name of the hospital?" She scribbled it down, and was grateful when he also provided the phone number. "Thank you, Officer, I appreciate everything." She hit the end button and sat there in a daze until she finally realized the house phone was still ringing. She checked the caller ID and was not surprised to see her in-laws' number showing. She picked up the receiver and said, "I know. I just got off the phone with police department there."

"C.J., you need to get here as soon as possible," Mrs. Singleton screamed into her ear. "They're saying Randy might not make it. He's asking for you. Just catch a plane. We need you here!"

"Ok," she managed to say before hanging up. C.J.'s mind was in an emotional whirl. "Oh my God, Randy! Lord, please have mercy on Randy." She cried and prayed until finally, she snapped when a big question loomed. "What am I going to do?"

Marc, and how this news would affect the new status of their relationship was the reason for that question. She was faced with a precarious decision— rush to the aide of Randy and the Singletons, or do what she was nearly one hundred percent sure Marc would want her to do— not go! She fell to her knees and prayed. "Father, I have a decision to make and I don't know what to do. What would

You have me do?" Suddenly, her spirit was flooded with messages of admonishment, comfort and guidance.

"How many times must I deliver you, sustain you, provide for you, give you victory after victory, close old doors, open new doors, and send people into your life to love and care for you? I have done all of this for you to realize just how much I love you! When are you going to believe My promise to never leave or forsake you? Don't you understand that My faithfulness, My mercy, My compassion, never fail and endures forever? When will you trust Me enough to know that any door I have opened cannot be closed?

But it was not for you. Now, you must be a channel of blessing, an instrument of My love, My forgiveness, My peace. Now, you must let My light, and My love be shed abroad through you to comfort others as I have comforted you. My grace is sufficient; My strength is always perfected in your weakness; Trust and do not lean to your own understanding; I will direct your path as you commit every step to Me. I am your refuge and strength, a very present help in trouble."

A few minutes later, she grabbed Geordi from the riding toy he was on and ran up the stairs to her bedroom, where she began packing bags for her and the baby. "Lord, I hope what I heard in my spirit is from You," she stated, as she frantically stuffed clothes into the bags.

Marc

Marc's phone buzzed several times during class Monday afternoon, distracting him, and filling him with concern when he saw it was C.J. calling. The minute class was over, he hit the return call button.

"Marc!"

He heard the urgency in her voice. "Honey, what's wrong?"

"Randy's been in an accident and they don't think he's going to make it. I got a call from the Little Rock Police Department, and from Mrs. Singleton. Randy is in critical condition and asking for me."

He groaned, and finally asked, "So what are you going to do?"

"Marc, I have to go. What else can I do? But I'm torn because I know how you feel and I don't want it to come between us, but you have to understand, I lived with Randy over twenty years. I can't help but have some kind of feeling for him."

She started crying and it almost tore his heart out. "Okay, listen, Honey. If you feel you have to go, then go. But don't try to drive. Just catch a flight. I wish I was there and could go with you but I can't get away now. Just remember that you're not alone. God is with you. And whatever happens with Randy, it's in God's hands."

After he hung up, he hoped he had said the right words, because the truth was, he would have been happier if she didn't go. Temptation rose up within him to give into those negative emotions, call her back and insist that she not go. But inexplicably, something—or someone—helped him remember she was the woman he had asked for and that she needed him to understand her predicament, and to love and trust her enough to put his feelings aside and provide what she needed, which was his support. But darn it, that was hard to do, and he had to dig deep into his spiritual reservoir to finally reach the conclusion that the right thing to do was pray — for Randy, his parents and C.J.

"Thank You for reminding me when I forget this Father. I'm sure this won't be the last time I forget." He was right—it was far from the last time.

Chapter Fifty-Five
C.J.

BEFORE HER FLIGHT, C.J. CALLED HER PARENTS AND ASKED THEM TO come to Little Rock to get Geordi. After landing she rented a car and drove straight to the hospital and was relieved to learn Randy was still alive. Randy's parents, who were huddled together in the waiting room, both with tears in their eyes, jumped up to hug her.

"I'm so sorry," she said in a broken voice. "With all the problems Randy and I have had, I never wanted anything like this to happen to him."

"We know that," Mr. Singleton answered. "Just go see him because he's been asking for you."

She explained that her parents were coming to pick the baby up, and put Geordi in Mrs. Singleton's arms and was amazed at how the woman hugged him close and kissed him before Mr. Singleton took him and did the same thing. She drew a deep, steadying breath and headed to ICU.

"Randy?" she whispered. "I'm here. Can you hear me?" A weak grunt was the only indication she had that he heard her. "Well, you hang on. You can't let a car accident take you out after surviving all those years in the NBA."

"Sorry," he whispered weakly. "So sorry."

"I know, Randy. We're okay, now be quiet and save your strength." She grabbed the hand that was not covered in a cast, and started praying. "Father, I know You have the power to bring Randy through this. I ask for Your healing power, Your comfort, Your peace. He's Your child, Lord. He asked You into his heart not long ago. Now, Father, have mercy upon him, in Jesus' name, Amen.

"Randy, I want you to start calling on the name of Jesus. Just repeat that name in your heart and know that there is enough power in the name of Jesus to meet you at your point of need right now, to help you, to comfort you and give you peace." She lost all sense of time as she stood there, continuing to silently pray, until suddenly monitors started beeping and the hospital staff was pushing her out of the room.

She walked back into the waiting room where she broke down and boo-hooed. "I don't know, something's happening," she managed to say in response to the questioning, frightened looks. "They put me out of the room." Randy's parents, assuming the worst, started crying too, and she was wiping tears from her own eyes and trying to comfort them when her own parents rushed into the waiting room. She could tell by their faces that they too, assumed the worst. "We don't know," she quickly said. "Please, just pray," she begged, looking at her parents, who nodded and sat down to wait with them.

A doctor finally came into the room and told them that Randy had lapsed into a coma. "He needs another surgery to relieve pressure on his brain, which will be difficult due to his extensive head injuries, but before we can do that, we have to stabilize him. So let me prepare you, the prognosis is not good and there may be some difficult decisions to be made. I suggest you go home and get some rest. There's nothing you can do here."

There was no way she and Randy's parent were going to leave, but eventually, her parents decided to take the baby and check into a nearby hotel. After transferring the baby's car seat to their car and seeing them off, she returned to the waiting room to sit with Randy's parents.

Marc

It was Tuesday afternoon and Marc had stayed in touch with C.J. as often as he could. Each time he talked to her, she sounded more stressed and weary. He wanted to be there with her but wondered if his being there would cause more issues for her to deal with.

The next time they talked, he confessed his struggle and was surprised when he heard her crying. "Honey, what is it? Has Randy taken a turn for the worst?"

"No, he's still in the coma. I really wish you were here, but I didn't want to ask you to come because of the situation and the discomfort you may feel."

"Well, I can handle the discomfort if you can. If nothing has changed by Friday, I'll fly in. At least I can give you a little TLC for a couple of days."

"I would love it if you'll do that, Marc."

"Okay, just hang tough, and I'll check in with you later. Oh! And I wish you'd go to the hotel and try to get some rest."

She sighed. "I know I should, but I'm reluctant to leave."

"Well, you're going to leave when I get there, that's for sure," Marc said, forcefully.

There had been no significant change in Randy's condition on Friday, and he flew into Little Rock as he'd promised C.J. He rented a car and drove directly to the hospital. The waiting room was full. He saw some of C.J.'s cousins, a weary looking couple he assumed was Randy's parents, a few guys he recognized as Randy's former teammates and others.

C.J. immediately took him over to Randy's parents. "Mr. and Mrs. Singleton, this is my fiancé, Marc Carrington," she introduced.

Marc saw a mixture of emotions—distress, anger and finally acceptance—cross their faces before they acknowledged the introduction. "I'm very sorry about Randy's accident. I hope he'll be okay." He was really at a loss for the right words.

"Well, C.J. told us she was engaged, and of course, we saw the ring on her finger. Thank you for your kindness," Mr. Singleton said.

One of the guys from the team walked over, and said, "How're you doing, Chief? Nice to see you again. We met at Jason Gilmore's house at a fish fry several months ago. I'm Kyle Bingham, Randy's friend and former teammate.. My wife and I came as soon as C.J. called us."

Marc nodded. "Yes, I remember meeting you Kyle. Good to see you too, just wish it was under better circumstances."

"Yes, I do too, Man," Kyle said. He turned to the Singletons. "This is the former Chief of Police of the Houston Police Department, and now he's currently working for the F.B.I., the Justice Department, and was recently appointed to work on a Presidential Commission on law enforcement," he informed the Singletons.

Marc saw their jaws drop and hurried to say, "Well, all of that is temporary. My long range plan is to set up my own legal and security consulting business."

"Oh, you're an attorney?" Mr. Singleton asked. And at Marc's nod, he said, "I need to talk to you if you have time. So how long have you and C.J. been engaged? "

"Not long, Sir, but hopefully, we'll be getting married before long. We didn't meet each other until she and Randy were not together, though. I just want to make that clear."

"Are you the one always sending her flowers?" This came from Mrs. Singleton, who still didn't look too happy about him being there.

"Yes, probably so," he answered with a smile.

"Well, you must care for her very much, to come all this way to support her. I appreciate that. She's like a daughter to us," Mr. Singleton told Marc.

"Yes, I do love and care for her very much," he answered, quietly, before Kyle pulled him away and across the room.

"I know this has to be uncomfortable for you, but I'm glad you're here for C.J. She's under a lot of stress over this," Kyle said in a low voice.

"Appreciate that, Kyle. So, are there any new reports on Randy's condition?"

Kyle shook his head, sadly. "It's not looking good. He's been in a coma several days and the doctors are not hopeful. They're amazed that he's held on this long." He shook his head again. "I've been fearful of something like this happening, but I just couldn't get through to him."

Marc's stomach sank, thinking about C.J.'s feelings. "Yeah, I know C.J. has tried as well without success."

Kyle nodded, then said, "Well congratulations, Man. I've been reading about your new ventures. You're walking around in high cotton. I'm happy to see it. If anybody can speak to the police issues, it's you."

Several articles had been run in Houston Newspapers about his new ventures, and he didn't know if that was a good or bad thing. One of the reasons he'd wanted a change was to get out of the public's eye. Maybe it was time to accept that evidently that was his destiny. "Thanks, Kyle. Just keep me prayed up. The issues are deep and complicated, and won't be easily fixed. The entire judicial system on all levels is reluctant to criminalize police behavior, but bad behavior on the part of some of them is a reality and if we don't get a handle on it, it's only going to get worse. I'm authoring some books on police procedure and community policing."

"So, you're an author now? That's wonderful, Marc. You certainly know how it should be done."

"Yes, C.J. suggested that I do it, and with her help, I've already finished one on police procedure, which includes crime scene investigations, police decorum and integrity. It's a training video and workbook for all levels of policing. And now, we're working on one which is a how-to guide for community policing, and will provide practical guidelines and programs for establishing and maintaining positive relations between police and community."

"Wow. Well since you implemented that in Houston, it's certainly helped. Of course, there will always be the human element and the bad apples who refuse to follow the rules."

Marc nodded. "Always—on both sides. We can't regulate human

behavior, which is why it's so important to educate the public while also weeding out police candidates who have over-zealous tendencies during the selection process. Now, we have way too many who slipped through and are now holding high positions. That's a different can of worms."

Kyle frowned. "You're right, the problem is deep. Not just in the police department, but the entire judicial system. I'll definitely be praying that what you're doing will help to bring about change."

"Thanks, Kyle, I need all the prayer I can get."

Marc coerced C.J. away from the hospital a few hours during the next two days, and he pitched in and helped Kyle get Mr. Singleton to his treatments—something C.J. had been doing before they got there. Mr. Singleton explained his reasoning for wanting C.J. to be the executor of his estate and strangely, after seeing how much they depended on her, Marc understood and agreed.

The doctors met with the family before he had to leave for the airport Sunday evening to fly back to Virginia. There was a decision to be made—they had to risk the surgery Randy needed to give him a chance or he would never regain consciousness.

Leaving C.J. was one of the hardest things he'd ever had to do, but he had to get back to work.

Chapter Fifty-Six

Randy

RANDY REMEMBERED GETTING DRUNK, TRYING TO DRIVE AND A loud crash. Everything after that remained a blur in his mind. Now, several months later, he was in a rehab hospital and was still barely able to function, but everyone was telling him how blessed he was to be alive.

Thank God C.J. had come to their rescue. Randy, along with his parents, relied on C.J. so much that every time she talked about leaving, they begged her to stay. His recuperation was slow and painful, and the doctors wouldn't even talk about when he might be able to go home, but whenever that happened he knew his need for C.J. would be even greater.

Home. Whenever he thought about home, it was C.J.'s home, which was the last place he'd felt really at home. But C.J. continually let him know in no uncertain terms that she was engaged to that cop and fully intended to marry him, despite the fact that he told horror stories and tried to discourage her by telling her that the cop was just after her money, and that he, like most cops had a reputation for being abusive wife beaters.

Of course, C.J. reminded him that he was the pot calling the kettle black. Nevertheless, he planned and plotted. He had lost count of the times he'd regretted all the low down dirty things he'd done to her, and actually prayed for God to help him find a way to get his wife back.

Although she was headed back to Houston and to that cop, he had no intention of letting her forget she needed to be there with him. He thought, planned and plotted trying to find a way to coerce her to come back to him. The only thing he came up with was a gigantic guilt trip, which had worked so far, but he had to perfect it before he called her.

The plan couldn't have gone any worse!

Cleah

Cleah never heard from her cowardly assistant, Carl again, and she certainly could have made use of his services now. But fortunately, she didn't let the fact that she was in hiding stop her from staying abreast of what was going on. She still had people around who kept her informed—people who didn't know the real story and believed her when she told them she was out of the country on a fact finding mission indefinitely. She hadn't lost her fanatical fascination with politics and regularly sneaked into Houston and drove around with her sister, who kept stacks of newspapers for her. She was troubled— almost to the point of insanity —when she considered all she had lost or missed out on because of her own careless stupidity—not because of what she'd done, but because she hadn't been smart enough to cover her tracks. That included keeping her husband. And yes, she still thought of Marc as her husband.

She was almost driven to violence when she read about Marc working for the F.B.I. Academy, the Justice Department and being appointed to a Presidential Commission on criminal justice reform. He was writing books, producing videos and making a name for himself that could eventually lead to where she had always dreamed they would be—The White House.

That silly woman, Catherine Stroman—the target of her violent aspirations—had no idea how to work the system to help propel him to where he needed to be. When she and her sister drove by the beautiful house in the lakefront community that Catherine lived in, and her sister told her about the rumor going around that Marc had plans to marry the woman, Cleah wandered if there was a way she could kick Catherine and that brat out of that house on the lake and take her rightful place there as Marc's wife. Her mouth almost salivated as she visualized being in D.C. with her husband, working on that Commission with him, going to dinners at the White House with him—until she remembered what happened the last time she tried to kick Catherine out—and the subsequent events that led to her downfall. No, she decided, best to leave Catherine alone because something about the woman filled her with inexplicable fear.

The fact remained that the only way she could get her life back in order was to become Mrs. Marc Carrington again. Surely with all the connections Marc had, he could get her out of the mess she was in.

But knowing Marc as she did, she could only come up with one possible way he would agree to help her—that was to threaten the reputation he valued so highly.

Seemed like a good plan. But sadly, she had no idea that when she tried to put it into action, her life would go from bad to worst and she would end up in a place she never imagined she would be.

Chapter Fifty-Seven

Marc

THREE MONTHS HAD PASSED SINCE RANDY'S ACCIDENT, AND MARC'S insistence that C.J. come home had hardened into stubbornness and anger when she refused. That had led to a rift and silence between them for the last month. He did remember God reminding him of the woman C.J. was and why he had fallen in love with her—more than once. But that didn't change the fact that this time he was right and she was wrong.

Another thing it didn't change was his misery. He'd prayed for God to fix things between them, although admittedly, most of the emphasis had been on fixing C.J.

That's why he made sure he was at ManPower Hour that Saturday morning. Perhaps the Pastor would say something to help him deal with the situation. Boy, was he about to get an ear full!

"Is your 'He Man-Master of the Universe' persona robbing you?" Pastor Robinson started by asking. "Is there anyone here who just knows that in your current particular issue, you are right and she is wrong?"

Marc felt the start of a cold sweat. He knew that once again, God was about to remind him of something he kept forgetting—if he wanted C.J., he had to accept her as the woman she was. He didn't bother to wonder how the Pastor always seemed to teach on what he needed to hear. He just zeroed in on what the guy was saying . . .

"Sometimes our ego, pride and arrogance will have us thinking we are He-Man-Master of the universe and everything revolves around us. So I want to talk from Galatians, Chapter 5 today. Hopefully, it will help somebody."

As Pastor Robinson read a passage of Scripture, Marc felt the sweat pop out on his forehead and wiped at it. This wasn't the first time he'd been pointed to this Scripture. His sister had told him several months ago that he should meditate on it. But the Pastor went even deeper now than his sister had, and continued with . . .

"There's a battle going on in us most of the time, namely, the flesh against the spirit of God. The battle of the flesh includes but is not limited to—sexual immorality, pride, egotism, hatred, jealousy, selfish ambitions, etc.

"But the fruit of the spirit listed in this Chapter includes but is not limited to—love, joy, peace, faith, kindness, goodness, faith, self-control, etc. You need to read this Chapter and study these lists on a regular basis. I know I'm not saying anything that you haven't heard before, but we need to be reminded and refreshed ever so often. That's why these times of man talk are so important. There's nothing wrong with being right, and let's face it, sometimes we need to stand up for what we believe is right, but we always need to examine our motives. The bottom line question is, do we want to be He-Man for fleshly reasons or for Godly reasons? So, if you're experiencing conflicts and altercations in your relationship, maybe it's time to ask yourself what's more important—being right or being Godly?"

While the Pastor answered numerous questions from others on the subject, Marc was examining himself, and unfortunately saw more fleshly attributes motivating his attitude and actions toward C.J. than Godly ones.

When the meeting was over he thanked the Pastor for the helpful message, left the church and drove home in a troubled frame of mind.

How could he apply this lesson to his conflict with C.J.? He'd had no problem moving on after Cleah, but for some reason C.J. couldn't move on from Randy. His dilemma—where did that leave them?

Was his ego getting in the way? Was he expecting more from C.J. than he had a right to? Was jealousy the root of his problem? He followed the Pastor's suggestion and re-read the Scriptures then fell to his knees and prayed, asking for God 's help and guidance. After he prayed, he knew he needed to call C.J. They had to talk about this. He picked up his phone and called her.

He had barely hung up from talking to C.J. when his phone rang and he was shocked when he heard who it was.

C.J.

C.J. had been in Little Rock since Randy's accident with the exception of two quick trips home to check on things, get her truck and more clothes and necessities for her and Geordi.

Thankfully, after surviving the touch and go head surgery and a series of other less severe surgeries to try and repair all the injuries in his body, Randy had eventually been moved to a rehabilitation hospital. Although his health was still fragile, the good news was that he was improving. Randy's parents were worn down and Mr. Singleton's fragile health suffered, and Mrs. Singleton was overwhelmed with worries over both her husband and her son.

To say that things after the accident had been crazy was putting it mildly and it was she who'd had the chore of wading through everything and setting them straight. Word had somehow gotten out that Randy had died, which brought all sorts of wild, far-fetched demands out of the woodwork— women demanding money for children Randy had supposedly fathered; dozens of people who claimed Randy owed them money; and still others who claimed Randy had promised to give them money or donate large amounts to their organizations—many of which no one had ever heard of.

Yes, it was definitely time to leave. Although they begged her to stay, she knew it was time—past time really—to get back to her own frazzled life.

Early the next Saturday morning after making that decision, she left Little Rock and drove the three hours to her parents' house in Riverwood to pick up Geordi.

C.J. visited briefly with her parents and couldn't help but notice their apparent relief. They loved the baby, but having twenty-four hour care for him for so long had exhausted them. She loaded Geordi into the SUV then wearily hit the highway to Houston. Her mind immediately rushed to all that was waiting for her to deal with at home—mainly Marc.

Marc. She sighed sadly. Needless to say, remaining in Little Rock so long hadn't set well with him and had taken a toll on their relationship. The excitement she'd been savoring over their engagement had long since departed. In fact, all the plans they'd been joyfully making before Randy's accident had faded into obliviousness.

She had questioned if staying to help Randy and his parents at the expense of her relationship with Marc was the right thing to do, however, their need for her help was so great that she couldn't bring herself to leave.

As a result, she and Marc hadn't seen and had barely spoken to each other in over a month, and his last words angrily spoken to her—"I don't have anything else to say to you."—caused her to wonder if she was still engaged, and worse, did she even want to be? She didn't even know where he was now—D.C. or Texas.

As she took the interchange from Interstate 30 to Highway 59 South, and noted that she had almost three hundred miles to go, she wondered if that was far enough to leave her old life behind and re-kindle the new one she'd planned with Marc. She'd made the decision to do that before and gotten side-tracked but now it was a matter of doing it or losing the future she wanted. Randy and his parents had consumed so much of her life that everything else that was important to her had almost gotten lost—Marc, moving on with the plans and vision for her business, clearing up the issue surrounding Geordi—crucial parts of her life. Yes, she had to express God's love to the Singletons, but did she owe them her life? Did God require that of her?

She thought about the words God had dropped into her spirit when she'd asked for help after hearing about Randy's accident. They had sustained her throughout all that had happened since, and she grabbed hold to them again—especially His question—'How many times must I rescue you from trouble for you to know just how much I love you?' And His promise to never leave or forsake her. She prayed for direction and wisdom on just how much she was supposed to give to this family, then re-focused her mind to thanksgiving, inserted a favorite CD, and pushed toward home.

She was a hundred and twenty miles from Houston when her phone rung. *Marc!*

"C.J., how are you? What's going on?"

"I'm fine, Marc. What about yourself?"

"Pretty good. Are you still in Little Rock?"

"No, as a matter of fact I'm on the road now heading home."

"What! Why didn't you let me know? Where are you now?"

"Well, based on your last words to me, I didn't think you'd be interested. Anyway I'm just out of Lufkin."

"Yeah, I'm sorry about that. Those words were spoken out of anger, frustration and jealousy. We need to talk so we can get this resolved once and for all. You're still about two hours away so if it's okay, I'll meet you at your house."

"Yes, it's okay, Marc, because we do need to talk. See you soon." She hung up and wondered exactly what the result of their talk would be. She was suddenly dreading every mile that took her closer to home.

Her phone rang a few minutes after she talked to Marc and she groaned when she saw who it was— *Randy!* She answered, but pushed the disconnect button before Randy completed his threat. That was the last thing she wanted to deal with now.

265

Chapter Fifty-Eight

Marc

AFTER MARC TALKED TO C.J. AND FOUND OUT SHE WAS ON HER way home, he was trying to figure out what direction he and C.J. should take, when at just that time, something happened that was almost too ridiculous to believe——a call from *Cleah!*

He started not to answer the call since it came from an unknown number, but he was curious and figured it could be someone calling about his consulting service. He immediately regretted answering when he heard her voice.

"Cleah. Why are you calling me?"

"I've been reading about all the things you're now involved in and I'm excited. Of course, you know I'm supposed to be there with you in all this."

"I don't know how you came to that conclusion, Cleah."

"Oh yes, you're fulfilling the dream I've always had for us, and I don't have any intention of missing out on it."

"In case you've forgotten, you've already missed out on it."

"No, I haven't, and you're going to see to it that I haven't."

"What are you talking about, Cleah?" He listened in amazement while she told him what she was planning to do . . .

"As you know, I've always planned for us to be married again, and now that you're exactly where I want to be, it has to happen. You're in a position where you have the right connections to get me out of the trouble I'm in, and I expect you to do that. If you don't, I will start releasing stories to the press about how you helped me do all the things I did while you were the Chief of Police, and then set me up to take the fall."

"What! Cleah, you know that's not true. Why would you do that?" He listened again to her ridiculous ranting, finally realizing she was apparently unhinged and actually planning to carry out her threat.

"I know it's not true, and you know it's not true, but the media won't care if it's true or not. It'll just be another hot, sensational story for them that will earn high ratings."

"Don't do this Cleah," he warned in a steely voice. I promise you will regret it."

"I am going to do it, Marc. I have to. So I'll give you a week to drop Catherine Stroman and to work some magic in clearing me. If I don't hear from you, you can expect to see your name in the headlines, and for something totally different than what you've been seeing."

"You are going to force me to do something I don't want to do."

"Marc, I can't stay in this God forsaken place the rest of my life. There's nothing you can do that'll be worse than where I am now so you'll be sorry if you think I won't do this."

Marc hung up with an astonished look on his face. How did Cleah have the audacity to threaten to implicate him in all of her illegal activities if he didn't pull strings to get her out of her mess, and on top of that, re-marry her so she could be a part of all that was happening in his life and in D.C.? The woman had lost her mind!

But the fact of the matter was that she was right. Although untrue, her allegations could harm the reputation he'd worked so hard to establish. He wasted no time in calling Harry to tell him about Cleah's threat.

Harry actually laughed before asking, "Okay, do you want her under the jail or just in jail? Marc, I've tried to tell you before that Cleah is lethal and is not going to stop until she ruins you trying to get what she wants. The time has passed for you to go easy on her. We only went part of the way before because you just wanted to stop her attack on C.J., but you should have turned her over to the authorities then rather than giving her the chance to run and hide. She's just like a snake and as long as that head is alive she'll still be able to strike. I say cut that head off by digging up everything we can and throwing the book at her."

"You're right, Harry and I should have listened. I can't let her destroy my life at this point. Go ahead and do whatever it takes to stop her once and for all."

"Well, I'm going to start by immediately releasing the story of her criminal activities to the press. That will destroy her plans to go to the press about you. Then, the District Attorney will get a big file on her, including the current location where she's hiding, and the fact that she attempted to blackmail you. So get ready, it's coming."

Marc sighed and said, "Okay, Harry."

A little while later, he arrived at C.J.'s house just minutes before she pulled into her garage. She hoped out of her truck and watched as he approached her. They stood there a long time looking at each other with amazed looks on their faces before they spoke at the same time . . .

"Cleah called and threatened . . .!"

"Randy called and threatened . . .!"

They fell into each other's arms and hugged closely. It had been months since they had seen each other. Anger, frustration and uncertainty had stretched between them, separating and confusing things. But that hug spoke louder than any words they could have said.

C.J.

C.J. and Marc unloaded her SUV, checked the house to make sure everything was okay, and ordered pizza because they were both hungry. While they waited for the pizza, she fed Geordi while Marc told her about Cleah's threats and that he already had Harry working on it. "I hate it, but Harry's going to throw the book at her for all the illegal activities she committed in her Council position as well as the additional charge of trying to blackmail a law enforcement official. She's going to jail for as long as he can manage it. Hopefully, by the time she gets out she'll be a changed woman."

C.J. shook her head. "Well, she basically forced you to do it, and I'm thankful Harry convinced you of that."

Marc nodded. "So how did Randy threaten you?"

"Oh! I didn't listen to all the mess he was sprouting. I hung up on him, but he was yelling something about killing himself if I didn't come back to him."

"What! Okay, I need to talk to him. Call him back," Marc said, angrily. "This is just the time for me to deal with him since I'm already angry over Cleah's threats. I might as well take care of both of them today. It's apparent to me that we're dealing with the strategies of the devil. Both of these threats had to be directed from the pit of hell.

C.J. hit the button on her phone to call Randy and handed the phone to Marc.

Marc didn't hesitate to start right in on Randy, who answered right away, probably thinking it was C.J. calling him back. "Randy, this is Marc Carrington. It's past time for you to understand that it's over between you and C.J. She is going to marry me and there's nothing you can do or say that will stop that. Now, if you really want to kill your fool self just go ahead and do it, but I'm not going to let you put the responsibility for that on C.J.

"I will help you accomplish your death wish if you don't leave her alone. And let me make something else clear. You will never be welcome in my home or anywhere near C.J. and if you dare come around, you will regret it. I will complete what that accident didn't accomplish or throw you so far behind bars that you'll never see the light of day again. Now, do you understand me?" He hung up and handed the phone to C.J. "I don't know but I think he got the message."

"I hate you did that, but I guess it had to be done," C.J. said sadly.

"It did have to be done. Otherwise he would've kept sending you on guilt trips. "I'm amazed at those last ditch efforts by Randy and Cleah coming almost simultaneously at a crucial time when we were both having doubts about us. It had to be the hand of the devil orchestrating that," Marc said hotly. "But that only makes me more determined. I'm never going to give up. What about you?"

C.J. looked at him as she thought about everything that had happened. "No, it must be God's plan that we are together, otherwise, we wouldn't be having these ridiculous battles meant to kill, rob and destroy us. Oh, Lord! Poor Randy probably didn't know what had hit him. If he wasn't already lying down, I'm sure he had to do so after you got through with him. And I almost feel sorry for Cleah——almost."

Marc went to the door to get the pizza while C.J. got plates and napkins out of the cabinet, and they sat down to eat. "Well, would you rather see Cleah destroy me, and us?" he asked, after he took a bite from a slice of pizza.

"Of course not, but I don't wish on anyone what she's about to go through."

"We're probably going to feel some pressure from the press, so get ready."

C.J. put her slice of pizza down and dropped her head in her hands. "Oh God, am I destined to be hounded by the press all my life?" She knew she had to get prayed up.

Chapter Fifty-Nine

C.J.

C.J. STARTED WORKING TO PICK UP THE THREADS OF HER LIFE FROM before Randy's accident, which wasn't easy. She'd thought the threats from Randy and Cleah would be the worse battles to overcome, but found out how wrong that was. She chided herself over the next months for even expecting that to be so.

Marc wanted to get married soon, but she reminded him of the marital counseling they needed to go through, which stretched longer than normal because of Marc's schedule. Needless to say, after the counseling started, she realized there would always be battles to fight. Thankfully, during the counseling sessions, Pastor Robinson kept driving home the continued need for them to trust God, keep Him at the center, make prayer the priority, and obey the principles of God's Word. If those things didn't see them through, then the marriage wouldn't make it. But he also gave them some practical advice that would help them. "My wife and I, who remind me a lot of you all, do something that helps us nourish our marriage," he told them. "We try to outdo each other by doing random acts of kindness for each other. It can be small things like flowers, a favorite meal, or an 'I love you' text message or note. Of course if serious issues are involved, this won't work, but it goes a long way in nurturing our everyday relationship. We might be mad as heck at each other, but we try to do this. It forces us to lay aside anger, pride, egos and anything that might be between us."

But first, they had to get through the battles to marriage. They had already been through too much to expect a fairy tale 'happy ever after' life, but they did agree that it was only stubbornness on both of their parts that kept them from calling it quits——that, and the undeniable fact that they loved each other too much to give up. But through it all, God gave them enough joys to keep them thankful and encouraged; and enough trouble to keep them praying and trusting Him.

The topic of her money was a big quagmire that almost sank them. Marc had deep rooted issues about C.J.'s money and how it might affect their marital relationship. C.J. accused him of being chauvinistic and Marc responded that her strong personality, backed up by her money would usurp him or cause an imbalance in their relationship. It took several sessions of counseling and much prayer, to get through that challenge.

While they were struggling through the money dilemma, Marc brought up the Geordi situation. "What about Geordi?" He asked with a frown. "Did you ever get that worked out?"

She groaned in frustration. "Well, I did ask my attorney to look into it, but then I got side-tracked with Randy. My brother also promised to work on it, but I haven't heard from him about it."

"That's not acceptable, C.J., and we have to get it settled. What do you really want to happen? If we have to give him up, I'd rather do it now than wait until he's older and the adjustment will be harder on everyone, including the baby."

"Well, Chuck asked if I wanted to adopt him, and I said yes of course, but I'm so afraid that one of them will have a change of heart and decide to take him that I'm reluctant to push it."

Marc gave her a pointed look. "I hope you understand that it won't be just you adopting him, it will be both of us and he will be as much my son as yours."

"Are you sure? I mean is that what you want to do?" she asked.

"Of course that's what I want. I love him too. But we have to pursue a legal adoption or I insist you let him go. Let me handle it, okay?"

With tears of fear in her eyes, she agreed. "Okay, I know you're right."

They were still working on his latest book, which he complained he needed because he had already started consulting with law enforcement agencies. C.J. compiled loose-leaf packages for him to use until they could get the books printed. But when he was in Houston, much of their time was spent on his project, forcing her to squeeze work on her own business plans into when he wasn't there.

But she was excited that things with her business were slowly moving forward. She asked Jason to help her find a suitable facility and he suggested that she lease rather than buy a place in case she found that the business didn't do well in the location. She was overjoyed when he showed her space in one of his buildings that she thought would be perfect. It was a large two-story center space with one-story spaces flanking both sides of it and already occupied by a diversity of businesses. The building covered a full block, was located in a high traffic area and had adequate parking. It was perfect!

Ron, who was a well-known architect, agreed to redesign the space for her needs, and went to work on bringing her vision to reality. Her cousin, Nita, continued to work on ordering the inventory and was also working with her husband, Ron, on the design and layout, and Marc gave his input on security cameras and other security matters. C.J. worked projects with the Bradshaws as often as she could to network and market her event planning, and was happy when requests started rolling in, even though she had to find appropriate venues for them until her space was ready. She nixed including a sandwich and coffee shop in her space since there were already a few eating places on the property, but everything else in her vision was a go.

The battles kept coming.

Marc

Marc was sweating the house situation, and rightfully so, because he knew it was going to be a doozy of a battle to convince C.J. to move. Randy's words about throwing him out of C.J.'s house which was bought with his money still bothered him. However, he also meant everything he'd told Randy about throwing him out if he ever came to his house, which he planned to buy. But the fact remained——C.J. loved her house and would not want to move.

He asked Jason to look for another house for him since he knew Jason knew what C.J. liked, and a few weeks later, Jason told him he'd found the perfect house, in the same neighborhood.

Marc felt like he was in the middle of one of those gulf coast hurricanes when he told her he was buying another house for them. He was afraid it could be the end for them because C.J. raised such a ruckus and stubbornly rejected his efforts to explain why he wanted another house.

"I just got settled into my house and you want me to move again? No! I am not moving, Marc, and I resent the fact that you went behind my back to buy another house. That was downright sneaky, and I hope you enjoy living in it alone."

Marc sweated. And pleaded. And finally got her to listen. "Babe, I can't live in a house that another man brags was bought with his money. You have to understand, it's a man thing. Randy believes his money paid for your house, and even though he may never get to tell me again to get out of his house, I'll always feel uncomfortable knowing how he feels."

But Marc and Jason had been very smart about it. Not only was the house in the same neighborhood, it was larger, similar in custom design to C.J.'s house, and was a lakefront house, but on the other side of the lake. When he finally convinced 'hurricane C.J.' to go——although kicking and screaming——to see the house, she walked in, looked around, and got quiet. Marc started to get nervous until she said . . .

"But Marc, I really love my house and finally have it just the way I want it. I really hate to go through that again."

He grabbed her and hugged her tight. "I know, Sweetheart, but you won't be doing it by yourself this time. I'll be there to help, and you know my sister and her family and my parents will come and help us. And I want you to know that although I'll be buying the house it'll belong to both of us."

She gave him a cynical look. "Okay, but I'm not selling my house. You men are fickle and I will not put myself in the same situation as I was with Ron. That's not to say you'll do what he did, but it was a hard lesson learned and I'd be crazy to ignore it."

He understood her point, although it jabbed at his ego a little.

When their wedding was only three months away, Marc moved into the house, and they started gradually moving some of her things in.

Another big victory happened shortly after he moved in. The attorney working on the adoption case for them called with the news that they were clear to adopt Geordi. Both of his parents had relinquished parental rights. C.J. immediately started planning a celebration. "This has been such a long time in coming," she said excitedly. "Wouldn't it be great if we could do it on the same day as the wedding? Symbolically, we could all be marrying each other and becoming a family."

But it seemed as if every victory was followed by a gigantic challenge. When he returned after he had been away almost three full weeks, which was happening more frequently, Hurricane C.J. had surfaced again.

"You want us to move into that house when it's apparent you're going to be gone most of the time? That's not fair to us, Marc. I'd rather stay in my house if Geordi and I are going to be alone."

"I'm sorry, Honey. All I can say is I hope you'll bear with me for a while. As you know, this work is important and I just can't walk away from it now. It's people like me who will have to get things on a somewhat balanced track and unfortunately, that will take some time and personal sacrifices. Hopefully, you can travel with me after we're married."

"And what am I supposed to do with my own business while I'm traveling with you? It's not going to get off the ground and run on its own. Honestly Marc, how much am I supposed to sacrifice? First you want me to give up my house, and now you're asking me to give up my business?"

"Well, it'll be a while before that's up and running full force. Hopefully by then, the travel will have slowed down. And remember, you can always hire a manager to handle it when you're gone. Can you please just work with me on this? Let's just play it by ear. If after a certain period it's not working out, I promise I'll give it up."

She was not happy to say the least, and it created another hurdle for them to get over on the way to their marriage. Then, at the worst possible time, the story about Cleah and her arrest hit the news, and in their effort to add sensationalism to the story, reporters dug up the old story about Randy and C.J.'s separation and divorce and tried to tie Marc and C.J.'s engagement to that break up. To make matters worse, they got in touch with Randy, who claimed Marc was the reason he hadn't been able to put his marriage back together.

To get away from the media harassment, C.J. took the baby and left town for almost three weeks. She visited her parents, then flew to California to help her cousin, Gina, pack and prepare for her move to Arkansas. Marc went along with that as long as she had no plans to cancel their wedding. After all, he was traveling too.

C.J.

Time seemed to snowball. C.J. returned home when she suddenly realized the wedding date she and Marc had agreed on was only six weeks away, She hired a moving company to come in and pack everything, asked Jason to work on leasing her house, and slowed the progress with her business so she could finish editing Marc's book and get it processed for publishing.

"Marc, after we get married——if we get married——because if

one more crazy thing happens, it'll convince me that God is trying to tell us something. Anyway, I'm going to start working full time on getting my business set up to open. That's why I'm trying to get your book finished and behind me."

"Thank you, Sweetheart. I appreciate that. But what are you talking about?" Marc asked with a frown. "There is no 'if' about it. We are getting married. Honey, you know we agreed that we wouldn't let any of these challenges come between us." He looked at her in frustration. "Everybody is afraid you're going to back out before it happens, and that's why they want to help with everything to make it easier on us."

Thankfully, it would be a small, private wedding, combined with Geordi's adoption ceremony, followed by a reception. To make things easier, C.J.'s cousins and Marc's sister took over the preparation for everything——under her direction, of course.

To the relief of everyone, things went smoothly. The wedding, adoption ceremony and reception with only family and close friends in attendance came off without a hitch.

Geordi went home with C.J.'s parents for a week while they went on a honeymoon cruise, then returned and hit the ground running. They went to Arkansas to pick up Geordi, then stopped by and spent a couple of days with his parents on the way back. After putting Geordi in daycare, they were in her place of business setting up, arranging and re-arranging things, ordering necessary furniture, decorum items and other practical things.

Marc spent the next few days helping her, but then had to report to D.C. for a meeting with the Presidential Commission on Law Enforcement Reform, and catch up on his other responsibilities. He had suspended his consulting and traveling activities for three months to settle into his married life.

C.J. had made herself accept things as they were for now. Her husband was trying so hard to please her that it would be ridiculous to fight him over his efforts to make a contribution to a worthy cause, be a good husband and father, and make a living at the same time, all of which he was determined to do. In fact, it almost brought tears to her eyes when she observed him with Geordi. Based on her experiences with Randy and Chuck, she was shocked to see a man embrace his 'daddy' role so joyfully. He had never hesitated to change dirty diapers, feed and bathe the baby, drop him off and pick him up from daycare, bring at least one toy every time he came home, spend time playing with him, love it when Geordi followed him around, and said he couldn't wait to teach him to hunt and fish.

Okay, he was the same with her most of the time, but after all, she was his wife. But it certainly circumvented a lot of complaints on her part. Truthfully, she spent several nights on the edge of the mattress of her side of the bed when she went to bed angry at him——until he quietly handed her a list of Scriptures about anger——especially the one about not letting the sun go down with anger festering in your heart. "If I'm going to be in bed with my wife, I want to sleep with my wife," he told her in a firm voice.

But since they didn't live in a fairy tale world, there were still battles.

Three months after they had been married, the phone rung as they were relaxing at home one night, and they both groaned, hating the interruption of their time together. Marc went to answer it, and silently handed the phone to C.J. who wasn't surprised to find Mrs. Singleton on the other end. Although Mrs. Singleton called her at least once a week to give her updates on Randy and Mr. Singleton, Marc barely tolerated the woman, and often said, "I don't think she'll ever get over the fact that you're not Randy's wife."

When she hung up, she had tears in her eyes and said, "Mr. Singleton died."

Marc hugged her tightly. "Oh, Honey, I'm sorry to hear that. He was the one in the Singleton family that I liked."

"He was the one who treated me half-way decently," she answered, deep in thought, and was already dreading the conversation she knew was coming with Marc. But he surprised her.

"If you want to go to the service we can go, so don't sweat that. I can deal with Randy for that little while, after all, you're my wife now."

"Yes, I think I would like to go, and Mrs. Singleton just said she hopes I'll come and be a part of the family, and also to bring Geordi, who her husband was so crazy about."

"Okay, we'll go. Just find out when the service will be, so I can make sure it doesn't conflict with anything else on our calendar."

"Thank you, Sweetheart," she said in a soft voice. "You know I was getting ready for one of our battles."

They went to the funeral, and Marc sat with her parents while C.J. and Geordi sat with Mrs. Singleton and Randy, who was in a wheelchair. It brought tears to her eyes as Mrs. Singleton, who tearfully told everyone that Geordi was her grandson and her hope for living, hugged the baby all through the service, and Geordi, who usually wiggled during church, seemed to sense her need and submitted to her hugs. Of course Marc and Randy ignored each other, and for that C.J. was thankful.

But the next week, C.J. received a fat envelope in the mail, and discovered that despite her refusal, Mr. Singleton had made her the Executor of his estate anyway.

Marc looked a little sheepish. "Oh, I just remembered, he talked to me about his need to do that, and I did tell him I agreed. I guess he took that to mean it was okay."

But he wasn't as accommodating when, a few days later, She received another fat envelope with a copy of Randy's will, and making her the Executor. In it, Randy left everything to her with the provision that she use it to take care of his mother as long as she lived, and to set up a 'Randy Singleton Memorial Basketball Scholarship' in whatever amounts she deemed appropriate. The remainder, if any, could be used in whatever way she desired.

That didn't set well with Marc, who grumbled that Randy had come up with a diabolical plan to keep her tied to him.

Chapter Sixty

Marc & C.J.

More than a year after the wedding...

THEY WENT TO EARLY MORNING CHURCH SERVICE, THEN HEADED to Roz's house for brunch and stuffed themselves on the tremendous spread of food Roz had prepared.

As they were leaving, Roz handed C.J. a shopping bag full of food. "There's a casserole for later today so you don't have to worry about cooking. Just put it in the oven until it browns. I also put in some leftovers from this morning for you guys to snack on."

"Thanks, Roz, but you didn't have to do this," C.J. said as she hugged her.

"I know I didn't, but I just appreciate how much of a blessing you are to my brother. This is nothing compared to how happy you've made him, and all you do for him, especially since you're so busy yourself."

"I do it because I love him," C.J. responded with another hug.

They went home, changed in jogging suits and sneakers and took a walk along the walking trail by the lake. They stopped in to say hello to Ms. Maggie and her husband then barely made it home before the sky opened up and rain poured.

It turned into a stormy afternoon, and they snuggled down

supposedly to watch football. Sheets of heavy rain, gusts of wind and rumbles of thunder raged outside but there was love, peace and contentment inside.

In fact, Marc was having one of those, "there's no other place I'd rather be," moments. He silently breathed a prayer of thanksgiving when his eyes traveled around the room to his family. His son played contentedly on the floor near him, and his wife, lounging on the other end of the sofa, had her nose buried in her iPad instead of watching the game.

Truthfully, the game wasn't holding his attention either. He looked at his wife and said,

"You know, for some reason, I'm sitting here reflecting on all the challenges we've had to deal with to get to this point, and thanking God, because you know what? I'm happier than I've ever been."

C.J. closed the iPad, and scooted closer to him. "Me too, Sweetheart. I never imagined the day I left home after the violent fight with Randy that I'd be this happy a few years later."

She'd been battered, bruised, homeless and nearly destitute. Where would she be if she had become embittered, vengeful, unforgiving and had abandoned all hope for the future? Would she have a loving husband and son? A promising business? A beautiful home full of warmth, love and the presence of God?

"It hasn't been easy, but through it all, God has been faithful. I could easily be in a prison of bitterness and hopelessness like Randy and Cleah. I thank God for answering my Grammy's prayer for a godly husband the blessing of children."

Marc nodded and reflected on the babies lost to him by the unloving, uncaring and callous actions of Cleah, and the long, lonely years he had yearned for a loving wife, children and a warm home. "I'm thankful that God has given me exactly what I wanted for so long. You and my son are the most precious things in my life."

He leaned over to kiss her, then said, "I think the washing machine just stopped. Want me to put the clothes in the dryer?"

"Yes, Honey," she answered as she went into the kitchen and prepared a tray of fruit, cheese and crackers from the leftovers Roz had

281

given them and then put the casserole in the oven. Geordi came running when she carried the snacks back into the family room, and they all snacked until satisfied.

A flash of irritation hit Marc when C.J. picked up her iPad again. He pulled her closer to him and said, "Put that thing down, honey. This is family time, and we have precious little of it so I'm not sharing." Between Marc's work and travel, her varied responsibilities and three-year old Geordi, their time together was at a premium.

"I'm just checking emails," she answered.

"Put it down!" He insisted, and proceeded to kiss her. He understood that she was just as busy as he was. In addition to being an excellent mother, she was helping him write, publish and distribute his books, take care of her own business, and look after Mrs. Singleton and Randy's affairs. She was currently working on a luncheon for a large group of ministers who would be in town for a conference in a few weeks, followed a couple of weeks later by a Christian Women's Symposium on domestic violence that her cousin, Nita was sponsoring. The Bradshaws regularly recommended her for events, and every event led to others since she worked so hard to make each one special. All this, while traveling with him as much as possible.

"Okay!" C.J. said, putting the iPad down.

The phone rung and C.J. ran to answer. She came back smiling. "Harry wants to know when he's going to get another cake. I guess I'll make it tonight. I gotta do it because he's been so good about arranging security for my events that I can't say no."

"No, you can't!"

The ringing phone interrupted them again, and C.J. answered. She gave him a regretful look when she hung up. "It was Mrs. Singleton," she answered his quizzical look.

"What did she want this time?" Marc asked in an agitated tone.

C.J. grimaced. "She's thinking about visiting in a couple of weeks."

Marc frowned. "Well, you know my feelings about that." He was still bent out of joint over the fact that Randy had also made her the executor of his estate—without even asking her.

"Well, Honey, beside Randy, we're basically the only family she has and you know how much she loves our son. And since she and Ms. Maggie became friends, she's enjoys running around with her and indulging in some senior activities. And by the way, that street runs both ways," C.J. said, with a smirk. "I don't like the fact that Cleah, through her sister, is still stalking you either. I can guarantee she has nothing good in mind. You need to tell her to get lost once and for all. Anyway, she'd better not come up with anymore of her mess, or she'll get more of what she's already gotten."

"Trust me," Marc said, with a chuckle, I don't think she'll ever forget. She's probably still shaking in her shoes because she thinks you're the one who asked God to bring her down. He gave her a hard look. "She might be right. Don't ever pray on me, okay!"

C.J. shook her head. "Cleah can't blame anyone but herself for her troubles. So I'm stuck with Randy and his mother, and you can't get rid of Cleah. I guess there's nothing we can do except deal with it."

"Let's forget them and enjoy our time together. You are going with me to D.C. next week, huh?" Marc asked.

C.J. looked at him with a scowl and refused to answer.

Marc's work with the justice department and the Presidential Commission he was working on seemed to require more and more of his time, while the F.B.I. Academy had approved his workbook and teaching video, and other agencies were signing on to use it, requiring more and more traveling for teaching presentations, as well as on-going consulting opportunities. It was a great day for their household when the box arrived with copies of his book. They celebrated and immediately placed copies in her bookstore.

Whenever he had to be away for a week or more, which was happening more often than they liked, Marc wanted her to go with him, and leave Geordi with his parents. C.J. objected to leaving her baby so often, and when she did, felt more comfortable leaving him in Riverwood with her parents. Marc frequently pulled rank, but 'Hurricane C.J.' would start blowing, and truthfully, the battle could go either way.

After the bookstore and gift shop opened a few months ago, it had hindered her being away because she had no one to oversee things. But one day, her cousin, Nita had dropped by with her sister-in-law, Monique, who had recently moved back from the Mid-East, and still hadn't found a job that she liked. When Monique, an avid book lover, walked around the store, she got excited and told C.J. that if she ever needed help, to let her know because she would love working there.

C.J. had already tried out several people in part-time capacities, but none had worked out well enough for her to consider them for full-time. She had looked at Monique and said, "As a matter of fact, I'm looking for help now. Are you interested?"

Of course Monique was, and C.J. hired her. She had worked out so well that C.J. eventually hired her on full time, and trusted her enough to leave her in charge when she wasn't there. But, she kept her time away to a minimum, since common sense told her that no one will take care of your possessions like you will.

Now, Marc drew a frustrated breath as he waited for her answer. "You don't have a reason not to go with me. You have things ready for the upcoming events, and Monique can take care of the store."

He grabbed her iPad and went to the bible app and found Isaiah 43:18-19, which was one of the favorite Scriptures they often relied on to help them through every situation. *"Do not remember the former things; neither consider the things of old. Behold, I am doing a new thing! Now it springs forth; do you not perceive and know it and will you not give heed to it? I will even make a way in the wilderness and rivers in the desert."*

Marc pulled her into a tight hug. "Thank You, Heavenly Father, for bringing us through all our former troubles; thank You for the new things you are doing for us, and help us to never lose sight or become ungrateful for anything You have done or continue to do in us, for us and through us; we trust that You are going to continue to make a way through every wilderness and rivers in every desert. We thank You and praise You for it all. In Jesus' Name."

They both said, "Amen!"

A loud rumble of thunder shook the house, and Geordi screamed and ran to her. He climbed into her lap and said, "Mommy, I don't like that boom-boom. I 'fraid of it."

C.J. hugged him and said, "I don't like it either, baby, but that's God's work and we can't do anything to stop it."

"Daddy can! Tell it to stop, Daddy!"

Marc's chest swelled in pride. "I wish I could, Son but I can't. Like Mommy said, that's God's work," he said, reaching to pull Geordi into his lap. "But I can hold you tight, and we can trust that God is going to keep us safe. How about that?"

"'Kay, Daddy," Geordi said, snuggling into his arms and yawning. Then, he said, "Mommy, get my blankie."

C.J. didn't move. "Who is he learning all this bossiness from?" She asked Marc.

Marc chuckled and said, "Not me! How are you supposed to ask for something, Geordi?"

"Oh." He giggled, then said, "I forgot. Mommy, may I have my blankie, pease?"

She got up to get his special blanket, which he tucked under his chin and snuggled closer to Marc, then yawned and mumbled sleepily, "Thank you, Mommy."

"You're welcome, baby." She got a larger blanket, went back to the sofa, snuggled closer to Marc, and covered them all with it. "Nap time!"

"Yeah, and I wouldn't be anyplace else," Marc said as he snuggled closer to her.

Epilogue

C.J. STEPPED OFF THE PLANE IN D.C. WHERE MARC WAS IN MEETINGS with the Presidential Commission on Law Enforcement issues, and headed down to baggage claim. She'd had to bring two large bags, since Marc, who had come a couple of days ago while she dropped Geordi off in Riverwood with her parents, had told her to bring some heavier clothes for both of them because it was very cold. And he was leaving D.C. for another cold city the following week.

She was waiting for her bags to come down the ramp when she was hugged from behind.

"Hey, beautiful lady! Waiting on someone?"

"Yes, so where is he?" She asked with a straight face while looking around.

Marc turned her around and kissed her, then said, I'd better be him, or the dude's in big trouble."

They laughed as they gathered the bags and headed to the car and his hotel room. Later, they met some of Marc's co-workers for dinner.

"So, do you all have children?" One of the women in the group asked.

"Yes!" They both answered. C.J. pulled her tablet from her purse and pulled up a collage of pictures of Geordi, and passed it to the woman.

"Oh, he is so handsome. I see both of your features in him," she exclaimed.

Marc grinned. "That's what everyone tells us," he said proudly, then looked at C.J. and winked.

Beyond the Break - Discussion Guide

1. If you had been C.J., how would you have handled finding your husband in your bed with another woman? Would you have shot him? Her? Both of them? Or packed your things and left?

2. What do you think C.J.'s reasons were for staying with Randy when he continued to cheat, get into all kinds of trouble, and get a vasectomy without her knowledge when he knew she wanted children?

3. What do you think happened to Randy after he was released from the team? Temporary insanity? Deep depression? Loss of hope? Immaturity?

4. Why do you think Randy was so angry with C.J. and why did he go into such a rage and beat her for shooting at him? Why do you think he tried to make her suffer even when he knew she missed on purpose?

5. What do you think was at the root of Randy's selfish immaturity? His parents? His fame and money? His wife?

6. Considering Randy's objection to a divorce and his stalling actions to avoid it, should C.J. have dated Marc before her divorce was final? Why or why not?

7. Was Marc wrong to aggressively pursue a married woman, even after she repeatedly asked him to back off?

8. Do you think political fanatics like Cleah exist?

9. Should Marc have ended his marriage to Cleah the first time he discovered she had cheated? The first time he found out she had aborted a baby? Would you have stayed with her despite public opinion?

10. What do you think about C.J.'s relationship with Randy's parents? Forgiving and Godly? unrealistic? Sub-consciously still in love with Randy?

11. Do you think Randy ever seriously regretted what he did to C.J., or merely wanted her back for his own selfish comfort and convenience? Or he just simply didn't have the depth to do it?

12. Do you think anyone would realistically go to the extreme that C.J. did to hide her identity by disguising her appearance and using her maiden name to keep a job?

13. Would you have legally pursued Randy for a fair and prompt divorce settlement or do as C.J. did and leave it in the hands of The Lord?

14. Was C.J. right or wrong to refuse to jump into marriage to Marc even after her divorce? Why and why not?

15. Marc and others accused C.J. of being both hot tempered and letting others take advantage of her. What do you think, and how should she have been different?

PRAYER OF SALVATION

God loves you!
You can ask Jesus Christ into your heart right now by faith through this suggested prayer.
(Prayer is simply talking to God)
God knows your heart and is not so concerned with your words as He is with the attitude of your heart.

SUGGESTED PRAYER

Lord Jesus Christ, I need you. Thank You for dying on the cross for my sins. I open the door of my life and receive You as my Savior and Lord.
Thank You for forgiving my sins and giving me eternal life.
Take control of every area of my life and make me the kind of person You want me to be.
Thank You that I am saved in Jesus' Name. Amen.